The Satanist

The Satanist

A novel

SANA MUNIR

PARTRIDGE
A Penguin Random House Company

Print information available on the last page.

To order additional copies of this book, contact
Partridge India
000 800 10062 62
orders.india@partridgepublishing.com

www.partridgepublishing.com/india

Contents

Dedicated to the precious memory
of my dearly beloved father Sirajuddin Munir
and my angelic mother Bano

When Satan chances us to see,
He doffs his cap respectfully,
For we have lessons to impart,
To Satan in the tempter's art.

- Fariduddin Attar (Persian poet 1142-1220)

PROLOGUE

His feet seemed to drag him as he approached the muted grey building that stood just five steps ahead. He was like an etching of ennui himself – his time seemed stopped long ago. The Nigerian rain had been heavy on him. Drenched right from the top – the lanky uncut hair down to the black ratty pullover soaked and clinging to his wafer thin body and from there to his bare feet that were no longer under his command, were carrying him to a destination whose destructive effects were known to him but he was most eager to go there and find what he needed the most.

The Church of Satan was not a picture of fiendish architecture - there were no skulls hanging or vile looking birds perched upon arches, there were no arches actually. It was a regular looking house with a regular compound and a huge door. The greyness of the architecture made it look sombre, ignorable and daft in the same glance. As he jerked forth after stumbling upon a *stone lying in peaceful slumber in the middle of the road, he almost thought he heard it groan like an old man who had been awaken from his sleep with a startle. As he turned around to spot the stone which had made him jump and lunge forth instead of walking the zombie-like walk he was walking, it was the first time for these deadly couple of hours that he had moved his head in some direction other than the pose of utter submission to whatever had taken the place of almightiness in his faith system. His head had been bowed for the longest hours ever since he had been treading on this wet road as cold as ice, under the fearful shower of a chilled November night, his hands were tucked securely in the puddles forming in the hip pockets of his jeans and as he walked his desolate walk with chin on his chest, he looked like a prisoner being taken to the gallows. The only difference being, there were no on lookers, no scaffold or grind to cast a frightful look upon and no guards to hold him tight. Yet, it seemed as if his limbs were forcefully secured and he was going to crawl on his death bed to hide under sheets of white. The two hour walk had surely burdened him but the craving of coming to this place had hit the crescendo now – just five steps away was the place where the coveted answers to all his questions were lying bare.*

The door was discouraging him. It was fastened. He knew the hour he had chosen to arrive unasked could be unwelcomed by the paganists inside. What if the door is not answered? What if he had to walk away? His hands, the second ones to defect after his feet, protested when he yanked them out of their slumber in the pockets. He brought his hands from behind up to the fore front, his shoulder blades cracked, so there was another limb protesting. The gaze of his eyes upon his hands was interrupted by a bolt of lightning that struck somewhere and lit a spark. 'Fire? Is that a sign of being here?' The spark was beaten to death by the impish droplets of water from above. 'Rain belongs to God,' he thought. Though the rain was persistent upon beating him down, he held his jaw and wasn't dampened.

Five steps, the five colossal steps were hard, so were his facial features. The only way to stop his teeth chattering like a sucker was to clench them tight. With shaking hands he lifted up a hand to thud on the door. Thud, not knock: to create more sound and wake up anyone inside, even Satan himself. As soon as his palm touched the brow beaten entrance gate, it creaked open.

This was a warm welcome which he had never thought of. He whimpered a sigh but could not tell whether it was reflective of relief or the appalling awe that had clutched at his heart like a tiny cold hand and had put the drumming rhythm of his heartbeat to a frozen still. Bewildered, he stepped inside the dark hall where the torpor of the walls and the altar could match his present demographics.

Chapter 1

HARRIS

"We've lost it," Obiyara yelled from the thick foliage behind them.

"We haven't, you did," he snapped back as he tried to catch the slug which had wiggled out of his hands as the shout out from behind startled him.

"Harris! Come on man, help me find it. You ain't no crazy, are ya?" Crazy was his pet word.

Obi was insistent this time to find the football that had disappeared into the woods since he owned it. Those that had belonged to Harris were lost in the dark woods forever.

Harris was no keeper and Obi was too young to persuade him to be one. "You lizard-brained *baturiya*! Leave the poor thing alone, and stop molesting it," he teased as Harris gingerly balanced the two ends of the yellow and leaf-green slug on the tips of two twigs.

"Why do you care so much?"

Obiyara looked at his friend, thought for a micro second and then replied, "That's my dinner," he kept his face straight after playing a prank on his friend's imagination but inside he was laughing his head off when Harris's head yanked to the other side to stare at the tiny creature in his hands. "It's delicious, the soup, with balls of boiled and pounded rice." Obviously, he was enjoying the amazement in Harris's eyes. At ten, both best buddies had enough glimpse into each other's lifestyle, but this was new information to Harris.

Harris could well imagine the latter taste. He had seen Obiyara's mother boil rice that she had separated from the chaff herself. In the summers, the rice paddy would be dotted with colourful heads bobbing up and down. The men, taking rest after toiling all season for the crop to grow well would enjoy a time out with bowls of wine churned out of barley and sugar cane juice. The women, wearing head cloths on their heads, a colourful turban really, baskets tied to their backs and a long yard of cloth called a wrapper wrapped around the length of their torsos falling down to their calves or knees would be singing songs to themselves or in groups, harvesting the crop with their bare hands. Sometimes, a mother would stop because the baby hanging from a sling across her bosom would wake up and wail for milk. And the mother would let nature flow to her off-spring from the pathway that would lead right to her own heart. Amidst such commotion, the crop would finally reach the farmers' homes. The fun part began later as the unpolished rice; fresh from the chaff would be boiled with water in a cassava pot until it turned soft, gooey and mushy. The ingredients then would be overturned into a huge wooden pail that was roomy enough to allow Harris sit in it and hide from Obi during a game of hide and seek. It was after all this that two ladies would sit across with the wooden container between them, sing a song in a language that Harris had grown up with – Hausa – but the songs still didn't make much sense to him.

"sakataye ai na zama mai kyan kamu
sakataye ai na yicikakken kamu
sakataye burin danake nai damu
yazamo na sanya zuma kashanye"

It was song sung to entice a lover stationed faraway, reminding him what he's missing back home. Harris remembered those words for a long long time for more than any other reason, what struck him the most were the environs in which the lyrics were sung: a small hut comprising of only one room, rounded instead of having slanting corners thus providing slumber space to everyone in the house. Obi told him the walls were rounded giving no corners to them to signify the rounded nucleus of the family where no one could be a miscreant or find a detached corner for one's self. The family Obi belonged to was large - his grandparents, mother, and uncle along with his three wives and seven cousins all lived thatched beneath the same roof. Obi, like Harris was an only child and he had lost his father to a disease as curable as dysentery. His mother had not found him a new father as yet. The compound around the house was a big court plastered with mud. The ladies in the house would batter up sand and dried grass to cure the floor and walls every week. When the water pots would crack, they would fix them with a muddy paste and leave them to dry in the scorching sun. Sand was a remedy for everything – skin rash, scalp-acne, sunburn, insect bites.

In the midst of this mud plastered compound were children of different sizes – one tied to the mother's back in a hammock like fashion and fast asleep, the others playing with a football and the girl trying her hand at raffia. The two ladies chose to sit down right in the middle and began their perilous task. The pestle jostling between them both came to a halt as soon as the song came to its end. The grains had transformed into a fluffy meringue and the ladies started to form small spherical bite sized morsels from it. Harris had a sensory refraction of the balls of fluff he had seen at Obi's house as his best friend spoke of it. Harris had a hard time imagining the white morsels dipped into a broth made up with the colourful little slug in his hands. In his imagination, he tried to chew it to feel whether its flesh would be tender as chicken or chewy as a sausage. He gulped back the curious whim to bite off its head and started focusing on the beady little eyes that poked out of the head. The timid little fellow looked lost. That was a sure put off for Harris's appetite.

In the axis of an uninhabited African jungle, two boys of the same age – ten – playing football was an uncommon sight. The residential area that belonged to the foreigners, the white man or more commonly called the *baturiyas* was in a close vicinity to the common man's bush land but the two landscapes gave a clear differential, almost hegemonic view of asymmetry. The houses that looked like cottages to the white but had the appeal of a mansion to the black person, the fact that the local Nigerian servant addressed the white man as Master, drew a thick line between privilege and desire.

"Its dusk, Mum would kill me if I am not home," Harris protested.

"Come on man, I am afraid to go in there," Obi pleaded.

Both the ten year olds wearing a pair of shorts each, bare chested and bare footed in the damp forest that was just twenty yards away from the place Harris called home, decided to go deeper. There never had been any news of a wild animal in the region, but the two were just kids, oblivious of the discrepancy of the skin, creed, race and religion. They shared the commonality of fear, excitement, curiosity and exploration. That was enough to form a bond of togetherness. The slug was shifted into an empty jam jar and the lid fastened tightly. Harris had taken pains to punch holes with his geometry compass into the metallic lid.

"Would it be a good idea to drop in a few blades of grass?"

Obi grunted in response and unfolded his legs from the squat that had allowed him a connection with the ground. The Nigerians had a strange relationship with sand which had a red tint instead of the murky brown dirt that Harris later came to get accustomed with. They would mix up the sand with water and rub it on their bodies like a coolant when the sun would be too hot or make huts with gravel and sand and give it to their daughters when they would marry them off to the man with the best prospects. The common African man would be happy with the bare necessities of life – a bed to sleep on even if it was woven with straw under a shady tree or a tent house made with discarded polythene sheets from Master's house to beat the continuous July showers. His celebratory moment would be the Friday lunch after the Jumma prayers or the Sunday lunch after church service. If neither, they would be idol worshippers and sat together each evening around the idol they preferred to kowtow to. People met, shook hands, embraced one another, talked of the weather, the prices of commodities at the big market, school fees going up and new marts opening up everywhere. Even with uncommon religious backgrounds, their issues of interest were common. "It's thee Nigerian vay of leevin'," Malam Yakubu told his pupils every time during the games class when the black kids would refuse to have Harris as their partner in the three-legged race. "Baturiya," they would whisper to each other. Obi, fortunately for Harris, took Malam Yakubu seriously: the Nigerian way of living was to embrace the baturiyas. Harris's best friend, Obiyara was from the Ibo tribe. He wore a small troll threaded into a string of black beads around his neck. It was to ward off the evil eye. Harris wore a small scrap of leather stitched and bound together to form an armlet – an Imam Zamin - which he wore on his bicep. It too was, Mum would say, to ward off the evil eye.

The troll swung around Obi's neck as the boys ran across the tall dry bushes and past the favorite dried old tree trunk that had been their 'bench' for as long as they could remember. Sometimes a chameleon would be hiding under the trunk-bench. The little reptile harmless and brown at that moment with the small hills running down its spine serving the best guise to gel with the rough bark of the tree, its beady eyes popping out of the head and giving him away to the two pairs of merciless hands who would sometimes pelt stones at the creature or push it with a twig to something grassier and watch it alter its shade from brown to green. The metamorphosis would be like the amalgamation of two metals fusing with each other and eventually the dominant shade would take over. Harris would never get tired of telling Obi how his Mum once confused the chameleon for a bitter gourd hanging in her vegetable garden.

"It swirled in her hands and that's when she found out," he chuckled.

"You should've listened to her screams," it was a humorous anecdote since giant lizards, green snakes and chameleons didn't bother them; they almost had been with them like playmates.

That evening, they didn't have time to look for a reptile hiding under the trunk, they had an important task to finish – find the goddamned football. The grass under their feet began to turn drier as they slowed their pace and started creeping instead. The deeper the woods became the more silence prevailed. The sky was hidden and engulfed by the tall tree tops which seemed to join heads together in deep conversation. The sun had yawned into the west and all that was left was the purple afterglow reflected on the lining of the clouds.

"That's not much light," Obi thought out aloud.

A hawk screeched somewhere. Harris tread in front, Obi followed.

"You couldn't have kicked it this hard," Harris hissed.

"I swear I saw it head this way, I ain't no crazy," Obi insisted.

The ruffling of their own footsteps had started to get submerged in other voices of the dusk coming from various directions of the woods which could be inhabited with wild monkeys and wild dogs who could be benign or bloodthirsty depending on the time span of famine that they had experienced. On the optimistic side, they could be confronted with a family or two of bush people camping out for free in the woods from where they could not be hunted out for taxes, bills or rental payments. The two boys' audibility had become stronger than any other of their sensibilities co-related together. There were squawks of the African negrofinch, the stout little black and white bird with an orange beak, timid and tiny, settling in its nest as soon as the sun would dim out its illumination; a deep throated sound of a group of frogs in the close distance and the constant whistling of the crickets and grasshoppers in a shrill note as if each was trying to out-voice each other. The ruffling of the leaves was lost amongst the condiments of the sheer silence that prevailed in the midst of the forest. The boys were leaning onto each other, rubbing their naked chests across the aged bark of gum trees that was as smooth as the leaves that protruded out of their heads like a splurge of water gushing forth a fountain's squirt. The long leaves from the gum trees hung silently in the half-night surroundings, denying to move or sway being heavy with the oozy whitish juice that Obi loved to milk out through tiny cuts in the veins of the leaf. He aspired to take up medicine.

"It is pure biology," he would breathe when the veins would give out the gooey sticky fluid.

"It is mutilation," Harris would tease.

While Obi would go on with the dissection of his leaves, Harris would secretively poke his pen knife – a gift from Dad – into the trunk of the tree and let the liquidized warm gum ooze out of the slit and gather in his palm. It was like milking Mother Nature herself, Harris's father had once told him. Harris had learnt very efficiently the art of collecting gum discharge in his hand, letting it harden and take form but just like Mum used to do with ice cream, not let it get stony in a long spell of ignorance; instead; shifting the sides and kneading gently like Mum did with her pizza dough and form a shape out of it. Dad had made a ring for Mum's finger, for a stud, he had picked a white pebble with blue stripes on it, the size of a chocolate chip. The pebble sat perfectly in the middle of the tiny hoopla that Dad had made. He remembered how Mum had squealed with pleasure when Dad gave it to her.

Maryam, Harris's mum, was a vagabond soul. She found pleasure in creating things out of nothing. She sculpted, wrote poems in a secret journal, she cooked, she planted seeds and watered them to make them grow into fruit bearing useful plants. To her, the cooking ingredients that she would put together to prepare a meal for her family, the words that were jumping inside her head waiting to be born and take form of an uncelebrated and unshared poem, the ceramic cement that she used to dough up to create a figurine and paint it afterwards and the seeds that she would talk to and cuddle near her bosom before burying them deep inside the soil, all of these were fragments of the omnipresent truth about her way of life – she believed in creation. She would mould the leftover sculpting material to form pendants and beads threaded together to give away as presents to the native Nigerian women who would come to sell fried yams or jars of Vaseline or lacy corsets to her doorstep. They would call her Madam and ask her to allow them to paint some henna marks on Madam's cheeks so that her anemic skin could be guised by the black flowerets or lines that they would adorn their own cheeks with. Maryam would put them off gently saying her husband won't appreciate.

"Waayo! Master like it Madam! Master like it for me!"

Maryam never ventured to find out how Magana, the frequent visitor to her home had gotten her flowerets approved by Master. Although she always tried hard to chat up Magana asking how the dance went last night for she being a maiden would be desperate to look her prettiest for the young men in her bush land who would ask her for a dance around the fire and pick her for marriage. She provided Magana a listener's ear for her girly problems and herself tried her best to brush up her local dialect and language. Waayo was one of those words one could pick up easily in Nigeria – it could roughly be translated into plain English as Oh! The other lady's broken English would improve day by day since a lot of Baturiyas had chosen this country as their homeland and the interaction between the white and black people had somewhat created a grey language. Hausa, the local language was difficult to adhere and acquire for the white or brown man, the blacks had decided to turn to learn English, pidgin however, but English. Magana was lucky to have found Maryam – although she was not interested in teaching Magana how to speak English, she was more interested in learning Hausa from her.

Magana was, by all definition of the word, beautiful. She had the perfect proportions on her vital statistics. Her skin was not the ordinary chocolate brown or coffee brown as was usually with other locales. Hers was a strange bottle blue hue, the sheer blackness transcending into a midnight affect that glowed from parts of her body that were consciously left bare – her shins and feet, arms and shoulders and her oval face with a sharp chin. Her lips were thin and her eyes were round. She pleated her hair in about thirty tight oiled braids. Maryam loved her choice of wrappers – the long yards of cloth that the black ladies wound around themselves and sometimes coupled with a head gear of the same cloth. Magana would choose the ultimate African patterns usually huge circles or big hoops in fiery shades of yellow, red or orange against a darker background. The affect of her miniscule clothing would be enough to tease the eyes since the darker background of the fabric would blend in neatly with the dark shade of her skin and leave the fluorescent hoops and circles of the textile pattern to snuggle up on the roundness of her perfect curves. When Maryam painted beads or pendants for Magana, she would always keep in mind loud vibrant colors to go around that midnight blue neck of hers that could awe-struck any man. Including Hyder.

And Harris.

To Harris, his Mum was like a strange puzzle. She never gave out much about herself. She showed love to women who were infatuated with her husband. She wore that ring everyday to show her life partner how much she appreciated his creation while she tucked away her wedding and engagement rings in some remote corner of her closet. A gum ring was good enough for her. Harris had so much gotten used to the hard and cold touch of that ring that whenever Mum lovingly cupped his face in her hands and told him he was her 'precious boy' his conscious and subconscious had registered to his memory the feel of that gum ring as well as the feel of Mum's touch.

Even now, standing against a tree, Harris could feel something cold and sticky clinging to his chest. It was the oozing gum from the trunk he had just rubbed his torso against. This leakage was not from a slit made by Harris's pen knife, it was a hollow hole probably made by a woodpecker which must have gotten its beak glued afterwards. It was not an uncommon sight to see a woodpecker whetting its beak alongside a stone or sitting on a tree branch after experiencing a misfire at a gum tree.

"Let's go," Obiyara mouthed to his baturiya friend when the latter turned to glance at him.

"It's your focking ball," Harris hissed. "It's your focking call."

Harris had learnt his first swear words in the Nigerian dialect. He knew Obi had the natural instincts to climb up a tree as gracefully as a monkey if danger would be near. He knew Obi's fright was tilted more towards his friend than himself. Their most horrific imagery was simple – wild dogs running free in a batch, hunting in groups, sometimes bonding up with a pack of hyenas.

"Let's get outta here," Obiyara hissed through his teeth, his jaws gritting hard together so much, they created a chiseling sound. The afterglow from the sun had faded from the usual orange-yellow hues into a darker grey-purple one, the only help they had was from the holes in their pupils, dilating and letting them see more despite the damp darkness that had crept up slowly and was about to devour the whole landscape into its scary appetite.

"Creeping time is over, lets run."

Obi agreed with his friend although the latter's fear was also extended out to making his father cross if he reached home later than usual.

Hyder Khan, Harris's father, was popular amongst not only the white people but also the locales that looked up to him as one of their own – he had a way with them. He knew how to flirt with the black ladies in the typical local way, how to chum up to the men and what advice to give to the younger lot who referred to him as Sir. Other than working for the petroleum ministry in the Lagos state, he also took bachelor classes for anthropology in the State University. The campus was collaged with an amalgam of creeds and cultures fused together like rosary beads threaded into one collective unison. Life on campus was so easy, like the rest of the fabric of the society; it was multilingual, multiethnic, multicultural and unisexual. Just like every other morning, Dr. Hyder was ready to drive himself in a graphite hued

Cadillac standing humbly right outside his house. The sheen on the bonnet a result of Garba the houseboy's toil since early that day, the splashes of water and soap suds around the glistening automobile a proof of the hard work Garba had been engaged in. It was such a contrast, Garba would often chuckle a deep throated laughter upon the sight of an out of place vehicle in a dusty compound, lined with a vegetable garden that sprouted French beans, okra, bitter gourds, radishes and baby aubergines – courtesy Maryam, the planter and the gardener. Around the fencing of the house she had planted more delicately the romantic hues of petunias, gladioli, hyacinths and marigolds. It was strange she should have an interest in a comparatively commonplace marigold as compared to the seedlings of exotic flowers.

"Arrey Maryam!" a voice would call out every morning in a motherly fashion. It was the voice of Mrs. Needi, a south Indian old lady who would come to pluck the marigolds for her morning pooja.

"Arrey Maryam, what happened to the gulab jamun dough? Did you put more milk powder in it?"

"Yes, didi, but it didn't work," Maryam grinned sheepishly.

"You younger generation, you want everything readymade. You give up too easily. And what did you do with the dough? Threw it away, didn't you. You people have no sanctity for food the gods send to us, do you?"

Mrs. Needi would keep complaining and once the *pallu* of her *sarree* would be full, she would mutter herself out of the compound and sail into the vicinity of her own verandah that was just across the road. That morning, Dr. Khan was jostling with his necktie in his bedroom when Mrs. Needi came in the sitting room to ask how Harris's flu was coming. "Did you give him ginger and honey tea?" "Err. No but he is taking his vitamins and is improving," Maryam knew what was coming.

"You think all your mother did to bring you up was wrong. Of course, we are outdated now. Why should you care what suggestions I make."

Dr. Khan smirked at the grumbling and kept looking into the mirror still fiddling with the strand of silk that he was trying to tie into a perfect knot around his neck. He knew Maryam would be smiling, listening to what Mrs. Needi had to say, helping her out with the flower picking and ask her a problematic question regarding a recipe to make the old woman feel better. He was right. Maryam was indeed smiling. She had a beautiful smile, not like a film star's smile which would reveal a perfect set of whites and melt a man's heart, hers was a girlish smile. She parted her lips to stretch them into a smile only when the joy came from within. Her smile was one for which Hyder had to wait – and savor. The one moment her lips definitely curved up was when he would bend down to take her by surprise in a quick kiss while she would be folding laundry, shining up his shoes or arranging his files one on top of the other in a sequence that had taken her weeks to memorize. She would look at him through her dark eye lashes and stretch her lips to complete a moment of mutuality. She would be pleased he was content with her shoe shining and household capabilities while he would silently glow with satisfaction for her being the compliant wife he had always desired.

Maryam found her meaning of life in extending out her abilities to satisfy her husband in every way possible and her need to love was fulfilled with Harris. She would whisper to her baby suckling at her bosom that he was her Savior. "You have saved me in so many ways," she wanted him to record her words in his subconscious for all times to come. "You have given me my life back, I had lost hold over it," Harris didn't remember the words or the moments when his mother had tried to persuade him to think of himself as a superhero who had helped his mother in times of distress like a young gentleman. What he did remember were the moments when he as toddler and a pre schooler had seen his mother hunched into a corner, bleeding from the corners of her delicate mouth, wiping blood splurging out of a nasal blood vessel or rubbing an ice cube on her cream-and-peaches colored cheeks to tone down the burns his father's hands had caused.

What he did remember were moments when his parents thought of him asleep or considered themselves inaudible behind a locked door and had no idea Harris was watching through the keyhole to see his father throw his Mum onto the bed like a rag doll and from there down to the floor, kick her and pummel her torso with anything that came handy – a phone set, a small lamp at her bedside which kept alight while she slept, his shoes that she had taken so much pains to shine, the trashcan that sat silently by his writing desk, the stapler with which she pinned up his loose papers – he could not wipe out images of the anthropologist tearing off his mother's clothes in an attempt to annihilate and obliterate. The look on his father's face during one of these violent sessions matched with that on the school bully's face who wanted to stomp down on each and every sign of a sandcastle or a mud pie which the children back at school would make during recess after having a rainy morning. There would be no sign of lechery on her husband's face when Maryam saw her ratty pullover tear down right in the middle or when her smug Capri lost touch with her skin. It was supposed to be a mere rip of her being. Harris saw and registered when his mother would plead her husband to not be the man who taught her what the word dishonor meant. Harris heard his father snarl and hiss in a fit of rage and ignore his wife's plea. Harris had had a hard time blocking away the image of his mother's bare torso. He couldn't look at her for days. He remembered the clattering sound his father's roughened, fossil-hunting hands made when they struck across his mother's face; he remembered the sound of the thud which his mother's body made when he thumped her against a wall and brought her down to her knees. He could clearly recall the changing hues of his father's face and the crimson lines or spots that would appear on Maryam's cheeks, jaw line and eyes that would turn blue and black the following morning.

Harris remembered his father had an awful snoring habit. He would hear him snoring after a violent episode in the room which had a joint wall with Harris's bedroom. He would know his mother was awake, sitting in a corner, licking the torn corners of her lips, trying to stop the blood from sticking around her mouth and harden the wound … just like his pet cat Whiskers kept licking its paw when Obiyara had cut its claws too deep. Harris also remembered how his mother managed to hide all the distress of the night before beneath sheaths of makeup when she came to press her swollen lips against his forehead and wake him up for school. She would keep the air light around him, knowing not he had seen her bleed and had dreamt all night of being her superhero. Even this morning, Mrs. Needi's mumbling hadn't stirred him and Maryam woke him up in the usual way. He sat right up and rubbed his fingertips into his eyes. Perched on the bed with night clothes hanging loosely from his thin frame, Harris was staring into the space in front of his eyes while his mother fussed around to clear the clutter from the floor to create walking space from his bed to the bathroom.

"What is a damsel in distress, Mum?"

"Where did you get that, sweetheart?"

"Mrs. Danap told us the story of Hercules yesterday. He was so unpossible, he rescued damsels in distress" his eyes opened wide, revealing the high level of interest that his favorite teacher had managed to invoke in him. The Greek mythology of a half-deity half-man unveiled a spark in his eyes.

"Impossible," she corrected.

"Yes, impossible. Was Hercules alive when you were a kid?"

"No, that was a long long time ago."

"Do you know any other superheroes?"

"No, but I know Cinderella…"

"I don't like girlie tales."

"They are lovely, Harris. Let me tell you one. Okay take your pick and choose from Rapunzel, Belle and Snow White."

"Mum, why are all of these girls sad and boring?

"Are they?" She was taken aback.

"Yes, they are losers until a prince comes to kiss them and take them away."

Maryam twitched her eye brows.

"Are all girls losers until a prince comes to rescue them?"

"No sweetheart. That's just how they make up stories."

"What happens after the prince takes the girl away?"

Maryam smoothed a curl on his forehead, smiled a sad smile, indecisive whether she wanted to weep or laugh, looked into the boy's chocolate brown eyes, the boy who meant the world and beyond to her, who was her Hercules, who, like the mythological Greek god had lifted her world and sky on his shoulders to keep her sanity intact, who being a fetus in her womb had once stopped her from slitting her throat with the hunting dagger in the tools' cabinet.

"They live happily ever after…" she breathed. "That's what the books say, don't they?"

Harris was not impressed. He grimaced, a tiny purse at the lips, a faint scowl apparent around the nose and eyebrows and for a finishing touch, a yawn. At ten, he had learnt about gender specific role assignment a lot more than girls and boys of his age did.

"Come to the dining table and see your father off," Mum said gently as she pouted her lips into one of the innumerable kisses she had blown to him ever since he had come to her.

Maryam left the room to go see if her husband was ready to leave, to see whether he remembered his wallet, sunglasses, reading glasses, carryall which held his papers together and the car key. She had been late since the moment she entered the living room, he was already hurrying out of the verandah to the compound where the Cadillac stood serenely on a puddle of wet crystallized red sand. Garba had hung his head as if he was counting the toes on his feet and a dressed up man was yelling at him for creating patches of mud near the car which could result in a speck or spot on the automobile. "Sorry, Master," the bushman had been psychologically conditioned to apologize for every logical or illogical reprimand. The man in a perfectly knotted silk tie and a corduroy jacket sped away in the car. Harris peered through the white blinds of his room's window and heaved exasperation. He was better off in his room instead of letting his father begin the day.

Harris went to school on foot. He had begged his parents to let him go to the unprivileged government run school near the house instead of the expensive private school twenty kilometers away that his parents had preferred to send him to for the first three years of his scholastic career. The classrooms in the expensive school were more generously dotted with white and yellow faces, urging a mixing up of the urban baturiya with the local Nigerian child, equal in social status. The kids were encouraged to share desks and benches with one belonging to another creed, race and nationality. They would just be Nigerians, sing the national anthem every morning, pledge their faith to the simple looking two toned Nigerian flag, play football or run races, dance to Michael Jackson tunes at parties or farewell meetings, out dance one another after watching Soul Train the other night on national TV. To them, Michael Jackson was more than a hero. He was a bond that helped the urban children of the private school cling together. He was to them a pagan they followed, irrespective of demographics.

Harris had started hero worshipping the afro American icon when he overheard his father chatting up his colleague Jacob Daas, an Indian Christian who was family to the Khans.

"Nelson Mandela patched 'em up with football – the colored and white South Africans," Uncle Daas proclaimed as he reached out for an onion fritter Mum had fried for the guys as they sipped whiskey from regular tumblers. "We have Michael Jackson," Dad drawled in his drowsy voice. Hyder had a thunderous voice, it was gruff when it was calm, it was rowdy when he was loud and it was husky when he was drunk. Harris did not like to look at his father's face when he was tipsy - his eyes that were usually oblivious behind the eye glasses he wore would suddenly pop out of his head, becoming the only features that would be noticeably scary with red mist in them and his eye bags puffier than ever. His mouth would turn down and he would often lose his head.

"In America they say, it was Jazz," Uncle Daas was mixing liquors and humming Bill Whithers. Despite his uncle's soulful voice, Harris had every ounce of his mental juices focused on the chemical process going on in front of his eyes. The honey, maple syrup and balsamic vinegar colored liquids getting mixed together were creating spirits of unknown hues and he could only wait to taste those liquids once uncle would cross the threshold of the house and Dad would go along, unsteady on his feet to see off his drinking buddy. He never got to learn their names anyway, but he had managed to take half a sip of whiskey from Dad's glass once he had gone to see off his friends. It was a stolen moment and a quick one too. He couldn't decide whether he liked it or not since it was bitter but it was a case of stolen mangoes so there was the element of sweetness, the element of have attained level one of manhood. He had sneaked behind the china cupboard and had stayed there as his father and his friends talked of bartenders in Las Vegas, sports, African women with big jubilees and complimenting backsides, the newest Nigerian dream of building a city under sea water. It was a cause of haunted dreams for Harris when he heard for the first time how people were expected to live in a city that would be built underwater. 'What if the ceiling broke and let in all the sea monsters and all the salty water?' Underwater, that jargon was registered in his mind forever. It was scary. It sounded like a threat of boarding school that Mum would use when he refused to eat the bitter gourds in his plate. Harris never explained it to her that her garden vegetable reminded him of the crocodiles he had seen at the governor's house. It was a privileged field trip arranged for the privileged few of the private school, to go see the privileged governor's house that sprawled on several acres of land. It was so big; he had invested in a natural habitat for his deer, zebras, tigers and crocodiles. And it also had a temple, to please the gods. The governor didn't wear a troll like Obi because he afforded to build a whole temple. But then, Obi was poor and he didn't afford to build a temple for his deity. Obi's gods would have to understand and be pleased with the troll alone. At school, there were many like Obi who wore the troll and a few like Harris too, who wore the Imam Zamin.

Finally when Harris's parents had succumbed to his desire of studying in a government school, Harris had found a friend. He found a certain kind of solace in Obiyara. He lived two crossroads away from where Harris had his mansion. Obi was a poor child, as opposed to the rich kids who studied with him, with money in their pockets and secret ambitions to go to Britain or America one day. "Aiee!" a bush land commoner could screech to hear such a plan, the land of the white man? Harris remembered Obiyara's grandfather, a fictional character who wore a white beard on his dark face, his silver hair shone like a skull cap on his head and his yellowing teeth crooked at all the wrong angles, worn out and aged, trying to leave his jawbone given a chance. He had freaked out, given a half minute chide to Obiyara, pounded the soil under his feet with his walking stick – a long sturdy old branch really - right after his beloved grandson had told him he would go to Amhericah to study medicine. "Arewa" he repeatedly said, meaning, here. Here. Harris remembered the way the old man shot glances at him, trying to outwit his grandson by saying the white man had come to live here. Study here. Obi would try to explain to him that the British had gone back to their land and that Britain was very far away from America but the old man was probably too old to learn a new logic. Obi had tried to explain to him by writing a few words on the mud plastered ground with his grandfather's chewing stick with which he cleaned his teeth daily. He wrote COLOR. "This is Amhericahn," he said. "I study this in school," he tried to explain with eyes wide open, hope gleaming inside them. Then he continued, COLOUR. "That is English. I no study English." Not impressed, the old guy had decided to shoot his grandson a bloody glance and turn around to leave. "Wawa," the grandfather ended his argument.

Wawa means stupid.

He switched his looks from Obi to Harris and Harris shuddered. He had never managed to pile together nerves enough to explain to the old man that he was not white, well, not racially at least since the color of his skin would surely defy his claim. He was white skinned but technically he was brown, Asian as well as third world just like the Nigerians. His parents also spoke of a British colonial history back home and took pride in having liberated themselves of the slavery. Harris had wanted to inform Obi's grandpa of the similarities between them but he couldn't. The old guy was tough. And creepy. He was not frightening though.

Not as much as his Dad was to him, at least. He dreaded being near his parents any time his father touched his mother because he knew he would hit him back for his mother's sake. He was too angry, too frustrated and too regressed with his conflict to become a superhero that it was hard to stay put. He desired to shove that anthropologist away from his Mum. His dad called him fidgety – he was always twiddling his knuckles. Even when the flu had allowed him to skip school that day, Harris wasn't going to mop around the house. His breakfast was usual – a bite of the toast, an uneaten puncture in the yolk of the fried egg and a sip of tangerine juice taken to swallow that bit of bread which he did not want to munch at all.

Maryam watched him from the corner of her eye, as he slid off the chair, without saying a word, slipped on his sandals and walked right out the door. It was trend in the Khans' house to not say good bye. It was also impossible for Maryam to not wait up for anyone crossing the threshold of the house. She would busy herself with cooking, dusting, cleaning brand new teapots and scrubbing Hyder's worn out sandals with boot polish. Garba would take care of the cleaning and just before she would expect Harris to be home, she would sail out into her precious garden and talk to the sprouting baby veggies, encouraging them to grow and grow well. Her favorite part of the day was looking after her garden and that was coupled with setting her sight on a tiny image of Harris, from the end of the road that led home. The image would keep growing until he reached her and she would put her hands on his cheeks to tell him every single day, how precious he was to her. That day, Harris was not at school. He had left to explore the woods alone and Maryam had no clue when he would return.

It was evening. Harris had come home just before sunset and had busied himself with school work. With that done, he started on a project he had promised to finish that very day. Hyder Khan was not home that evening. Maryam knew he had to go recce the canyons at the coast of Lagos, the city of their dwelling but she knew it couldn't take up so much time. Khan had considered a telephone set to be useless in the house and had not installed one. Although he had chosen the Central Lagos to be his area of residence, which meant he had a house in the vicinity that housed the Emir's palace, the central mosque and the main market, thus the hub of activity and importance. Hyder was very conscious of the image he carried. He was a baturiya but he wanted to be a respected, honorable baturiya. His house was one he had bought off the market and the main attraction was the fact that it had belonged to some army officer during the colonial period so it had been built with European standards of lifestyle in mind.

Not many houses in Lagos would have a half acre of garden in front of them; neither would they have colonial furniture upholstered to perfection lined up in every room. But Hyder Khan was different. And lucky.

Waiting for him, Maryam sat in the love seat near the huge Italian window that opened into the patio in wait of a screech of tires, a slam of the door or sight of a familiar stranger loosening the perfect knot of his neck tie and letting his chic corduroy jacket hang loosely on his arm. Harris was back after an expedition in the woods. He had come back empty handed for it was not the same without Obi. Cross legged on the kitchen floor, he was busy making a necklace out of metallic bottle tops that were placed on the thread about an inch away from each other and so they jingled quite serenely upon movement. It was supposed to be a present for the donkey that the school gardener brought and tied up in the playing ground every day. The donkey, Mosy, was important to Harris.

"Mum, do you have any more bottle tops?"

Maryam was not listening.

"Mum?"

"Yes, darling?"

"Do you have any more bottle tops?"

"No, they are all I got over the week."

Harris wasn't done with Mosy's embellishment and he wanted more tops. Mum was engrossed in her own handiwork – applying lacquer to a gracefully painted figurine. Usually they would be of idols that the Nigerians worshipped. She never made them bigger than her thumb. It was just not the Nigerian gods that took her fancy; it could be Apollo, Narcissus, Atlas holding a bit of the sky on his hands, Hades the demon of Greek mythologies and ironically the brother of Zeus and sometimes it would be Freya, the goddess of love. Mrs. Needi had almost a collection of Ganesh, Hanuman, Krishna, Rama and Kali that sat silently on her bed side dresser. Maryam had a gift and she wanted to keep it compact. Right now, the small sculpture of Cupid asleep in a motherly palm was what had come to her since Harris had shown faithlessness in commercial notions of love. Harris had been watching her eyes grow intense every time she pinned her sight into the small figure that she gingerly held in her hands. It was a good time to sneak into the larder and pull out a crate of colas. He carefully opened two dozen cola bottles and poured their contents all into the kitchen sink. Mosy had to be adorned. Tooth or nail.

Maryam's eyes were digging into the figurine in her hands, brushing and poking into minute corners of baby Cupid's curls swirling on his forehead or his tiny toes that curved at the most infantile bends with a thin brush so that every millimeter of that tiny fragile statue could be preserved under a sheath of transparent luminous lacquer. She was trying to lose herself and her concern about Hyder into the white cement that she had chiseled up to form the shape of a Greek god.

For ever since Harris remembered, he had never watched his mother sleep. His father was never home before bedtime. Harris had realized something was wrong with his family when the English teacher, Malam Yakubu had told them to write about family activities they did at home. Obi did not have a father, he had died of dysentery. He could not be taken to the nearest hospital for his grandfather did not trust the baturiya doctors. Harris never really had an opportunity to feel Hyder Khan had ever shunned his responsibility of being a father, a beacon at the filial bay to him. To him, fathers were there to get money and work and come home after their kids' bedtime. Malam Yakubu had given him an F for his essay of a hundred words. When Maryam had to see the teacher for that year's scholastic result, she was given the disgraceful composition. She kept it in her journal, folded in an envelope. Harris eyed her the way back home, from the corner of his eyes that changed shades of brown with his thoughts, as his pulse raced. Maryam didn't talk about it, she kept her sight on the road and switched the car radio from the regular station playing Michael Jackson to Lou Reed.

The crooner was singing about heartbreak, a lyrical theme that she did not really enjoy listening to.

Name: Harris Khan
Form: Fourth
Composition: My Family Activities

"*I like to play explorashun with my friend Obi. My mum tells me to do activities with Obi. She likes to listen to Michael Jackson. I broke one string of my guitar yesterday. I want a new one now. Mum says she will fix it. I like the drum more. Obi plays the carimbo drum. Its taller than him so he climbs on a stool to reach it. I love the beat. It is like the thump in my chest. Mum says her heart beats like mine. The drum goes from slow to fast and then it keeps going like my heart.*"

Chapter 2

HARRIS

The ornament had been well lauded by Obi and both of them had gone sneaking around the bushes to the donkey that stood there aloof from the crowd at school. They had put the necklace around its neck and had stood there admiring their contribution to art and nature for a long time.

School was Harris's favorite place. He got to spend time with Obi and the stuff other than studies going on kept him at bay from all the tension back at home. Harris had found many ways to stay away from Maryam and Hyder. He felt hurt and dejected by both his parents. Maryam pretended too much in front of him and despite expressing her love so much to him, she never told him the truth. She always lied about the backache she had or the swelling on her forehead. Why couldn't she trust him? Hyder had himself created a chasm of mistrust between himself and his son, although he didn't know.

Harris had found the filial bonds he coveted in Obiyara. To him, he was more than a friend, he was family. They spent the day at school together and after homework, they both met up at the woods. It was always Obi who walked the distance from his comparatively poorer neighborhood to reach to his buddy. Lagos had lately become a wonderland sort of a place. Things were changing fast and many residents were being pulled out of their homes and the lands that they owned to construct more and more buildings and bridges and leisure parks. While Lagos itself was the hub of all political and economic activity, the two islands that faced one another had a lot going on in them with respect to social uplift and immigration. People from other states who afforded a richer experience of life were pouring into Lagos, particularly with Victoria Island in mind. The other island that was connected to VI, the Lagoon Island was mostly filled with the locales. Lagos was growing upwards but the tycoons and businessmen, they still needed janitors and sweepers in their mansions, the restaurateurs and hoteliers still needed waiters and bellboys and the land reforms could not completely root out the locales from the island of opportunities.

Obi belonged to one such lucky family who had been allowed to live in their bush land without much turbulence. He was the Nigerian kid who had seen Lagos transform in front of his own eyes. He had seen the engineers build the shiny steel fence around the creek that separated the two islands from Lagos, he had seen cranes lift up heavy iron rods to build a bridge over the creek to enjoin the two islands together, he had seen the Atlantic ocean show its might completely to gobble up kilometers of land from the Victoria Island and the Lagos coastal land itself. It was a strange justice of nature – the men of the empire kept taking land from the poor and the ocean kept taking land from the empire. Things had changed favorably for Nigeria but years ago, as a toddler, Obi's favorite toy had been a bicycle tire's tube which he kept rolling with a stick as he walked around the lanes and streets, and even now, his favorite toy was the same tattered tube which he took out every day, took it with him to Harris's place and from there they both went up to the woods to play football or to hunt chameleons.

Harris admired his friend for reasons beyond his age. He had opened eyes in Nigeria. To him, Nigeria was his country, the only place he had seen and been exposed to. To him it was difficult to imagine a country with people of the same color everywhere. Yet, he had experienced his share of racial discrimination, a fair share rather. He had learnt the meaning of baturiya at an early age and had despised that word. He was a Nigerian, why couldn't his classmates see that? Obi had accepted him and had embraced him. He had no problem with the apparent class difference between them. He had no alter ego issues with the apparent difference in the colors of their skins. He understood that there were things that couldn't be altered like socio-demographics and then he understood there were things that could be changed with education. Obi had a progressive mind; he was the kind of Nigerian that made Nigeria stick together.

It was recess when the boys had sneaked off to the remotest corner of the school playground to find Mosy. Like all donkeys, he was lost in some philosophical pondering when the boys showered their admiration at his embellishment – the necklace of bottle tops. This had been Obi's idea. The rationale behind this gesture of sheer kindness was that they both wanted to take a ride on Mosy's back. Obi said his grandfather had told him that animals can easily sense kindness and affection. So, they had decided to give him a gift that no one else ever had given. They had brainstormed hard on this one – it was a brain teaser. What do you give to a donkey? They had made a list of the requirements of the animal and had come down to nothing except grass and water. So they tried hard to imagine what could be special and Obi had thought of adorning it with opulence.

Harris had the artistic thing going on at home so he had taken responsibility to create something nice and durable. Mosy, the protagonist in this scenario was a school gardener's vehicle and had seen very little in the world. Its owner's job required him to move from the government run school's playground to his home every day and back next day. It had not seen many pranksters as these and was quite a simple fellow. While the boys contemplated on who should go and be the first Don Quixote, Mosy, tied by the neck to the nearest tree kept its eyes lowered figuring out some truth about the world. Harris wanted to go first and Obi was amiable. So very tenderly, Harris got ready to climb over Mosy's back and he did, with a little help from his buddy. Mosy had been carrying his master to and fro the school and was well accustomed with the daily route. Sitting on his back meant that it was time to move. Obi had already loosened the noose around the tree trunk and Mosy was ready to take flight. And it did.

With the speed of a mule, Mosy started running on the lane that led to the nearby neighborhood where the gardener lived. At first Harris thought of it as immense fun since his hands were holding the mane on Mosy's neck and back and the air that was going past him was slapping into his face. It was a moment of sheer joy for the boy who had dreamt of going on this exotic quixotic adventure for long. He was laughing a full throated laugh. Obi was running on one side, his stride matching well with the stride of the donkey. They were both looking at the road ahead and would glance at one another; it was a moment of sheer joy in the youthful years of boyhood. Both of them kept laughing with their mouths open, the air entering and leaving their lungs on its own as they cackled their joy out into the air. They both patted Mosy on its belly's sides and that was their mistake. Encouraged by the continuous pats he was receiving as a token of the boys' appreciation, Mosy started to gallop.

Now the scene slightly altered – Obi got left behind and Harris got way ahead perched atop Mosy. The animal had taken speed and Harris clung to it by wrapping his arms around its neck. It was exhilarating, to feel like flying especially when he hadn't expected it. His concern was Obi but that was on a very small proportionate scale. Harris was living a dream and he didn't care at all when or where the donkey might take him.

Marooned, Obi was perplexed at the turn of events. He had tried to follow Harris and had put all his energy and effort into running after him but he had lost sight of the two adventurists. He was worried about having to answer many questions at school and at Harris's home. He knew his friend was a very special being to his mother and he couldn't let anything happen to him.

The donkey had faithfully and obediently done its day's job and had taken its rider home. Home being the place where he knew his water trough was and where his master's wife would have made a fresh bed of straw for it to sleep on. Little did the poor fellow realize that it was still late morning and the trough was empty as it had left it at morning and the straw was yet to be fetched from the market. After all, it had come home earlier than before.

Harris had felt embarrassed and clumsy as Mosy had led him into the grassy compound of the gardener's house. He had climbed down from his imaginary saddle and climbed down from the high horse he had been straddling in his imagination for the past few minutes. In front of him was a brick house. He couldn't see what was inside since the door was ajar just a little but the kitchen which was built outside the rest of the house, having a joint wall with the house and an entrance door which opened into the compound was full of noises. There was something fragrant going on in the pressure cooker that was whistling away, someone was busy doing stuff with the mortar and pestle and the tap was running in the sink. Across the kitchen door, at the other end of the compound was the water trough and that is where Mosy had taken a stop. He looked around and saw a girl of about his age standing in the doorway, looking at him, as if asking, "Where did you land from?"

He kept still, waiting for someone to tell him where he was when the girl ran out of the doorway into the kitchen and a few seconds later a lady appeared from the kitchen. She was round and big and her face was kind but her voice was shrill. She called out, "Hey you, who are you? Haan?" Harris didn't know what to say. It was so embarrassing, he wanted to run away. But something held him and fixed him to the ground he was standing on. The lady reached close and put her hand on his shoulder, "Boy, you lost?"

Yes! That was it! He was lost!

"Where is Mahmud? The donkey bring you here?"

Harris had no idea who the hell Mahmud was.

He managed to gather some gall and said, "I was sitting on the gardener's donkey when it started to run and brought me here," he stuttered a bit.

"You from school?" she had gotten half the story.

"Yes," he said.

"Waayo, you boys. So naughty. No good. Mahmud the gardener, he knows you are on donkey?"

"No," he bleated.

"Okay, now Mahmud, my husband, he come in the afternoon when school closed, but today he come late because you stole his donkey," she was in the middle of the sentence when Harris cut her off.

"Not stolen, I borrowed it."

"You very clever, boy," she laughed a shrill laugh. "I like eet, but you stay here till Mahmud come home, then he take you home. I don't know where ees school, okay?" she was the sort of person you would get to like immediately. She was plump from all four sides and wore two straight lines of henna on her rounded cheeks. Her head dress was a mismatch for the long robe she wore that covered her from her neck to her toes.

Harris looked at her thoughtfully and then looked at the girl who had now appeared in the kitchen's door and was staring at him with a finger in her mouth.

"You Zainab, come and sit with him, see he no make more mischief," she called out to her daughter.

Zainab was obedient although anyone could see she was feeling a bit shy of the baturiya boy. He was a baturiya. And he was a boy. He could be rude to her. She sat down on the steps in front of the main doorway and gestured him to sit too.

Harris followed orders and sat down. The girl was wearing her hair in eight or nine little piggy tailed braids and a robe just like her mother. She looked at him for a while but knew there was a gap between them – she couldn't speak his language and he couldn't speak hers. Well, not so well. Hausa was taught at school but he had changed it for Spanish. So his vocabulary was quite limited. The girl put her chin on her knees and stared at the ground. With the index finger of one hand she was writing something on the ground. Harris had nothing to do and nowhere to look so he followed the patterns she was making. She was writing "yaro" which meant boy. He knew this much so he poked her with a finger and wrote on the ground, "yarina" which meant girl. They both laughed out loud. She wrote, "Zainab" and looked at Harris who in turn traced his name on the ground. She wrote again, "fitina" which meant naughty and he wrote back, "kyau" translated as pretty. She laughed again.

"ka ya sata mahafinisa jaki?" she asked encouraged by his Hausa skills.

Harris knew jaki was donkey but the rest just whooshed past his head. The girl had asked him why he had stolen her father's donkey.

"Um, it's a good donkey, yeah," he tried to sound as if he understood. Zainab's face showed signs of confusion. She didn't understand a word. So he gave it another try.

"ta ye kyau jaki."

She erased the confusion off her face and smiled. He had told her it was a good donkey and that reply made her understand that there were limitations between them so talking was out of question. Suddenly she gestured him to wait for a minute and ran inside. He followed her with his eyes but the curtains on every door blocked his vision. Then a few minutes later, she came out grinning from ear to ear with a polythene bag in her hands. She sat down next to him and opened it gingerly just like one opens a treasure.

He peeped over to see what was in there and gasped at the contents of the bag.

There were marbles. Of every shape and size of every color as well as sheer. She piled up some of them on the ground in front of them and shaped the pile into a triangle. Then she gave him five marbles and kept the same for herself. They started a game of marbles which felt far far better than playing billiard that his Dad had tried to teach him in the VIP lounge of the Lagos Polo Club. Hyder wasn't a rider but he loved to watch polo. He was an exclusive member of the club and he went there often. Sometimes if his friends weren't there to accompany him, he would take Harris. Harris's only attraction there was the horses. Their beautiful discipline and their charm made him admire them. The horses wore their jockeying paraphernalia and stood like gentlemen waiting for their turn and as the match started, they would all look like players and the jockeys became a blurred vision. The adventure he had had in mind for Mosy had a lot to do with the love for horses.

Playing marbles was fun, but the Hausa girl kept beating him. He was enjoying it though. After several friendly matches, Zainab grew tired of winning her own marbles back. She gestured a hopeless sign to him and he smiled sheepishly. Then she thought for a few moments quietly. She said, "kuna jin yunwa?" Harris knew yunwa meant hungry and he thought about it. He wasn't. So he gestured no. She pulled a face and ran into the kitchen. He paid a little heed and realized the whistle of the pressure cooker had subsided, the mortar and pestle were no longer making noises and the kitchen was comparatively quieter but the aromas coming out of there were delicious. The big lady appeared with a plate of rice in her hands.

"Boy, you eat?"

He couldn't say no so he gestured yes and received the plate with a thank you. It was a common household cassava plate, some metallic sort with yellow red and orange patterns painted on it. He noticed Zainab's plate was plainer. She came to sit beside him.

"Eets jollof rice, yes? You eat at home? Your ma cook?" the lady was asking questions rapidly and was expecting answers in the same speed.

He looked down at his plate and saw yellow colored rice with specks of white and tiny dots of paprika visible along with bits of meat. There were some tomatoes and onions to eat raw with it. So he decided to call it a yes. It did look a lot like mum's biryani.

"Yes, thank you very much. I like to eat this," he said politely. The lady smiled and went into the house. It was closing time at the school by now. He ate his food and his mind started wandering and guessing what must have happened to Obi, would Mr. Yakubu have noticed he wasn't there after recess? Would mum be expecting him home any time now and go crazy to find out he was missing from school? Would Dad come home for lunch an hour later and swear to kill him when he found him? Had Obiyara reached the school back safely or had he wandered here and there to look for him? His mind and pulse both raced with the enormity of these thoughts and he kept eating thoughtlessly not knowing or noticing that what was looking like paprika to him was actually African bird's eyes chili and was making his throat burn, his eyes and nose were all pouring water and Zainab was laughing at him.

He stopped eating and stared at her. She offered him a glass of water and he dunked it down his throat all in one go. Then he ran a few paces ahead where outside the kitchen there was a tap which he turned and washed his face and eyes several times with the water.

"me ke faruwa?" the lady heard the splashing and called from inside, asking what was wrong.

"Chili ma zafe!" the girl answered back, zafe means too much.

The lady came out.

"na ka?"

"No, ga yaro," Zainab replied when her mother asked if the chili had been too hot for her too.

They both looked at each other and shared a laugh. Poor baturiya boy.

Harris felt embarrassed and started at his plate of jollof rice again. This time he took smaller bites and small intervals too. He was still wagging his tongue out in the end but it was all win win. His insides were replenished. The girl cleared the plates and went in the kitchen. Harris had a very happy meal. It was not like his dining tabled lunch like every day, there weren't any utensils, not even a spoon to eat but it had been lovely to share a meal with a friend.

He took out his hand and asked, "aboki?" he needed a confirmation of their being friends.

The girl took the hand shyly, shook it and said, "aboki," so they were officially friends.

CHAPTER 3

MARYAM

Maryam had been waiting for Harris for almost an hour now. The walk from the school was no more than fifteen minutes and that was a calculation she had made having kept in mind Harris's inquisitive, curious nature which would make him stop every five or ten steps to bend down and look at some marvel of nature otherwise easily ignored by others.

She loved the memory of him having brought a couple of snails back home one rainy day. He had tried to keep them as pets but the poor fellows were so scared of the glass bowl he put them into that they wouldn't come out of their shells for quite a few days! Maryam had had a hard time persuading him to let them go for some things weren't just meant to be.

"If it is not happy with you, would you keep a stranglehold on it?" she had asked him gently.

"Why doesn't it like me?" he sulked as Harris was experiencing the first blow at his ego.

"Maybe because you are two very very different beings. Maybe because the snail finds its comfort in someone else and your goodness, your charm and all of you, does not fit his moulds of liking," Maryam had trailed off the subject, talking about something that had been bothering her for years instead of pampering her boy's ego whose feelings had just been rejected by the snails.

He had let them go after Maryam finished her monologue, but she kept wondering whether he knew what she had talked about or not. She spoke very little; there was no one to talk to anyway. Garba, with his broken English and Magana with her little crush on Hyder, were her two permanent pawns of socializing. Hyder had an image to carry and having his wife going places and running about town was not good for the image he had managed to carve out for himself in all these years. Those things mattered to him – his image, his status, what he wore, where he socialized.

Harris unlike his father had found his roots in the earthy, warm culture of Nigeria. The pompous environs of a private school hadn't suited him so Harris had begged his parents to allow him to go to the government school and they had agreed. After all, Hyder himself was educated in such a school and had made it from the bottom up to where he was. He expected Harris to do the same as well. Every afternoon, Harris reached home around quarter of an hour after the closing time but today it was almost an hour. The lunch that was waiting for him at the table was cold as stone by now. She had made him lasagna today; it was his favorite sort of pasta. The casserole dish that had come bubbling and sizzling out of the oven topped with four types of cheeses, fragrant with the aromas of rosemary and thyme, had turned into a shriveled up dried patchy layer of skin. She was worried. There was no phone in the house with which she could call the school office. She shook the anxiety as much as she could but her breaking point came as the clock struck three. Hyder not coming home for lunch was frequent but Harris was late for the first time. Her world had gone crazy like the top spinning in her head giving her all sorts of terrorizing ideas about what might have gone wrong. She almost cursed herself for letting Garba go earlier than usual since the chores were all done. He had, like always asked for her leave, "Madam, I go now?" and she had, as usual replied in affirmative because Garba did not have to be reminded of any assignment. He remembered Tuesdays and Saturdays were laundry days, Wednesdays and Sundays were ironing days, and he dusted the furniture, mopped the floors, cleaned the kitchen and washed the Cadillac every day. Just like he had done today. Even if Garba was at home, she would have sent him to check or at least taken him along. She grabbed the door keys that hung silently beside the main door and dashed out of the house. She had no idea what way the school was but it was no hard thing; she could ask anyone on the way.

She ran past a local guy and stopped to ask for directions. He wasn't too sure but the community school was just a couple blocks away, he responded, she thanked him and moved on. She ran across the woods where Obi and Harris played every day, she passed the community mosque from where men were dropping out after saying their afternoon prayers, she crossed the residential block and the building of flats that was situated just ahead of the school. The gate was opened, a big signboard read, "Model Secondary School, Lagos". She entered the gate and saw the faces of many children, black, white, brown, yellow – she looked at all of them but the face she was searching for wasn't among them. She asked the custodian staff if they had seen Harris, but none of them gave her an affirmative.

"Haven't seen him at recess too, Madam," they were all sure.

Did that mean he had been missing since morning? Maryam couldn't take it anymore and the anxiety that had been giving her heart somersaults for long finally gave in and she had to sit on the ground, her nerves collapsed. She was crying and asking questions to the air all in one go. Someone tried to be helpful and brought Obi from the classroom to the lady that was weeping and creating a scene, the baturiya lady in her sweatpants and sweatshirt, her hair long and brown but very plain, her eyes pouring hard, her mouth swollen. The lady that was the focus of attention of every parent and child at school at present. The lady who never showed a tear when her body was bruised with kicks and her face was swollen with black and blue marks. The lady that smiled for her son even when her lip was torn and her tooth was loose. That lady had broken down. Obi came to her and greeted her; he bowed to her with his feet, stomach and chin on the ground, the traditional way to greet one's parents in his tribe. The baturiya lady cupped his face and asked him where Harris was. Her hiccupping stopped upon seeing his face. He sat up crossed leg and told the whole story. There was a buzz in the crowd.

"Foolish boys," someone mumbled and walked away.

"He will return," a mother patted on her shoulder and tugged at her daughter's hand to move away.

"I asked the gardener if his donkey had returned, but he replied in negative," he added. She asked Obi to take him on the route.

"Mrs. Khan, I was left behind," he said, his eyes puffed up. He had obviously been crying in the classroom, praying to his gods for Harris's return.

"Take me to the last spot where you were with him," she said standing up. Her tears had stopped falling and she wiped the ones standing adamantly on her cheeks.

So they started walking. He took her to the point where he had fallen down and Mosy had galloped away. She walked the road on which the donkey had sped off as per Obiyara's observation. There were houses on the route and good looking houses, nothing like a house a gardener would own. She walked on and the road split into three directions, ahead, left and right.

"Mrs. Khan, we don't know which path to take," Obi was the sound of reason.

She knew she didn't know the way. She was herself like a zoo animal out on the loose, she was out of a cage and didn't know where to go but she had to find her son. She looked at Obi, put both her hands on his shoulders and told him to go home.

"But I can't," tears welled up in his eyes again.

"Obi, you don't want your mother to end up on the roads looking for you, do you?"

He dropped his head and walked back to school.

She said a silent prayer in her heart and took the road that led to the left. It was a residential block. The same as the one she had already been walking. Things weren't encouraging. At the end of the road was a small three storied plaza with shops and small offices. She went back to take the right path. It was a good one hour since she had left home. She thought of Hyder and wished him close; he would help her to find him. The right path looked very different as it was populated with government offices, a kindergarten school and the local veterinary clinic. She was wearied. She decided to go back home and tell Hyder what had gone wrong, he would find their son. She ran. There were children walking back from school, women carrying handbags, all going back home, all of them were startled by the woman who was running on the roads, madly.

She could have gone home on a shorter route but since going to school and then back from it was the only route familiar to her, she made a detour. Upon reaching the school, she saw Obi standing outside the gate looking around, as if he was searching for someone. She went up to him and asked him why he hadn't gone home.

"I won't go without seeing him," Obi replied. The hoarseness in his voice told her that he was obdurate this time. She sighed. She wanted to see her precious son too. She was full with emotion at the moment. Her only reason to live, her son was lost, her husband wasn't close to her and she knew he would wipe her tears and bring her son back if he was here, she felt so helpless, alone and unfortunate. She hid her face in her hands and prayed for her son to return. Her trance was broken by a loud shout from within the school, hoping for the best and dreading the worst, Obi ran inside. Maryam was reluctant. She didn't want to excite herself with a shout from a crowd of children. She took baby steps; after all, she had to reach home to tell Hyder about the situation. In a moment, she saw Obi beaming and pulling something with his left hand. The right one was being used to wave out at her, she lunged forward to see what he was pulling and what his object of amusement was and to the sooth of her nerves and heartbeat she saw Harris.

She ran, her face broke into a smile and her eyes had tears falling down. The reunion was beyond words, she had him cuddled, she covered his face with kisses, much to the embarrassment of a ten year old boy who would be teased as 'baby' and 'mama's boy' many days after. She thanked Obi, gave him a kiss as a prize and he grinned. She looked at him, if he was hurt but he seemed fine.

"I am okay, Mum, let's go," he was getting super conscious of the stares he was getting.

Someone patted his head, someone yelled, attaboy. They started walking back home. She was so relieved and listened to his adventurous story on the way home. She promised to bake a cake and a pie for the gardener who had brought him back to school. She hugged her dearest son several times and when they both turned the corner of the road that would lead them home, she saw the grey Cadillac standing in its place, gleaming from the long distance. She was so happy she hadn't lost their son and could proudly give the father his son.

"Just give him a hug when you see him," Maryam was preparing him for a big welcome.

"Does he know?" he asked nervously.

"Not yet, but when he will, he will grab you and love you," she smiled and ruffled his hair with her hand.

Harris never looked forward to see his father. Just a casual hi was fine. He couldn't answer his questions accurately and he didn't enjoy talking to him either. The mother son duo walked the rest of the walk silently. As she reached close, she saw Hyder sitting on the porch.

He saw them and his face turned red and twisted.

"Where the hell have you been?" he growled.

"Oh Hyder, Harris was lost today, I went to school to look for him," she started.

"Lost? What do you mean lost? He is very much here isn't he? I have been sitting here like an idiot for the past hour and a half and here you come loitering about as if it were a joke to you," he was roaring by now and it wasn't even his drinking time yet.

"Hyder, I was worried, he didn't return for an hour," she tried again, weakly.

"He is a boy for God's sakes! Let him grow up and stop treating him like a baby. I have been wondering where the hell you have gone sitting on the steps of my own house just because madam had a whim to go running around town in skimpy dressing," his eyes were ablaze, his voice loud enough for the neighbors to hear.

He doesn't care, she thought silently but couldn't help gaping her eyes wide open in surprise.

"And the lamest excuse for a wife that you are, you cannot manage a house even. What have I asked of you? To keep put in that house and you cannot even manage to put a damn hide-a-key somewhere near?" he was storming away.

But there is a key under the periwinkle plant, she thought silently. I told you when I put it there. She had lost voice.

"Now get your ass inside or will you keep inviting stares standing here?"

Am I the one who is inviting stares? She looked down at Harris who was looking up at her. His eyes apologized. There were tears welling up in them. He was so desperate to go inside that the brief moment between the mother-son seemed to agitate him and he held the boy from the nape of his neck and pushed him in. She was pained! She knew how hard those hands were, she had never touched her boy except for cuddling him and that man's hands roughening him in front of her eyes tore her being to bits. She protested with her eyes, couldn't say a word but the pain in her heart spread across her face. She looked at her husband is disbelief, dismay and displeasure. He banged the door shut and shoved her in. Her face that had been questioning his hitting her little boy turned red and the grip of his hands on her upper arm would leave a mark. Harris ran to his room and shut the door. He was scared, hurt and angered. He wanted to break a thing or two. Maryam had seen him run.

"Lunch?" she asked like a loyal servant. She never gave him the pleasure of thinking he had hurt her. She knew it maddened him more but the more beatings he meted out to her, the more stoic she became.

"The hell with lunch," he grunted, went in the bathroom, slammed the door and one could hear the shower running.

Harris had gone straight into his room and had flopped down on the bed. He wanted to cry out loud but he couldn't. He let the tears flow quietly. He heard the door open a bit and knew it was Maryam.

"Mum, I told you I ate with Zainab, now I am sleepy," he said with his eyes fixed on the ceiling.

Maryam came in silently, she wanted to cuddle him, take him in her lap and tell him how sorry she was, she wanted to kiss his face, cup it in her hands and promise him his father would never touch him again. Instead, she left and softly shut his door. She knew her son was disturbed with this atmosphere at home. She was ashamed of it and she was up to her nose with it. She just wanted Harris to enjoy the affection of a father just like she had. Although Hyder was far far behind Dr. Ahmar in grace and in character. Dr Ahmar being Maryam's father, dead for half a decade now. Hyder came out of the shower, dressed casually in a tee and jeans and stormed out of the house just like he had thundered his way in. She saw the Cadillac speed away as if it were a fire engine. Like most days, Maryam sat down at the dining table, stared at the dishes for half an hour and then cleared the table. She was used to being alone but she couldn't get used to dine alone. Her heart ached for her son.

Despite her strength, she couldn't cover the quaver in her voice. Garba looked up and said, "God is with you, Madam," and he silently left. The words rang in her ears for hours afterwards, hours that she sat like a statue on the same dining chair, her head crannied in the hook of her arm, buried deep in the cushion of her elbow, her sweatshirt doing a great job of absorbing all the moisture that she doled out of her eyes. She was re thinking her decision of stop taking Hyder as a husband and to work on him as a project. Any woman would leave him, discard him and divorce him for the way he treated her but she thought of her rootless self and looked back at her life – if there was family there was Hyder alone, if there was love in her life it was Hyder, if there was a father to her son, it was Hyder. She found herself tied up with so much baggage that taking the spiritual way was the only one left. She wanted to change him, she was an optimist, she was an artist, she saw beauty in everything, she had faith in kismet, she believed in fate, she believed in the good he had in him and wanted to bring that out, she wanted to show him so much stoicism, so much forgiveness, so much strength of the marital bond she shared with him that he would crack his hard shell and become the man she had fallen in love with. She ignored the scent of roses on his collar every night he stayed out of town, saying it was a meeting out of Lagos or something else. Sometimes, he didn't even have to tell her anything because he would find one excuse or the other to yell at her, storm the house and leave like a hurricane so as to avoid any questions. On such days Maryam was left with having to do nothing but sit and carve sculptures. She did it to kill time but she also did it because that is what she had studied for, that was her passion and also because that was the only thing that had attracted Hyder to her and her to him when they had met up. He was a finder and digger of sculptures and she was a creator. Their interests were both so intertwined. They had met in Lahore, in her father's house at the state University's campus where her father, a botanist had invited two young men at home to discuss with them the ancient Missouri Pincushion Cactus, which had been thought of as extinct but some group of anthropology students in Canada had discovered one of its kind growing in a valley in Nunavut, bearing the harshest cold climate known to human population living near the arctic.

Dr. Ahmar had a routine of sitting out on the front yard of his humble abode every day. It was a huge expanse of a house but with miniscule architectural frills. The part of the lawn he sat in on the cane-woven chair, was placed diagonally at the rear end of the grassy plot and around him was a flurry of potted plants – plants of all shapes and sizes in earthen pots of all shapes and sizes were available there, almost giving his surroundings the look of a hothouse or as the locales would dub it, a plant nursery.

"Pull out the weeds around the primrose shrubbery and put in some manure," his constant suggestions would keep flowing from the vagabond's corner in which he had perched his chair while lifting his eyes up from some glossy book he held in his hands, tilting his chin a little bit down to get a view of the gardener's actions from above the rim of his reading glasses.

"And plant the petunias in place of the dog rose," he would go back to the glistening pages of his botany book. The gardener neither nodded nor shook his head and kept trudging forth with a shovel in hand. His lack of communication did not bother the professor at all since he knew his words were being taken seriously and followed religiously. The gardener would speak only if he needed money or a leave. Head bowed, his wrapper which was really a three yard long piece of cloth tied around the navel to hang loose till the ankles (a dhoti) was scrunched up between his loins and his kurta, the long white starched shirt was allowed to mingle with the soil beneath his feet. A moment after the other he would take off the loosely tied turban off his head and wipe his brow, and then roost it back up in its place.

This was a routine day. On special occasions, Dr. Ahmar as his friends and students called him, would have guests to show around his collection of fauna and flora in the front and back yards of his government maintained house as well as the bottled miniatures that rested on window sills or hung from air vents in the walls indoors. Dr. Ahmar was a professor of botany at the state university and lived in an on-campus residence. Since the rooms were in plentitude and the beings in his family shrunk to a mere number of two, he had decided to give most of the space in his house to the first infatuation of his life – plants. In the evening, Dr. Ahmar's students especially those who had their origins in foreign towns and villages and were boarding at the university's on-campus hostel, they would come to see their teacher and relate the latest gossip doing the rounds of the campus or even the headlines on the evening paper that was cheaper to buy from the hostel canteen. The canteen was more than a place to eat. It was a place of gossip, of sharing personal lives over a cup of kashmiri tea that had been simmered on a slow and steady flame to release the earthy aroma and maroon color of the dried up shriveled leaves into the boiling water. The leaves that would appear dead and stale in a metallic tin would instantly come to life and start swimming around the boiling water until at last, the cook would add cold water to the maroonish liquid and turn the color even darker. The chemistry of the process would be beyond comprehension but as a few pods of cardamom would be thrown into the mix and a ladle full of rich full fat milk added to it, the tea would boast of a pinkish hue and thus the cook would be satisfied, that his toil at managing to get the absolute blush for the rich contents to be poured in a cheap earthenware teacup has not gone in vain. At a mere two rupees the tea would be enjoyed with a pinch of salt or a teaspoon of sugar or both.

Back at Dr Ahmar's home, the young men would not be served with the Kashmiri delicacy but a chilled bottle of Pakola would always be ready at hand. It was mimicry of Coca Cola but it was green in color the bottle a shade of bottle-green and it vaguely tasted of vanilla, hence the description of the soft drink as ice-cream soda.

Dr Ahmar was a naturist. His pagan was nature and the versatility of it. His gardener was a Christian, his house maid was a eunuch, his best friends were Sikhs and his wife had been an Afghan. Diversity should have been his middle name. Pakola was just a safe hit – coca cola was a drink of the infidels as per the moral police on campus and Dr Ahmar was too engrossed with his green housing theory to get bothered by the issues of infidel drinks and otherwise.

Dr Ahmar had very few interests in life – plants, books and his beloved daughter. The rest of his time was taken up by his socializing activities which mainly comprised of young men or students instead of his own peers. That fateful evening, his daughter had come to join him for his evening tea in the front yard and watch the gardener toil away lovingly with the soil and the manure on a hot summer day when the university had been shut down for the winter vacation. The on-campus boarders had gone back to their native hometowns and the university campus was quieter than usual. Other than the early morning buzz of the truck that arrived to collect flowers from the botanical garden of the university and supply them to flower shops around the city or the tinkling of some teenager's bicycle who would be running an errand for his mother by visiting the on campus farms to buy a kilogram of tomatoes or a half kilo of potatoes, there really wasn't much audible.

The day Maryam had met Hyder for the first time was something she could not flame out from her cherished memories. It was a day in December. The winters are not very cold in December in Lahore. It's just pleasant enough to miss the otherwise boiling sun that keeps glaring eight months out of twelve. The professor was sitting in his usual diagonal angle, reading a book about cacti – his latest obsession. The climate of Lahore was not suited for the plant but he was adamant to find a way to grow the cacti locally. And not just any cacti, he wanted to have the difficult and rare ones – the rarest kind and most precious too. He was lost in the poorly Xeroxed copies of the literature he had received via the sole fax machine in the registrar's office and the cloud of steam rising from his glossy white mug has dispersed into thin air, leaving behind a murky colored skin on top of the pool of tea that kept still in its container – unattended, untouched.

Maryam, swinging her childhood swing on his right side had clenched her mug of tea with both hands after emptying the vessel and looked around satisfactorily at her world – her father who was best left undisturbed while lost in a book, her house that was in the midst of paradise somewhere... punctuated with nature at every footstep and the insides of her house that were littered with her painting canvases, intimations of Greek statues and sculptures, the vagueness, the imperfection somehow attracted her. Books that belonged to both the book lovers and a very stingy number of old fashioned furniture dotting the house. Dr Ahmar's cane woven chair and Maryam's swing too were decades old but since they served the purpose loyally, they were part of the house.

Maryam had practically been brought up by her father – a recluse by nature but a humongous romantic. He recited out poetry aloud for his wife while she sat knitting or listening to classical folk music on the radio. He wrote her love letters when she would go back to the North West Frontier Province clamped up with Afghans from across the border. Maryam was never too keen to go see her maternal family – she would stay back with her Dad and draw I-love-you cards for mother to be sent along her father's blossoming flowery letters to her mother. Maryam became totally dependent on her father after her mother passed away in her youth, leaving Maryam to be an only child - a child that was pruned with care and showered with love. She had lost interest in the conventional subjects taught at college and had diverted to painting and sculpting alone.

While Maryam lived a life of contentment, swinging on her childhood swing, holding a warm cuppa in her hands, destiny had decided to let her tread on a path yet unknown to her, a pathway of dreams, of love and of realities unexpected. The mug in her hand was empty, the gardener had done his day's work, Dad was still engrossed in his book and two figures that had been seeming like images out of a black-n-white English movie from a distance, had come closer enough for her to curl her brow together to wonder whether the two guys were actually headed her way. One of them was pointing towards their house's direction while the other looked skeptically ahead and then threw down his head on his chest for the briefest of moments, pulled at his necktie and touched the brim of his hat. He wore a pair of spectacles and there was something about him that immediately took the fancy of the young girl who had kept her eyes fixed on one of the young men who kept minimalising the distance between her abode and his oozing charm. Once they entered the garden that had been tended as an infant, Dr. Ahmar looked up from above the rim of his glasses, immediately recognized the two and stood up, greeted them like old friends though they were the same age as Maryam. One that had been given no importance by Maryam's artistic eyes was introducing the one who had sparked an interest.

"Hyder Khan, he has just completed his doctorate in anthropology from Toronto and has come back to Pakistan," the unimportant man spoke and the young lady settled in a corner watched and listened. Hyder took off his hat for the botanist and admired him for his research papers published far and wide in Canada about the heritage and metamorphosis of soil in South East Asia. He spoke in a way Maryam had never known before – his eyes affixed, his voice gruff, his hands firm in the pockets of his trousers and his jaw straight, his words carefully picked and his facial expressions text-book perfect with everything the botanist was saying in response to his admiration. Maryam at that moment had quite forgotten herself and had not realized she was staring at a man.

"I apologize for being such an inconvenience, but could I have a cup of tea, please sir?"

The man back from Canada had definitely learnt his social etiquette well while he was abroad but had not forgotten the social necessity to win new friends over a cup of simmering hot tea in a contrast to the coffee-culture grown popular across Canada. He had had enough of his Second Cups and Tim Horton's for the past two years that he was in Toronto and back at home, he wanted to enjoy just the age old tea.

The professor laughed at the candidness and assured him it was no big deal.

Maryam, rather self conscious upon being addressed indirectly, walked inside, clutching her mug in both her hands as a toddler would clutch at her teddy bear upon the arrival of some unknown stranger making her nervous. There was something about him that made her forget herself, made her heart race and set her mind in a whirl. Whatever it was, it was mistaken for something spiritual, something long lasting, something life threatening. That evening ended at an early note when the cup of tea was sipped down and a few small packages of cacti saplings and dried samples were handed over to the botanist who received them with much joy and asked his benefactor to frequent his visits to him as long as he was staying in Pakistan.

"That would be kind, eh, Professor? Since I am about to leave for Africa for some research in a couple of months, having found a new friend in you would be a solace to my otherwise lonely being," Hyder Khan shook the old man's hand and walked away.

Maryam couldn't sleep that night. The shining armor of a prince charming in her head had somehow transformed into a Savile Row suit and a brimmed hat, the Anthropologist had suddenly taken the place of her favourite sculpture the Thinker in her subconscious and she had for no apparent reason begun to think what life could be like beyond this campus. She thought of foreign lands, of the snow capped peaks and gushing falls in Canada and the African desert lands and deep forests she had read about. Her brightly hued contentment faded into a bleakly dull realization that she had spent her entire life in the same vicinity of one city. Maryam felt vulnerable and lonely in one night. She wept for no reason and nursed her heart that ached for reasons unknown. She thought of the dark stranger and his chiseled face and in the dark of the night, lying in her bed, she felt her own facial features with the tip of her fingers just like a sculptor would feel up his model – the lines of her lashes, the curve of her nose, the corners of her lips, the hollow of her cheeks – all of it seemed faulty. She curled into a ball and imagined talking to a man whose voice could slither down her hearing organs to her heart and tickle her flesh with tantalizing tics. The night was unendingly long. Maryam didn't know that this was just the first of many such nights.

And days.

What she didn't know was that the new spark of interest in her being was enflamed much higher and intense in Hyder himself. She had maddened him up. Hyder Khan had gone back that night to his rented out room in the midst of the liveliest neighborhood in all of Lahore - Anarkali.

The neighborhood, famous for its name, was christened after a Mogul courtesan who had made the grave error of falling in love with a crown prince. Legend had it, the courtesan, for committing such an act of blasphemy, was made an example out of and was buried alive. Anarkali in Lahore, was as twisted as the braid of a dancing courtesan, as glossy as her tinkering anklets, as titillating and enticing as the rise and fall of the courtesan's heaving bosom – it attracted men and women alike for shopping in its bazaars, haggling at its footpath-stalls, eating out at its various eateries named after the cook instead of the food item of sale – phajja for the trotter soup, Feeka for the tea stall, Achha for the rice pudding known as kheer. Anarkali never slept, it kept welcoming people throughout the evening and at night.

It was justly named Anarkali; she wouldn't turn away her loyalists. At morning however, the streets seemed to sleep. Other than the sounds of a vendor selling daily vegetables piled neatly in a wicker basket fixed firmly on the back holder of his bicycle, a strange serenity would prevail. Or the sheer silence would be broken by the punctual milkman who would just ring the ding-a-ling-ling of his bicycle in front of every door behind which his customer would be awaiting her perfect measure of milk. Sometimes it would be a silent commotion of cell phones beeping as two lovers would exchange text messages or multi-media messages with the guy standing below the girl's window and the girl peeping cautiously from behind the cheap curtains of the jharoka, trying not to get the attention of any other person.

By late afternoon, the screeching of a rickshaw, driving back home a couple of kids from the neighborhood could break the sounds of silence and the rattle of marbles being played by the wearied pupils in the corner of the street. Daytime Anarkali was nothing like the nighttime Anarkali and those who knew life as a Lahori would, loved the latter facet of their favorite mistress – the one that she revealed once the sun had set and the bling was put up in every nook and cranny of her being, every part of her presence glowed and glistened and she would welcome all to her court, tease them, appease them and once she had worked her charm, most would walk away satisfied but with a vow to come again.

Hyder Khan, upon reaching his room in Anarkali, changed his attire and transformed from the urban foreign-returned baboo to a kurta clad desi. He wanted to fill up his insides and his walk from his room took him to a falooda shop glistening with sequins, tinsels and artwork. The blocks of pure milk ice cream; full fat, creamy and rich; topped up with rice vermicelli, chopped almonds and given a final bath of chilled condensed milk gave the customers a delight that no other dessert could. Hyder Khan found himself smacking his lips in the midst of his love affair with the silver bowl that he held in his hands while sitting at the cheap plastic table and chair the Falooda shop owner had gracefully arranged in a line alongside the pavement. Nobody gave a damn really, that the pavement was being used for business than as public property. Nobody uses the pavements in downtown Lahore for walking anyway.

The bowl full of falooda couldn't block away the images of the girl he had just seen. He had seen his score of girls, of course, but the girl, petite and svelte, with a creamy complexion, don a white tights that showed off the curves of her calves perfectly, her honey colored silk shirt with sleeves covering her delicate being right up to her wrists and her collar bone was a shade too much in conformity with her creamy complexion, her eyes wide open in askance and the bangs around her face flowing gently around her face, forming a frame around her oval facial structure were all parts of his comfort at the present moment. Her flowy flowery sash dropped just from the shoulder down on her arm and her embarrassed drop of eyelashes in a hurry to put it back in place were all sources of his discomfort. Like Anarkali's visitors, Khan too had made a vow to go see her again and find out what was troubling him so much.

He did go back to see the old man, to chat him up and also to catch a glimpse of the girl who had put his nerves into a twist. Sometimes she would appear for a moment and then not be seen for the couple of hours that he would keep sitting with Dr. Ahmar, waiting for her to show face. Between the garden and the indoors, she would have chosen a spot for her sculpting, which she usually did with ceramic cement. So he would be sitting in the garden, talking of rare plants and fossils he had come across and also noticing how delicate the girl's wrists were and how beautifully her fingers moved, curled and curved in the most noticeable positions. He had dared walk up to her one day, leaving Dr Ahmar with some photographs he had taken at Nunavut with the Pincushion cactus growing wild.

"May I ask who this is?" he had been the politest person she had spoken to.

"It's the Thinker, by Rodin," she replied.

"Is this plaster that you are using?" he touched the surface that was still wet but it kept its smoothness and didn't imprint any fingerprints.

"Um, yeah," she knew the original casting of the Thinker was in bronze but her medium was plaster.

"That's interesting," he looked around it, she had worked her way from the bottom up and the lower half of the statue was complete and she was working on his arms now.

"You are doing it backwards?" he spoke with an air of admiration.

"Doesn't really matter either way," she shrugged. To her, it was no big deal.

"Rodin was French, wasn't he?"

"Yes, he was and I am fan of his," she replied.

"Are you? That's interesting. So the Thinker, what does it mean to you?"

Maryam could have given him a long answer, the origin of Dante's Divine Comedy and Rodin's expression of interest in creating different scenes from the epic poem, Thinker being one representative of Dante himself, perched atop the commotion going on in the gates of Hell and watching with his chin on hand. Some thought the sculpture was a reflection of Adam and some thought it was Rodin himself. She chose to give a simpler reply.

"It's a reflection of anyone in solitude," she rubbed her hands on a small towel that hung on the edge of her easel.

His eyes squeezed and his head tilted to one side. He was slightly amused. "Do you have your moments in solitude?" he probed.

Yes, and I think of you, in the same pose, she thought silently.

"Who doesn't?" she chose her words carefully.

"And what are your thoughts in solitude?"

She stared at him blankly, she had already replied to that question, only he hadn't heard it. She had no idea how loud her eyes were talking, the flicker of her lashes, the quivering of her lips and the words on her tongue that weren't allowed to escape the slit of her mouth, they had all reached to him. He was reading her, while she had chosen to keep as silent as a closed book; he had stood there with his eyes piercing reading every tiny show of emotion on her face, noticing how hard she was trying to keep her secret disclosed.

His eyes softened and he looked back at the Thinker.

"I mustn't keep you from your work. It's an assignment, isn't it?" he let her go from his gaze. It was almost as sudden and cold as letting a dance partner fall on the ground instead of catching her when she leans back putting all her weight in the air.

She breathed reprieve and just nodded, her eyes shut.

That day before he left, he didn't just suffice to glance at Maryam, he waved a bye to her and put out a thumb to wish her luck, to which she had smiled and nodded. This was only one of many discussions they had had about the noted sculptures and statues in art. His favorite were the enormous Buddha idols, the standing, sitting, reclining Buddha those that were placed on mountain tops, whom you could see from afar but only have his blessing when one would climb hundreds of steps in Thailand, Sri Lanka and Japan. They shared a lot as his visits became frequent and Dr. Ahmar didn't seem to mind. Hyder was a gentleman. He did want to know although about the certain twinkle in her eyes when she saw the gentleman every time. Also, the smiles she would be smiling the day he would have been there and the sadness in her eyes when it would be a few days since his visit. The professor's observation was not just limited to plants. Maryam was his most protected, most cherished flower and he knew every jostle of thought going inside of her.

"This young man, Hyder, is a fine fellow," he started the conversation one day as they both sat in the TV room, watching news bulletins and sipping cocoa on the floral patterned couch.

She just looked up at her Dad, who hadn't taken his eyes off the screen.

"Isn't he?" he prompted.

"Um, yeah, sure. He likes you a lot," she tried to sound as casual as possible, her heart beating like the loudest of drums one could imagine.

"Well, I would say, I think he likes *you* a lot," he put his cup down on the coffee table that was right next to the sofa. Maryam forgot to blink her eyes. He knew? She gulped.

"Question is," Dr Ahmar continued, "do you like him too?"

Maryam was flabbergasted. She shuffled in her seat and fidgeted with her hair and cracked a few knuckles on her fingers.

"I see," the professor chuckled.

Maryam couldn't help but blush fiercely, the cheeks that were already cream and peaches went aflame. She picked up a cushion from behind her back and buried her face into it. Dr. Ahmar smiled and continued to watch TV.

"I like him, Maryam; it's just that he doesn't seem to be an affectionate man. He seems tied up in his own world," Dr. Ahmar commented.

Maryam lifted her head out of the cushion and stared at the ground thoughtfully.

"He seems to be one who has either lost a lot in his past or has suffered a lot. In either case, he is running after one thing and trying to run away from the other," he picked up his cup of cocoa and started sipping again.

"Dad," she spoke after a long lapse, "I think he needs his life to change."

"And he wants you to be that change?"

"I don't know. He hasn't spoken to me like that but he talks of going to foreign lands, Africa. He has been to Canada; he told me he wanted to be a pirate once. It all shouts out one thing to me, he wants to create a new life," she spoke eloquently.

"Yeah, and he would want a partner to start life anew," he said rather slowly.

"If you don't like him," she started and was stopped in mid sentence by a wave of Dr Ahmar's hand.

"It's not that, my child. I don't know him too well. Apart from his scholastic credentials and his brainy disposition, of course. But then again, if I would try to know any man as a match to you, I am afraid I would never find any, I would never find anyone as good." He smiled sadly; Maryam saw the hint of tears in his eyes. Her heart broke. "It better be the one you like," he said.

"It would be better that way," he conclusively repeated the sentence as if to convince himself more than her.

The next time Dr Hyder came to see the professor, Dr. Ahmar was sitting in his usual chair in the usual corner of his garden when the suited guy from Canada made one of his various visits a month later. It was during one of these many friendly meetings between the two men that the stranger who had soaked every bit of the young girl's heart in love, drenched it in emotion and had set it on fire with passion had proposed to her during a stroll in her father's garden where she would later marry him. She was never the one for a pompous show on a wedding. She wanted a quiet affair, in her father's house, with a few loved ones and the one she had vowed to love forever and to live forever with. She drove off with him in a rented car to his rented apartment in the middle of the old city.

"It's not going to be like this forever, you know," he was clearly embarrassed by the vacant room that offered nothing but a mattress thrown on the floor with a cheap cotton spread to cover it, a black and white television placed on the floor with a perfect tilt to face the mattress and a wooden chair. "My old room was better furnished but it would have been really small for both of us. It's just a few months before we go abroad you know." The apartment had two floors but with only one room on each floor. The top floor was frighteningly empty and voice echoed if one even whispered in it.

"The room upstairs is a bit eerie, I will arrange for some potted plants in there to make it alive," the young bride commented to her newly wedded husband. "But your room is okay," she finished her comment and looked around at the empty walls where some color of paintings could be added. Her artistic designing was interrupted by a touch of two hands on either side of her waist from behind, someone pulling her closer and whispering into her neck, "You mean our room," it was the voice of the man who had pulled her heartstrings as soon as she had heard him speak. It was dark outside already and a soft musical voice was being played in some tea shop or house with the gentle lyrics entering their humble abode with a certain musicality that charged up ions in the air around them. The atmosphere offered perfect condiments to let souls enjoin as they are meant to and as achingly waited by two persons deeply in love with each other.

It was a good three months that they had stayed there until it was time to fly to Nigeria. He had helped her to pack, there wasn't much really, except for two travel bags, their life really awaited them in Nigeria. Once there, Hyder was given his coveted post at the ministry of petroleum and the state university had come a few months later. He was very proud of having found a wife and took her along every social gathering amongst the expatriates, be it a dinner, a one-dish party at the community center, Eid celebrations at the Muslims' homes or Deewali at the Hindus' or Christmas at the Christians'.

Within days, his pride seemed to evaporate. He became more uneasy in her presence and every time before leaving the house he would tell her to keep the conversation as little as possible. She was very very conscious of her speech, her looks, her clothes, her accent, her level of information. She was conscious of the image he had, how important it was for him to create an impression upon others, how hungry he was to outshine others in conversation, jokes, information and style. Every time someone tried to speak to her, she would try to respond as intelligently as she could but Hyder would cut in saying, "She cannot speak English very well," and carry on with the rest of the conversation. Sometimes the men would tell Hyder how lucky he was to have found a gem and had brought her out in the rough and he would say, "She is herself from quite a rough land," and laugh with them over the smart jokes he could crack.

At Mrs. Matthews' dinner table on Christmas, when they were given a serving of five cheese ravioli, he had not looked at how well she was managing and had instead called out to Mrs. Matthews in the kitchen to please bring a spoon for his wife since she couldn't manage a fork and knife. Back at home he would gently shove her in an abyss of invisibility and the doom of failure, hold her hand in his and tell her how much she still had to learn to be a good wife, how much she still needed to do to win his love as a husband. At first, she believed him, knowing he was the guy who could love her the most. She tried to please him but his need was of turning her into a mere shadow where she herself would not be recognizable but merely regarded as a shade of him.

She sometimes fought hard with herself to keep her self-respect and her sanity intact but more than often he made it impossible. Then she started to understand the pattern – he would degrade her whenever someone else was present there. Be it the community center, his friend's house or their own living room. He made sure no one could think any good of her. He started to shrink in size for her. He wasn't that prince in shining armor. He was quite plain. He was insecure to the last limits of that word. She understood but she decided to work on it. On him, on her, and more importantly, on them.

It was the third month in Nigeria when he had taken her to the annual dinner at his university. That was the last date of the after-marriage courtship. The women were all glossed up, the liberal ones in haute couture, the conservative in long gowns. She had carefully picked a cream colored dress that covered her from shoulder to toes, it was not form fitted and had a lace frill that hung loose from the hem of her neckline. She looked beautiful – almost like a Greek goddess. Hyder had worn a dark suit paired with a white shirt with a silvery grey cravat, the same shade as his eyes. He looked stunning, too. They both looked together like a couple out of Hollywood's black and white films. She smiled at him when they were in the car, hoping to squeeze out a compliment from him and all he said was, "Isn't your lipstick too loud?" she had shamefully rubbed off the scarlet color that was so becoming with her attire and just left behind traces of the reddish hue, enough to make her acceptable amongst the dressed-to-kill ladies at the university. Once they reached, he introduced her to his female colleagues who would flirt endlessly with him in her presence and he would retort back in the same boyish manner, he would tell them how beautiful they looked in those mini dresses and how well the glossy tint in their hair looked. When they would leave he would whisper quietly to her, "It's the culture here, we have to blend in," his words rang aloud on her audibility. "We?" she had dared to question. For months, she had been a sponge, absorbing everything he was telling her... she was working her way up backwards just the way she did her sculptures; she wanted to gather enough information before asking questions or retorting. She had found her moment and had dared to ask, "WE are not blending in, Hyder. You won't even let me breathe." She was flustered but her tone was calm. His eyes showed amazement, he hadn't known she had a voice. He hadn't known she had a brain that could register things. The color had drained from his face and he had managed to choke out a smile when Samuel Daas had come over to them, asking them how the food was at the state university's annual dinner. They had both smiled although both had lost appetite. That night as they drove home, he was silent. Maryam knew she had upset him and planned to make up to him when they reached home. When they entered the bedroom, she had planned to throw her arms around him and follow the cliché formula of kiss and makeup. She was waiting for him to turn around after loosening his tie in the mirror, the moment he did, her eyes got ready to greet him and her arms were in mid air to go around his neck when she felt something hard strike against her face on the right cheek. Before she could understand what had happened, the same force got her on the left and the slapping went on both sides one after the other until she had lost count. The last number she remembered was eleven. By the time it stopped, she saw him standing above her, his legs apart and her in the middle lying in a curve on her side, he was spitting abuse at her, and he called

her an ungrateful bitch and kicked her bottom with his
boot repeatedly. He left the room, slammed the door and
began to watch some TV in the living room. She lay there
for a long time, thinking what had happened and she was
surprised to realize that she had just been beaten by her
husband. She had entered the dreaded company of many
women whom she had pitied all her life, she had become
a woman who was treated like crap by the only man she
had loved and had saved herself for, her dreams built over a
lifetime of chastity were brought down to a crumble.

She wasn't crying, her eyes had dried out with disbelief.
The glare of the TV shone through the slit of the door, the
voice of the newscaster filled up the room. After several
minutes, she managed to get up but her walk was crooked,
his kicks had torn her muscle and she couldn't stand up
straight. She hobbled down to the bathroom when she
heard the bedroom's door open and close, the beep of the
air conditioner as it was turned on and someone flopping
down on the bed. She was standing over the sink, her hands
holding the rim of the basin for support. When the silent
commotion in the bedroom ended, she looked up in the
mirror and saw her eyes puffed up and one of them was
wearing the black and blue shiner like that of a beaten up
boxer. She touched her face gingerly but her skin burnt.
She ran her index finger's pad around the boxer's mark and
couldn't feel a thing from the numbness. Her eyes were
small from the puffiness and that is when she let go of the
tears welling up inside her swollen eyes. Her eyes smarted,
it hurt to cry. She tried to stop crying but the salty water
was adamant.

As she sat at the dining table that day when she had almost lost her son, his indifference had reminded the pain of his first slap. The bruises, torn skin, the black and blue marks, the pain, the burning sensation, and the sting – it was all forgotten, it was all unimportant. What she hadn't been able to erase from her mind was the disbelief of him being that sort of man. She felt her love draining away, she felt the respect she had for him and the admiration wither away. But it didn't happen after one beating. The tower of dreams was demolished bit by bit; the land of love was cracked up inch by inch. Every time he hit her, she found strength in herself. A year after she had arrived in Lagos, and a few months after her face had been treated like a punching bag, she missed a cycle. It was great news to her. She wanted to tell him in the best possible way, hoping the news she would give him would soften him, make her loveable to him. She baked a cake, took it to his study and cleared her throat.

"Whatever this thing is, take it away, I don't have time for it," he had glanced up from top of the rim of his spectacles.

Her heart did a flip flop but she still gave it a try.

"I am pregnant, Hyder," she said and his eyes shot up.

"You are pregnant? Well, isn't that just great?" he jumped on his feet, hugged her and kissed her cheeks. She felt so warm and so thankful inside, her eyes gave out on her.

"Don't spoil the moment, come here," he took her by the arm and made her sit on the footrest of the reading armchair in his study. He himself bent down to look into her eyes,

"You need to take care of yourself, you are not just one being anymore… you are carrying my child, okay?"

That was an interesting angle for Maryam. It was *his* child that was in *her* womb. And she was a baby bag.

"It's our child, Hyder and we will love him endlessly," she put her hand on his cheek and corrected him gently. He nodded. Her hopes had come true, his behaviour did change a bit and breathing in the same room with him became easier. One day Maryam was in her garden, tending to the vegetables when she heard him calling from inside. She was seven months pregnant and hers was a big baby, moving and especially walking was getting difficult every day. She was big with the baby and walked with her hand below her bump to support. She was going indoors to see what he wanted when he came out in the doorway, his face ablaze. He saw her and pulled her inside, something she couldn't bear and let out a whimper. He shut the door behind her and with his thumb and index finger, he pulled at her earlobe, he used all his force on that delicate sag of skin and pulled it like he wanted to rip it off. "Can't you hear me, are you deaf? I have yelled a hundred times, where the hell have you been?" she couldn't say anything since the weight he was putting on tugging her earlobe was intolerable and had tilted her to one side.

She took hold of his wrist and shoved it away from herself saying in anguish, "Hyder, stop hurting me!"

Her words made him a little startled and his hold loosened, that's when she pulled away from him.

"You measly whore, how dare you push me?" he hissed between his teeth and to establish his manhood, he pushed her back. The big balloon that she had become lately, she lost balance easily and fell on the ground. His push had sent her straight on the floor, she fell on her back. She howled in pain as the baby inside her squirmed with pain, the baby squiggled and wriggled inside her and she wept, screamed, consoled it, ran her fingers across her belly all at once. Hyder saw the scene, grunted in dismay and left her. Many minutes later, after she had lost all hope of him coming to help her get up, she managed to sit up, she pulled the dining chair that was lying at about two feet away, and she held its seat for support and got up. She walked very painful half a dozen of steps to the couch in the living room and sat. The baby was kicking and disturbed. She lifted up her shirt and started to give a dry massage to her stomach. She sang a song from her childhood in whispers and tried to soothe the baby. Tears kept falling from her eyes and water dropped from her nose but she kept singing. Her ear had hurt for weeks at a stretch. Hyder got out of his study an hour later, dressed and walked out. That night she slept on the couch. Not because she was waiting up for him, but because she couldn't move her back stiff from the fall. She wished her father was there. But he had gone.

Dr Ahmar had died five years after her marriage. She was in Nigeria. The people at the university had tried to create some contact with her the day but in any case, the burial was done without even her getting a phone call from any one. The time some family friends made contact with Hyder through a telegram, it had been a fortnight since his burial. He gave her the news with a heavy heart. Maryam had mourned for a long time. She didn't give up on her home or

Hyder or Harris though. She just couldn't speak or smile or stop thinking about her father who was her entire family, her dearest friend. And with him under six feet of soil, she felt a part of herself die. His letters were a great deal of support to her wounded heart. She never disclosed her pain to him, she couldn't bear the thought of him grieving over her heartbreak. Whenever her strength to deal with Hyder's temper and his tantrums was withering away, she would think of happy days back in her father's garden and the thoughts gave her hope. She had sworn to herself, the day Hyder would take her to Pakistan to visit her Dad, she would never, ever, come back. The thoughts of the garden and the solemn swear too diminished with the news of death and she realised, she had signed up for a lifetime in Hell.

She was again sitting on the same couch which had taken her in when her back was stiff from the fall in pregnancy. Tonight after Hyder had sped away in his beloved Cadillac after shoving her for insubordinate behaviour and Harris for getting lost, she was neither nursing any wounds nor was she waiting up for him, but these memories all came haunting back. She had forgiven him all the times he had hurt her, he had stripped her to hit her skin and not her layer of clothing, he had ripped her esteem and respect but she couldn't let that happen to her son. He had touched him harshly today and her soul was ablaze with anger – part on him and part on herself for putting up with so much violence. She couldn't let whatever had happened to her, happen to Harris.

Chapter 4

HYDER

Hyder was driving across central Lagos towards the outskirts where the residences weren't too expensive. He wasn't sure what he was most angry about. He was upset that Maryam had left the house without asking for his permission. He was also upset that he had to wait at the doorstep for over an hour but most of all he was upset that Maryam had not apologised to him. She was forgetting her place and needed to be pushed back. He was the man in the house and he needed her to be treating him like God, taking punishments silently and thanking him for everything she had – her life, the air she breathed, the minuscule portions of food she ate, the bed she slept on. To him Maryam's most extraordinary quality as a young girl when he had met her was the characteristic of listening. She listened to him quietly as he spoke of his ventures and his knowledge, her eyes widening at the newest information and her lips stretching into a smile at the funny incidents. He hadn't wanted a wife to share his life with, he had wanted someone to wait on him, someone to throw herself at him, someone to mould, deform and rebuild like a sculpture. He had wanted a statue. She had fitted the description perfectly but her voice, her words, her briefest questions that left him speechless, they had turned things around. She had stopped throwing herself at him, she had stopped taking invitations for a carnal relationship from him, she never went in the room if Hyder was awake. She would dust the furniture at eleven at night and clean the sparkling kitchen counters after that and wait until the lights were put out.

The disinterest maddened him. He couldn't understand why a girl like Vikki, fifteen years younger with the looks of a supermodel was ready to throw herself at his feet, show him love so relentlessly and guilelessly and the woman who he clothed and fed had no interest in him. This anger tossed and turned in him until some drunken evening, he would see his friend, Samuel Daas, trash talk his wife and the relationship of marriage and force himself onto her. She who couldn't scream or fight back for fear of waking her son would have to succumb. As much as she hated herself for it, she was scared of him. How, how, she questioned herself, could she love him even now? How? Is love supposed to be headless, mindless, blind, deaf and dumb? Well, dumb it is, she answered herself. Her being was rotten from the core with pain, anguish, despise and a wounded self respect. But she stilled couldn't help staring when he wore a white shirt that suited him with elegance, she couldn't help cooking the cuisine he would prefer even if Harris would disagree at the table, she couldn't help wishing and praying that her sombre patience and endurance would one day change Hyder and some day his shirts would stop smelling of that rose scented perfume.

Hyder, although was unaware of what went on inside her heart and mind. All he knew was that she didn't want him. His ego would flare up and inflate in his drunken mind but in the morning, her face would spit cold hatred at him and things would go to square one once again. Why didn't she need a man in her life? She was young. Did she have a lover? He had kept tabs on that mental idea as well. He had dropped at home at odd times, sent Garba on a month long vacation and left her alone on weekdays and weekends and Christmas holidays but no one came and she never left the premises of his house. So that was out of question. His mind boggled. He could not come to any conclusion.

Driving in the fast lane, these thoughts were again coming to him. He was driving on the freeway, the road which would lead him to Vikki. It was not Friday, the day Vikki was supposed to meet him every week but he had decided to see her. He had tried calling her up at her flat in Central Lagos but it had gone unanswered. He was not sure whether she would be home or not or maybe have company that could ruin his image that he was so conscious about. The events of the day had grown a lot of hatred and anger in him and he wanted a soothing evening. It was almost five in the afternoon when he reached the flats and parked his car around the block to not be noticed. He walked his way up the stairs that led him to the fourth floor. He had been here a few times but only to pick her up and take her to VI. Today, he planned to just stay with her for a while.

He recognized the door he had rapped on so many times in the past and read her name written with a marker on the door – Victoria Jonathan. The door had opened when he knocked at it and she was there.

"Hey," she was startled.

He came inside and shut the door with his foot behind him and grabbed her to an embrace. She laughed at the spontaneity but hugged him back, her arms closing perfectly around his shoulders and his around her waist. They were in love. All notions of being the other woman in a married man's life came to a dead halt when they were together. They seemed so right for each other, they could say so much to each other with a gesture, a look or a smile that words wouldn't do. He inched away and put his hands on her shoulders.

"Can I stay here for a while?" he asked her.

"Do you need to ask, Hyder? Come, it's not fancy but its home," she tugged at his arm and pulled him to sit on a couch. The apartment was smallish, with one bedroom, a bath and a small kitchen that opened into the sitting room. A window opened into a small balcony that overlooked the street. The sitting room was furnished modestly, it was almost barebones with a TV set and a couch in front of it, a dresser with many candles on it, all of them the same size and black in colour, it looked as if someone burnt them all at once and blew them out all at once.

On the floor of the sitting room just between the TV and the couch, a star was painted with black. A five pointed star on a tiled white floor was in plain sight. He just looked around him and paid attention to the skinny girl who had put her head on his chest, had curled into a small kitten with feet tucked under her legs and arms wrapped around her beloved.

"What were you doing before I came?"

"Ah nothing, just watching some news, nothing's on really," she drawled.

"Hmm, I can see that," he said, reaching out for the remote controller.

"What brought you here?"

"You," he said without looking at her, flipping the channels.

She smiled. Straightened up and sat back.

"Doesn't your wife ever ask you where you have been when you spend hours with me?"

"Can we not talk about my miserable married life? I came here to escape it," he was sulking.

"Aww my baby, don't worry, we will make you a happy baby in no time," she joked.

"You got anything to eat?"

She chuckled, "You mean other than cereal boxes? I think not, but I can manage a quick suya," she said thoughtfully.

"Okay, I will help," he said getting up from the couch.

"Great," she led him to the kitchenette.

The beef chunks were taken out of the tiny freezer she had and dumped in a wok with spices and salt. Hyder chopped up some veggies and they too were popped in after half an hour during which Vikki had put some rice in the rice cooker to be boiled until fluffed up.

It was a meal they both enjoyed on the couch with bottles of beer she produced from the fridge. They tuned on a movie the network was playing – some Indiana Jones. They laughed at the same lines and spent a good two hours watching the age old classic. As the movie ended, Hyder stretched like a huge mountain cat and Vikki watched him, she wasn't sure what he wanted.

"Think I should go now," he said looking at his watch, it was around nine and the drive would make it a good half hour more before he would reach home.

"Okay," she breathed as she came forward to kiss him the cheek. He got up and walked towards the bath. It was a very small bath but very dutifully kept. There was a dried flowers and spices bouquet on the toilet's tank, a couple of towels folded on the edge of the small bath tub with bottles lined up with the same sort of liquid. It was some oily thing and the bottles weren't marked either. He got curious and opened to smell the liquid and in a flash he was transported to the land of roses. It was rose oil, the mystery was finally solved. She did actually fill up her pores with the sweet scented oil. He smiled to himself and while washing his hands, he noticed the same star he had seen on the living room floor painted on the mirror. As he stood back, the star was enveloping his reflection's face. There was something different about the star. He didn't know what but it was not like the star he used to get in his notebooks back at school upon doing well in a class test. He didn't give it much thought and left.

Vikki had given him a peck on his mouth, he just needed some pampering tonight, she knew. He wasn't in a mood to romance the woman he loved and Vikki knew his mood swings quite well. To him Vikki wasn't a mistress; she was a woman with whom he could be himself without any pressures on his mind or soul. She didn't ask for more than he gave her, she didn't expect him to give up anything for her sake and she loved him and showed it shamelessly. It was the first time he had landed at her apartment and was pleased to have found her home.

It was his inherent desire to make a comparison between the two women in his life, one who had been shut up in his house for the past ten years and wasn't supposed to go out except in his own company and there was the other woman who didn't have the same moral compulsion to wait up on him and entertain him on her sofa with a bowl of sticky rice and suya yet she did. Hyder was still stuck on to the spoon-fed humble meals his mother made for him. To him the only form of woman acceptable in his life would be someone like Nisreen. A woman who raised her children on her own, who never questioned him of his whereabouts, what he studied or who his friends were. A woman who couldn't read, write or ask for her rights.

CHAPTER 5

VIKKI

As soon as Hyder had left, Vikki had gone into her room and undressed for a bath. She filled the tub and poured the rose oil from one of the bottles. She climbed in the tub, rested her head on the edge of it with a carefully folded towel under her neck, closed her eyes and let the water do its magic. To her, it was a ritual, to dip herself in rose water each night before going to bed. Tonight she had been expecting a few guests, not Hyder but some others who were frequent late night visitors. She was still expecting company. Vikki wanted to empty her head from all sorts of thoughts as the prime motive behind this daily ritual was to relax. But she couldn't stop thinking about Hyder.

The question she often used to ask herself was, where was she going with all of this? However pure her feelings were for Hyder, and however burning was the passion he had for her, the truth would always be biting, she was the other woman, she was the home wrecker. She wondered what would happen if his wife ever found out. She never even had a glimpse of his wife, she didn't know whether she had ever run across her at the super mart or at the ladies club. She had no idea how meagre the relationship was between Hyder and his wife. Of course she hadn't tasted his beatings and didn't quite understand how on earth could a woman not respond to the amount of drive and passion a man like Hyder had, how could a woman not be happy with the opulence he had to offer in both ways – monetarily and in terms of social status. She bothered herself often trying to riddle herself out why Hyder, if so unhappy with his marriage, would continue with it. She had asked him the same question a few times but he had winced about having a son who couldn't live without his mother, he had claimed of being a pitiful man who couldn't throw a woman out on the streets knowing she had no family and no friends in her surroundings. "She wouldn't be able to survive here and to whom shall she go back in Pakistan? Her father had died five years ago," he would run his finger across her cheekbones while patiently answering her questions.

Most of the talking they used to do right after they had made love. It was usually at the apartment Hyder had rented out at the suburban area of Victoria Island. "Someday you would buy me this island too, wont you Harry?" she joked, it was a coincidence, her name and the island's, were the same. "If that's what you want," he would joke back.

Vikki had a load on her heart. She often thought she was the reason Hyder was so distanced from his wife. She believed her level of companionship with Hyder, whom she lovingly called Harry, had a lot to do with the disinterest he had in Maryam. Despite all her noble thoughts, she was unable to separate from him. She loved him with every fibre of her being. He was that forbidden fruit of the garden of pleasure that made him so covetable to her. Her relationship was wrong with him on so many levels.

One. He was baturiya.

Two. He was married.

Three. He was her teacher.

Four. He was fifteen years older.

It was hard to ignore all of these stinging truths about her relationship. Yet, as they say, it was complicated and Hyder never bothered about these things so she could live with a lump of guilt on her heart as long as her love was accepted and responded to. It seemed impossible to her in the beginning, when Harry was teaching her at the university, a classroom of twelve students, five of them girls and the rest guys. Hyder would look at her while lecturing but something pulled his stare away. It was disturbing, since she, like many other of his female students had a crush on him. It had taken her many weeks to muster up the courage to go up to him and say something but the moment she had chosen to just pass on a friendly remark, say something about his looks or the lecture he had just delivered, she had somehow broken all barriers and had come down with emotion, she had squeezed his hand and guided it to the curve of her throat where her heart beat like it would explode. It was as if some electric current had passed from his hands to hers and if she wouldn't take him to the depths of her emotion, the peril of walking up to him would go waste.

She had scurried down the corridor after making her first verbal and physical contact with him and it was the last time she ever had to hold back. Vikki was a passionate woman whose expression of love knew no bounds. She would caress him and run her fingers through his hair as he would lie down with head in her lap, she would listen to him when he talked of coral reefs found under water near Lagos or the canyons that were being unearthed underwater near the Lagos seashore, kissed him and caressed him when he needed attention and pampering, she let him be silent when he didn't want to talk and she let him rant when the politics, the traffic or his wife would become too harsh to bear. She knew her strength against Maryam was the fact that she made him feel like a winner all the time. She never held back, be it love or lust. When she was with him, both seemed to be one and the same anyway.

It had been half an hour since she had been soaking in the sweet scented rose water and it was almost time for her to rise. She dressed in her night gown and wore her favourite neckpiece – the huge metallic triangle with an eye in between. The eye touched all three sides of the triangle and was very similar to the eye that was painted on the urn that stood silently in the corner with a pharaoh standing sideways but his eye looking straight out of the urn. She was half prepared and curled up on the sofa like a little kitten waiting for the guests to arrive. They had to be here before midnight and it was already eleven o clock. She got up to light all the candles on the dresser and opened the door to the balcony. The night was still and stuffy. The moon was not going to be visible till tomorrow so the candles were a perfect condiment to the darkness of the night. She started doing a little shuffling of the minimalistic furniture in the living room. She pushed the small table on which she had shared a meal with Hyder a little time ago, she shoved it into a corner and thus left the place in front of the couch bare. The star painted on the floor was obvious now and more prominent. She picked up the candle stand from the dresser and placed it right in the middle of the five pointed star. She sat down on one of the triangles, cross legged, closed her eyes and began to meditate. Thoughts ransacked her brain. She had been through the exercise a lot of times till that day but every time it was as challenging as the first time. To empty her brain. How was that possible? Her thoughts chased after Hyder and his wife and his son. She squeezed her eyes hard, shook her head several times and restarted. Okay it was better than before. Her focus shifted to the pain her fingernails were causing to the palm of her hands since she had squeezed them tightly in a bid to focus, she released her grip and exhaled, accidentally opened her eyes and shut them back hurriedly.

After a few trials and errors, she was there. The place where there was nothing. Her brain had managed to turn off her conscious switches and had left her in the remote corner of her brain which was devoid of anything but herself. It was like staring into space with not a flicker of light visible to the naked eye. Then she heard a sound. A distant peal of laughter of a small girl. She couldn't see her but the sound of her giggles and cackles was so clear and crisp as if she was sitting next to her. A smile spread across her face. She heard footsteps, small footsteps of the little girl running across dried grass and heavier ones following her. She consciously allowed her subconscious to visualise the person with the heavy footsteps. The brain took the command and she saw a heavyset woman, in a Yoruba dress, blue and yellow flowers on her clothes, wearing a bright grass green head dress. She sprang open her eyes. Her breathing was heavy and the churn in her stomach made her feel sick. This was the seventh time her soul searching had taken her to her mother. Although what she wanted was a peep into her future with the help of the eye symbol she wore religiously – and not a glimpse into her past. She sighed. "What a waste of time," she muttered.

A few minutes later, the doorbell rang. It was almost half past eleven now. She rose and opened the door for the guests she had been waiting for. They were two guys and two girls. All of them seemed to know one another well. One of them was a more familiar face, it was Nuoko, the tall guy from her class. He was the only one who bent forward and gave her an embrace which she returned. The other guests were all part of the gang. There was Sarah the doctor, Evelyn the waitress and Joseph the assistant engineer working at the VI coast. It was hard to think how these people had all become one group but somehow they were. Nuoko produced a bottle filled with wine coloured liquid and asked her if all was set. She indicated and all of them took positions on the floor, each one of them sat on the corners of the star, around the candles that burnt away silently in similarity with the silence outside. They all seemed to meditate with their eyes closed for about ten minutes when Nuoko said, "now," and they all stretched out their hands to their sides and held each other's hands.

"We swear upon the darkness in the north that we stay loyal to the most powerful infernal force in existence; that we are Satan, one that bends our hearts and minds to the path that the flesh desires. We swear upon the darkness in the south that all that the heart desires is not man's vileness but is man's nature; that we are Satan. We swear upon the light in the world that there is no good without evil, no good without bad, no light without dark; that we are Satan." They had all chanted in one voice, holding hands and closed eyes, bowed heads. Then Nuoko had gotten up with the bottle in his hand, unscrewed the cap and poured a little thin drizzle on top of Evelyn since she sat at the downwards pointing triangle of the star and she was the starting point of this session. The drizzle went on gently from her head to her outstretched arm, her hand with which she had firmly held Sarah's hand to Sarah's arm and her head, thus the drizzle continued on until it reached a circle having covered Evelyn, Sarah, Joseph and Vikki. Nuoko was left, he sat in his place and poured the remaining contents on his arms and head as well, put down the bottle and held his hands with Joseph and Vikki on his either side. They sat there for a while and then opened their hands. Nuoko produced a small dagger, a very tiny one, almost the size of his index finger. The handle of the dagger was shaped in a triangle instead of the cross-like shape usually daggers have. He started the ritual with himself and cut a small slit on the palm of his right hand and then on his left hand. A small trickle of blood appeared from both the cuts. He handed the dagger over to Vikki who also carefully inserted the dagger vertically into the midst of her palms and the dagger was passed on, the loyalists continued with the pattern until all of them joined hands to become one entity. They stayed like that for quite a few minutes. They blew out the candles, one after the other, Vikki put the tip of her tongue to the wine coloured thick and warm liquid Nuoko had just poured on her arms and hands to make an additional circle to the circle of human hands they had already formed.

"Goat?" Vikki asked.

"Lamb." Nuoko replied.

They all chatted up each other, the candles were blown out and the lights turned on, Vikki proposed a round of beer which was readily accepted. They all kept their floored seats and outstretched their legs, holding their bottles of beer, Nuoko being the alpha male as usual and Joseph, the stout assistant engineer smiling at the jokes Nuoko shared with the ladies. Minutes after midnight, the guests started to leave one by one. Nuoko was the last one to leave.

"Any success?" he asked her.

"It will take time," she said.

He shook his head. "He is a big fish," he said, "could be helpful."

"I am not going to rush him or force him," she said flatly.

He bent down to plant a kiss on her cheek, walked out the door, turned around as if he remembered something and said, "Is it real between you two?"

"As real as can be," her voice exuded pride.

He smiled and walked down the corridor that would lead him out of the building.

CHAPTER 6

HYDER

It was a weekend. The beach was spotted with people. Most of them black but not necessarily locales. There were tourists, holiday makers, honeymooners, gangs of friends and couples. There were loners too but as legend would have it, once at VI, they all would see a happy ending when the night came to its pinnacle. The sea was quiet that night in a deep contrast to its environs – music exploding from the beach bars, six or seven shack like structures in a row with very little distance in between, so much so that the open air customers of two adjacent bars could easily mingle with one another. One was exclusive for the expatriates and white flesh shone through the happy beach shirts and skimpy swimwear of the gents and ladies alike. There were blondes and brunettes, some wearing red hair and some ebony black. Some danced with glasses in their hands and some just danced. Some smoked for ecstasy and some just smoked. The exteriors were decorated with Christmassy lights and the interiors glowed with a nightclub fever.

Away from the baturiya-exclusive bar, at an equally robust and lively bar, Steven's, at the end of the road the ladies had ironed the afros to a straight smooth silky tuft of hair on their heads, they wore glistening leather on their bodies and high heels on their feet. The men were equally stylish as they wrapped their arms snugly around their ladies in hats, Levis jeans and FCUK tees. No one could look lesser in opulence for they represented the urban Nigeria. Or to be more accurate, they represented the classiest uptown in Nigeria – the Victoria Island in Lagos. Victoria Island or just VI as it was lovingly called, was the jewel of Nigeria as it stood apart from Lagos at one end since a creek separated it from its motherland and at the same time, a thin strip of land joined it with another island Lagoon which was less populated and didn't share the glow and shine of VI. On the south of VI was the Atlantic Ocean with all its might and glory.

The ocean broke its waves at the coastline of VI and the party doers didn't notice. One man sipping his whiskey from a tumbler sitting at the far end deckchair of Steven's noticed the waves. He watched them move from a couple of kilometres away and the gush they made as they reached the coastline made him smile every time they landed at his feet. From where he was sitting, he could not decipher the words of the lyrics that were blaring out of the hifi system at

Steven's. Neither did the cheers of the crowd really perturb him. He wasn't there for the waves. He wanted to party alright, but he was waiting for someone. He had driven all the way from central Lagos to VI just for the person he was waiting for. He lit a fag and exhaled a loop of smoke.

His legs outstretched ahead of him spoke of elegance. His hand stitched animal skin boots were unfit for a beach however classy he may have wanted to look, his silk socks spoke for themselves and his pure white silk shirt atop the grey striped trousers were not a good choice for either coming to a bar or to a beach. His look on his face was soft – his eyes steely and gray just as his hair that was swept up by the coastal wind, his complexion fair as much as mistakable for being a European, his mouth was full and the skin on his lips was moist and had a hue of pink in it. The slim bar of tobacco in between his lips that parted every time he inhaled and exhaled smoke, made him look like an actor posing for the camera shot taken for a TV ad or something like that. The person he was waiting for must be worth dressing up for.

This was not new to Hyder – the bar, the beach, the wait, the dress-up or the night that was young and inviting. This was his weekly excursion to meet up the woman he had found too late in his life but still loved her endlessly to the smallest bit of his being.

She had a scent. He hadn't really figured until late whether it was perfume or mist but she smelled of roses. Especially as she embraced him his clothes would have that linger-on aroma of roses for the rest of the day. She must either bath in that perfume or it must ooze out of her pores for all of her bare parts – the arms, the legs, the shoulders on which her tops or dresses were hung by two spaghetti straps, her hair and the back of her neck where her black skin was soft, all gave out the scent. He could feel it as he thought about it and a smile ran across his lips. She was here.

"Hello," she called from behind.

He laughed the gentlest of laughs.

"Sir?" she called out again to tease and he had to look back.

She was there. In her totality of being the woman he loved and could never tire of. She seemed to be new each time he had her, each time she left her whiff on him. He was smiling and so was she, don in a flame red dress that fell from her shoulders leaving them bare down to her knees, flirting coquettishly with his eyes as the breeze kept sweeping and swinging the hem of her dress, allowing teasing glances at her coffee coloured shins. He stood there taking it all in watching her walk her walk, come to him and give him the embrace which would leave that scent on his shirt that was so easily familiar to Maryam as she did his laundry.

"Not too long?" she asked sweetly.

"Is always worth it," he smiled back, taking his stuff from the table beside his deck and they both got ready to leave.

"You brought the keys. Didn't you?" he asked.

"If I didn't, would you punish me, Sir?"

They shared a laugh. Her hair glistened in the nightlights around the bar. At the peaks they always shone and they still were.

They walked down the beach, his arm encircling the back of her shoulders and her hands holding her clutch. Both of them would just glance at each other, smile and keep walking towards Hyder's car that would take them to his apartment which he shared with Vikki. Anyone could see they had stars in their eyes just like two teenagers allowing themselves to follow the instincts of their love-hormones for the first time. They were a couple. They shared feelings, emotive drives and as of late, an apartment. The apartment was no lean meat for it cost him 45000 dollars a year. And he spent a night every week there, went home in the morning and left for office.

If soul mates did exist, he had found his but that was the wrong place and the wrong time. But the excitement and the desire was too strong to be denied. Vikki was his student and they had spoken to each other several times at the state university. He had felt her presence in a strange way in the classroom. Her eyes were too intense and very piercing. He couldn't stop himself from looking at her during the lectures and had to pull and tug at his eyeballs to focus on some other face as well. She had an air around her. Her dangling bracelets and hoops of earrings twinkled or shone in one way or the other and brought his attention back to her. After weeks of confusion, Vikki had taken the first step and had caught him alone in the corridor.

"Sir?" she had called after him.

He had turned back to see and had found her walking towards him. He gathered himself and waited for her to reach. He enjoyed watching her walk, coming to him.

"Sir, you forgot this," she handed him a crumpled piece of paper which he had thrown on the floor during class as garbage. It was bill for a purchase of ten Naira.

"Oh, thanks," he extended a hand to take it from her when she squeezed his hand with hers and let the crumpled paper fall again. He looked quizzically into her eyes and saw intensity there. She led her hand to the middle of her throat, her pulse was racing, her heart was beating fast and her skin was moist. He was charged with ions immediately. His eyes changed colours of surprise, disbelief, happiness and content. It was like an electric circuit completed when his heartbeat too started to match the rhythm of hers. So, it was going both ways.

"Meet me at VI tonight, Steven's on the beach," she whispered in his ear close enough to make him feel her breath on his ear lobe.

It was tantalizing.

Like a bite of the sourest pickle that keeps you smacking your lips a long time afterwards.

It was sweet.

Like a slurp of a stolen mango that makes your mouth water every time you think of it onwards.

They met up, they fell in love. He had told her he had a
kid and a wife but it didn't matter to her as long as it didn't
matter to him. "Keep her," she had said. It had been a year
since that crumpled paper fell on the ground and a year
onwards, they were still meeting at Steven's and going down
to their own apartment instead of some pricey hotel room or
cheap motel room. Hyder Khan was managing things well
between the house near the woods and the apartment at VI.

Hyder had found some mental solace in Nigeria. Some other
of his needs and desires were being fulfilled too. He was
minting money well from his two jobs and had earned the
respect of the people around him – baturiyas and locales.
Hyder enjoyed what he did – he loved the elements of
nature that had to be dug up, societies that existed before
his existence and finding clues to them through a statue,
a fossil or a sedimentary rock. His passion for history was
culminated in teaching Anthropology to the students of the
state university. His class was small, just six students who
found their interest in the unorthodox Anthropology subject
as their major for graduating. Nigeria was going through
the adolescent phase of yearning for modernization and the
parents who paid the fees for their children's college did
not see much of a brighter future for neither Nigeria nor
their kids if they would take up Anthropology. Medicine,
engineering, English, finance – these seemed to be the more
sensible approaches.

"Sir, shall we find good jobs with this major?" his six students
had asked him this question many times individually as well
as collectively.

To this Hyder had always answered that if they will be good at what they do, success won't really have to be sought for it will follow them. "Anthropology is being interested in others. If the significant You isn't happy with that, you better find a new interest," Hyder never minced words. "The foundations of a modern state are always based on the ethnography and culture of that place. You cannot convince the people of Nigeria to think and behave the way you want them to unless you get down into their roots and understand them. To speak their language and know their ways of living isn't enough to touch their psyche. When they consider you one of their own tribe, their own kin, only then can the masses be brought together collectively and the wave of modernism be introduced."

Hyder's dilemma was that Anthropology in Nigeria was discarded as the gift of colonization - that part of national history which they didn't want to forget for it was their drive. It was their id and it was their ego. He was a baturiya and the colour of his skin made him even more doubtful. The 1980s was Nigeria's rise as the petroleum hub and the political upheavals the oil brought along with it crashed its economy and its morale. As Hyder Khan was delivering his lecture in the state university of Lagos, the economic capital of Nigeria, a military dictator in the corridors of power had inched away to make room for yet another one. There was chaos, expatriates were haunted and the locales were terrorized. Many expatriates who shared a common social circumference, had left Nigeria for good. Some of them had sought refuge elsewhere and most of them had returned back home.

To Hyder, Nigeria was home. Like all patriotic Nigerians, he called it Naija. He had built a career, raised a family and found his comfort in the NairaLand. He had made friends and had created a social circle there. He had strong bonds that couldn't pull him away from that country. One of them was the rapport and celebrity-hood he enjoyed in the university he taught at. It's not like he hadn't seen difficulties. There had been days when Hyder could not go to the university and there were days when he could not return from there until it was late afternoon and the traffic had subsided then his students would have taped branches of trees all around his car and he had taken a safe passage to drive through the woods and reach home. He had to take a month long break from the office of the ministry of petroleum where he worked as a researcher and an adviser and had to face financial crunches at home. All of these reasons were not enough to pull him back to his roots. He was hopeful that things would get better and they had. The bloodshed stopped, the curfews stopped, being baturiya no more was a crime. He resumed his job at the ministry and had regularly started University where the strength of the students had become thicker than before.

Since the Anthropology majors were such a small group, he enjoyed a personal relationship with all of his students. There was Nuoko with whom he could talk about life back in Pakistan and ask him questions about wooing the average Nigerian woman since he was the hottest guy in class – tall around six feet, lanky and thin, he wore sleeveless shirts paired with the regular denims he wore almost every day and tied a bandana around his head. For a guy who didn't change his appearance ever, it often occurred to Hyder how he had managed to acquire the status of the alpha male and it had transpired many months onwards that Nuoko was not just the punk that he appeared to be but he was also a thorough gentleman who just sat at the back of the room with his head thrown back, sometimes his both hands entwined and cradling the back of his head, listening to every word being spoken and then when the ladies approached him he knew when to just smile and throw his head down at some smart remark and when to bend down just a little to whisper one of his jokes into the ears of softly scented girls.

One of these ladies was Vikki, short for Victoria who was going through the hippie stage long after the hippies had sobered down. She wore huge beaded necklaces around her neck, short skirts and tank tops with massively loaded anklets, armlets, waistbands and hoops in her ears. Her hair was unlike other girls – it was an Afro alright but she had it cut regularly so it just nestled softly around her head like a halo instead of being the tree-gone-wild look of most Afros. Her hair was brown, in the sunlight the edges of her halo-like spikes shone golden. She was one of the smart ones and very skinny. She would often be seen at the parking lot leaning against one or other vehicle parked, her tiny frame curved and arched at the absolutely perfect angles, gossiping and sharing a fag with Nuoko. Some even thought they were a couple and just were reluctant to admit. They were both standouts of their batch, and could be a good match.

Then there was Mustapha who was going through an immature phase of idealizing his professor. He volunteered to go with Hyder each time it was a recce time at the outskirts of the city or to other states of the country like Kano, Zaria, Abuja, Sokoto or Jos. Mustapha made it easier for Hyder to have a travel companion who could be bossed around for a week or so – there would be no question of who would drive for twelve straight hours on the intensely crowded highway with immensely huge oil tankers, caterpillars carrying twelve to fourteen cars on their backs, lorries and eight-wheeled trucks loaded to the top, no question of who would sleep in the state sponsored lavish hotel room with open access to the bar downstairs or who would get the chance to watch the Nigerian girls dance to the beat of the drummer in the club.

The girls usually danced in pairs or solos and they were, by all standards, no mean feat. Buxom ladies with glowering skins, tinselled up with glitter and shine, heavy dark hair plaited and allowed to hang like ropes from their heads that would shake with every move of their bodies were a scene to watch. The 4x4 stage in shape of a circle didn't give much leg room but did it allow the girl to shake like Tina Turner and show off? It was a sure bet. Hyder enjoyed those nights alone – no one to accompany or please, no one to watch or keep an eye on. He had the days to himself as a workaholic and the nights to himself as the young boy who had missed out his guilty pleasures in life. Sitting at one of the tables in any bar of any state he had had to go to, with a tumbler of whiskey or gin in his hand, he would easily forget who he was or where he had come from. The next day would always be pre-planned and Mustapha could take care of it for him.

Mustapha's room would be booked at one of the small inns close to the petrol stations. His rent was paid by Khan. His job would be to keep an eye on the car, sleep, refresh and drive down to the hotel everyday and keep Hyder company till his project would be over. Being a student, Mustapha worshipped his teacher. He had taught him so much about his own civilization that his ancestors hadn't been able to. He believed they had a spiritual connection for their religion was the same and that made them 'brothers'. Mustapha planned on getting a doctorate's degree just like his idol and wanted to teach for a living. He knew Hyder did more than recce the ruins- he wrote papers and researched, he wrote books and earned royalties – he was a character out of his imagination, he was a living example of how he had planned his future and he wanted to keep a close call, a certain proximity of being able to watch and learn. Little did he know, his idol did not have it all, as he suspected.

CHAPTER 7

HARRIS

Harris, if anything, had inherited the adventurous streak of his father. He had an almost dangerous incident the day before but it had left only positive impressions on him. The ride on Mosy, the feel of the air entering and exiting his body on its own, the filial warmth he felt while staying at Zainab's house, the gardener's wife with her matter-of-fact tone and most of all Zainab. The only reminiscences he had from his 'getting lost' accident were the ones mentioned above. The rest that had followed was something he wanted to push out of his mind and he had years of practice in doing so. He was conditioned to forget pain, to bear it as if nothing had happened, nothing was bothersome. Unknowingly,

Maryam had transferred her endurance into him and that is what terrified her the most.

To pain, endurance is a blessing; to cruelty, it is an extension.

He was at school and it was only mid morning. Malam Yakubu was taking the English lesson and was teaching Gulliver's Travels. The class had read the part of the travelogue-cum-fiction where he was the giant and omnipotent among the tiny Lilliputians but today he was explaining to the class how the man-mountain turned into the tiniest being in the land of giants where he was afraid of being overstepped and was treated like a plaything. Malam Yakubu lectured them about the powerlessness of humankind, how much they were dependant on God's powers and His theatrical skills to lead on a life. He was taking on serious lines and then coming down to funny questions,

"You Edet, how would you like if someone twenty times your size made you wear a girlie frock?"

There was laughter, the girls hid their mouths behind fists or opened palms and giggled, they glanced at one another and kept giggling, the boys guffawed. Poor Edet, just smiled sheepishly.

"What would you do Obiyara, if your master made you prance like a monkey all day to earn money?"

More laughter. Obi stood up and replied politely, "Malam, I shall ask for a lion's share in the money he made or else go on a strike," this time the loudest cackles came out of Malam Yakubu's mouth.

Harris was not enjoying the class. His mind was wandering elsewhere. He wanted it to be recess so he could take a trip to Zainab's house. He wanted to stay there till home time and then walk back home so no one would notice. He was a little embarrassed to go there though since Mum had not baked the promised pie and cake and he had nothing to offer to Zainab. He had, although taken the music player he had, which Dad had bought for him on one of his trips abroad but he hardly had used it. He could give that to Zainab. Obi had begged to borrow it but he hadn't budged. Since yesterday, he had developed a new sense of spitefulness against all the presents his father had ever given to him: the slingshot which was his favourite plaything when he went out in the woods with Obi, the penknife that had six other gadgets in it, the big Eskimo coat for the winters but it was never cold enough in Nigeria to wear a warm coat, the fake laser gun that made all sorts of weird noises and sparked a red coloured beam when you hit the trigger. He smiled at the thought of the laser gun because when he had brought it, Hyder had told him it was real and had poked it to the side of his ribs, funny, he could still feel the poke as he spoke of it. It was a hard poke and then it got harder. Suddenly he blinked his eyes and realised the poke was not imaginary, it was Obi's elbow that was about to grind a hole in his sides. He frowned and mouthed a small 'ow' to him when Obi rolled his eyes and pointed towards Malam.

Malam was standing there smiling, looking at Harris with interest.

"Would you like to share with us, Haris?" he said with the gentlest of voices. He had a Hausa-Fulani accent and always called Harris not with the correct pronunciation of his Arabic name haa-ris but he pronounced it as if it were an English name, Haris. Harris didn't seem to mind.

"Excuse me, Malam," he stood up nervous.

"Were you thinking for an answer to the question I asked or should I repeat it?" Malam was never offended with the students. He had the patience of a seasoned fisherman.

"Repeat, please, Malam," he was quite embarrassed.

The class was quiet, awaiting the answer of the only baturiya boy in class.

"So, Haris, if you were Gulliver entrapped in a world of powerful giants that didn't treat you like a human equal to them, what would you do?"

Harris looked at Malam's face thinking whether he knew what had been going on his mind lately. He took no more than two seconds to answer the teacher's question out of a book in his curriculum.

"I would run away," he answered.

"I see," said Malam, and turned to the rest of the class.

"You see, that is exactly what Gulliver did. It is the only logical way out. Good boy, Haris, sit down please," Malam nodded at him.

At recess, when Harris told Obi he was going to see Zainab, Obi ruffled all his feathers, put up a fight with him, implored, begged, warned, threatened and finally gave in.

"You watch my back, Obi," he said to which Obi only sulked.

All the winding way that the Gardener Mahmood had taken him, Harris had Malam's words ringing in his ears – the only logical way out. He believed if he did run away from home, Hyder wouldn't miss him at all. That was established yesterday when he had not even said a word of concern or care upon knowing that Harris was almost lost. What a stone for a father, he had thought that night. Mum was a different issue. Mum would go crazy but she will learn to live without him. Wouldn't she? He looked back at the memories he had had with his parents and strangely, he couldn't bring to mind any special occasion or day with both his parents on his side, happy and together. There were selective memoirs with Dad and others with Mum. His favourite memory with Dad was one when they would go fishing. There was lake that ran on the outskirts of Lagos, the border that was joined with the Ibadan state on the North. The Kemari lake, it was called. Hyder and Harris would dress up for the occasion, it would happen just once or twice a year, during summer or winter vacation. They wore their khakis, special fishermen shirts that they would buy off the hanger in the Sunday super market at a mere five naira per piece. They were always over sized but Hyder always told him fishermen are just like that. They had all the technical paraphernalia of fishing, the lines and rods and wicker baskets to bring home the catch, jars of salt to wash the fish with, boxes of bait and nets to fling. It was quite an occasion, this fishing thing and Harris loved it. Hyder would usually be in a good mood, they would have a neatly and generously packed picnic basket with all the stuff Maryam knew the boys would be happy to see – egg, lettuce and tomato sandwiches, grilled sausages wrapped in mozzarella cheese and buried in a small muesli that she would have especially baked by the baker who sold bread every night on a basket atop his bicycle. She would make popcorn and stuff them in small brown paper bags so they could stash a bag in their pockets and munch on until the catch would come by. Harris had begged her to go along many a time, but she had just kissed him and begged excuse. "It's a daddy-sonny time, my love, I would just be a nuisance." She did want Hyder to bond with his son. Hyder was a good sport with the boy, indeed. The road trip would cost them two hours to and two hours from the lake. He wouldn't leave the spot until the boy wouldn't get lucky once or twice. The lake was filled with cod, natural bred cod. Sometimes if they got lucky, they could spot an eel or two slithering along the shore.

"So, sonny, let's do this," he would keep the spirits up and celebrate every catch. It was a bit strange for Maryam although, to think that a man so restless and so jumpy could go fishing, sit at the lake's edge for hours at a stretch and wait for some action to happen. But then, there were many facets to his personality that didn't really gel with one another. The fish they would catch were cleaned and washed there and then, cured with salt to keep their freshness until they reached home. On the way from the lake, Hyder and Harris would listen to Michael Jackson songs, competing at who knew the lyrics much better. They would both win to most songs. Harris would enter the house triumphant and loaded with stories to tell,

"Oh Mum! I caught four today and one of them is a big jumbo size!"

"I saw an EEL! I thought it was snake and jumped up, totally destroying my line and almost breaking my rod but dad caught it with his bare hands. His bare hands mum! It is a fish he told me. Is it? An eel is a fish?"

"We caught just a couple today. Dad said it was too sunny for the fish to come up. Damn!"

"I saw turtle eggs near the lake! Dad showed them to me. There were mounds of soft soil everywhere. Dad dug one up and showed me two dozen eggs in a pit. They were all the same size! Can I keep a turtle at home? A small one? Pretty, please?"

Whatever the number of fish they would have caught, the pitch in his voice was always the same, high and excited. She would feel her blood rush faster to see the twinkle in his eyes, the colour on his cheeks. That night, he would go to bed as happy as a boy on the beach. That night she would smile lying in bed. Harris cherished the days of fishing, of going to the local cinema with his father. Although Hyder did not appreciate much his son's buddy, Obiyara but to the cinema, Harris would often make him tag along and he would have the best of times in the company of his two favourite buddies. Zainab was the latest addition to this list.

Harris was walking down the last lane that would take him to Zainab's house. His mind was cluttered with reminiscences, happy memories, sad memories. the previous day's incident had left him confused. Didn't Hyder love him? The turn on the street took him to Zainab's house. He stood there for several minutes, taking in the entire scene, exactly as it was yesterday, the trough empty, the kitchen door ajar and different sounds and smells coming from there, the main door shut tightly, except for one thing – there was no Zainab. He waited for a while and then walked up to the kitchen and peeped through the opening of the door and saw Zainab's mother, bent on a large dish kneading flour with her hands. It was just like mum used to need flour to make chapatti or parathas. He knocked on the door politely and her head jerked to see where the knocking had come from. The next few minutes were a bit chaotic, the source of chaos was the fat lady who hadn't really understood what was going on and had rather based her case on assumptions.

"Wayo, you boy, you come again? You steal donkey again? Wallahi Tallahi, you so bad. Your Ma no teach you nothing? My husband again come home on foot today?" she had stood up, hands on her hips and her loud voice was just going on and on zooming above his head, he was looking for the slightest chance to speak but so far there had been none."You go to school so learn, no steal. I nice to you, give you food, you keep stealing? You no good. Ba kyau. Fitina. I not forgiving you this time. Where is jaki, the poor animal, he afraid since yesterday, you hurt him again?" she had come to the door by this time, pushed him aside and stepped into the compound to pat the poor donkey. She couldn't see any.

"What, you lost donkey? Wayo, my husband, my jaki, my husband, my jaki," she was squatting on the ground now, mourning for her donkey or her husband or both, although she needn't mourn for either. Harris was confused, he was agitated, he didn't know how to tell her that her donkey and husband were both fine and together. He couldn't see a way so he squatted in front of her and put his face in front of hers. She stopped as she was startled.

"I did not steal the donkey, I came here on foot. I have come to play with Zainab. Can you please tell her?"

She kept staring at him. then she said in a very low voice, "Why you not tell me before?" he remained silent but she smiled.

"Zainab not home today, my boy," she said lovingly, "she go school," then she added, "she no run away from school." And gave her a motherly stern look.

He ducked his head. And smiled. But he was sorely disappointed. "Why was she home yesterday?"

"It Friday then? She go Muslim school, holiday on Friday. Your holiday, Sunday?"

"Yes," he understood. But he was still forlorn.

"Boy, what your name?"

"Harris," he said.

"Haareez, okay, why you run from school?"

He didn't know what to say. So he posed a question of his own. "If you can speak English, why can't Zainab?"

The lady looked surprised but then she said, "Haareez, I sell fried kosay and yam on the roadside when I young. Talk to baturiya people, bad English, I know," she grinned and continued, "but okay for sell kosay and yam, you know, no problem. Mahmood marry me, give me home. I stop selling." What a beautiful story, he thought. It was the best love story he had ever heard, the perfect happily-ever-after ending. So it did happen. It was not just Rapunzel who got her happy ending. "No teach Zainab broken English, people laugh," she answered his question.

"Can I stay here for a few hours? Until home time, please? Recess will be over, I cannot go to school so late. Malam won't be happy," he made some puppy dog eyes at her.

"Ha okay, you stay. But last time you run and I nice. Okay?"

"Jeez, okay," he grinned.

"I make doughnuts, you eat?"

"Yes, please," he said happily and sat on the steps where she had summoned him yesterday. The fat lady too got up and went in the kitchen to prepare something to serve to her little guest. Harris ate the doughnuts and planned to make his next visit on Friday. So he came on Friday, and the next and the next. It became a punctual habit for him, to bunk school after recess on Fridays and enjoy a meal with the happy family. He played marbles, ladders and snakes, steppoo and even dolls with Zainab. It was quite an experience. Such that playing pirates and adventurists could not give him. if Obi was strength to his growing masculine side, Zainab was helping him develop a feminine side. He gave her small presents – the jukebox, story books in Hausa lying spare in his room, a jar of apple jam from Mum's larder. Zainab, on the other hand, was learning English from him. Good solid English. She could even speak a few small sentences at the end of a month. Harris was a patient teacher. He corrected Mrs. Mahmood's English too and she would pat his head, lovingly, sometimes give him a treat of doughnuts, plantain chips or warm fuzzy kosay – the Nigerian version of a fritter. He enjoyed sharing the Hausa-Fulani culinary palette which would replenish him, more than feed him. It wasn't the food it was the ambience and the condiments of filial love that came along the cassava plate. It was about a mother screaming at them if they accidentally spilled water on the floor, or a playmate laughing if he got curry on his nose, or the fat lady telling him bunking school every Friday, no good for him.

"What your Ma say if she find out?"

"She won't," he would answer.

"You come in evening, with your Ma. She did well with you, you good boy. If you not stop cheating school, I will tell her. I," she threatened.

He simply smiled. He wasn't sure whether it was Zainab he liked more or the company of her mother, who would yell, screech, tease, laugh and scold him and also express her love without hesitation. She was a woman with a voice, she never had a sore lip or a bruised eye. Harris always made sure to leave the sanctuary of Mrs. Mahmood's house before her husband came back. Not that he wouldn't welcome him, he just didn't want to create an imbalance in the perfect serenity of the house.

Chapter 8

HYDER

Summer was long time over. It was December. The cool nights of Nigeria had turned colder. The air was heavier and the nights were quieter for the companions of the darkness – the shrill notes of the frogs, the hoot of the owls and the squeak of the mice had all subsided with the weather until summer. The afternoons were pleasant enough for a stroll. Maryam's vegetable garden had stopped sprouting hues and colours and nothing but the sugar-snap peas hung silently from the climber and a few patches of radishes were dotted with green heads bobbing up from the ground. She would wrap a cashmere and talk to the plants silently, as if ware of their slumber and trying not to disturb them. One evening she was doing just the same, thinking what fickle excuse would Hyder make this time for staying out. She always hoped his lies would be so convincing that she should not have an ounce of a chance to doubt him. But each time, the scent on his clothes defied him. the rose oil was the loyal connection between Maryam and the other woman.

As she contemplated on the whereabouts of her husband while stroking the dried up bitter gourd plant, Hyder and Vikki had just entered their apartment. The room smelt of tuberoses courtesy the air freshener. There was the usual air of expectation hanging between them. Hyder turned to lock the door but not before hanging the DO NOT DISTURB sign outside, lest the room service people should bother them asking if they needed more towels or the valet parkers in search of a fat tip, bring the car keys up to their room instead of handing them down at the counter. It was that sort of apartment – with the fringe benefits of housekeeping and valet, chauffeurs even if you would prefer. Vikki threw her bag over the sofa, fiddled with her high heels and peeled them off her feet.

"Something to drink maybe?" she asked him in the most casual of tones.

"Yeah," he flopped down on the three seated sofa and put his feet up on the table in front of him, tuned into the sports channel and fixated his eyes on the screen. His boots were speckled with the sand from the beach and specks of it fell in the edge of the table. Vikki came in with sparkling water for both of them, put the cans on the table, moved back a foot or two to pull back the curtains from the glass wall that showed all of Victoria Island to them with its hustle, bustle, glare, glitz, glam and shine. Every building was lit up, she stood there for a while, taking the scene in, the moonlight was dim and the moon looked faraway, the huge disco ball perched on top of the snazzy nightclub two streets away seemed bigger, glossier and more titillating. She was swallowing up the scene in big gulps, trying not to miss anything, the pomp and show, the dizzle-dazzle was all a source of joy to her. Her breath was warm against the cool glass pane against which she stood, thanks to the change of weather. Her exhalation made a small pool of mist on the glass and the scene had blurred a bit from that angle. She heard someone take a couple of steps behind her. She smiled, knowing who it was. Better still, she knew what he was going to do. So she closed her eyes and waited for the moment which arrived pretty soon. His hands crawled up her waist to the more swollen, fleshy and taut parts of her torso and his face dug deep in her neck that smelled of roses. He swept back her teasing hair with the point of his chin, that tickled her and she let out a laugh.

The lovers needed no invitation further and once on the couch, they taught each other with compassion and savoured patience the art of being one, body and soul. Following nature's clues, they fit each other to become one complete whole. There was no hurry to any motion, there was no existence in their world but them. Later, they had found themselves breathless and limp, squeezed into each other on the sofa, each wanting those coveted cans of sparkling water to run down their throats on their own. Vikki had her head resting on his chest, her body all curled up like a fur ball, her arms around him. Hyder had once again put his feet up, he had put the sports channel and was watching Nigeria beat up Sudan in a friendly football match, his hands supporting his head like a netball holding a big ball.

"Harry? Could we talk?"

"You have never asked me before, my love. What is it?"

"It's a request," she paused.

He took his eyes off the TV and looked at her. His face was pleasant. He wore a bitten mark just above his Adam's apple which would not disappear for a couple days. She felt responsible.

"Okay, first of all, you will need to wear a cravat on your neck for the next two or three days 'cause I seem to have bitten a bit hard," she said touching the mark with her fingers. He took her hand in hers and told her not to worry about it. "What was it that you were saying?" she certainly had his attention.

"I want to take you on a date-ish," she said after a pause and it was obvious she had pushed the words out of her mouth before she could think and rethink about her choice of words or fumble for appropriate vocabulary.

"Vikki," he shifted uneasily in his seat, his composure was disturbed, "you know that's not possible," he spoke in the gentlest of voices, stroking her cheekbone while he spoke.

"It's not anywhere near other expatriates, Harry, there's no one you know over there," she was imploring.

"What is the place? And why is it so important for me to go all of a sudden?"

Now she couldn't push the words out of her mouth, now she needed to thoroughly think, rethink and then play it strategically.

"It's my place of worship," that was the simplest, briefest way to say it.

"A church sermon?"

"Not really," she replied, "More like a party."

Hyder was confused. "Vikki, why are we going the religious way? Surely you have not planned a surprise wedding ceremony?" he could be cruel and not know. "I cannot give you an answer until you tell me what's going on?"

Vikki had prepared a whole monologue, she even knew what kind of questions the guy could ask him and she had thoroughly done her homework, but in his presence, under the skewed observatory of his sight, close to the warmth his body exuded, she was finding it difficult to speak.

"I have been keeping a secret from you Harry," she almost whispered, her hands folded in her lap, her eyes swept down for the briefest of moments.

He knitted his brows and waited for a few seconds for her to continue but then he had to prompt her.

"It's about my faith, Harry, I didn't bring it up because at first I was scared that you would not approve but now I know that things like belief systems and faiths can't come between us, can they?" she had finally spoken from the script.

"Vikki, what are you getting at? You are a Christian, I am a Muslim, what difference does it make? What's really on your mind, Victoria Jonathan?" he stressed on the name. He was partially right, it was a Christian name.

"On the contrary," she paused, pursed her lips and gave it a go, in the name of the Dark Lord, "I am a Satanist," she exhaled heavily as if she had let a huge stone off her breast.

"I don't understand, Vikki. You are a Satanist and so you worship Satan?" his tone sounded as if he had heard something ludicrous and incredulous.

"No, Satanism isn't necessarily Satan worshipping but it's close to it," she was eager to explain.

It was obvious that Hyder didn't like what he was hearing. "Okay, it's the last fifteen minutes, let me watch the match and then we will talk," he said. He tried to keep his composure cool but she could sense his uneasiness. She knew he had only bought some time to get his act ready, to become the same cool guy who could shrug off problems and scary thoughts. She knew it wouldn't be easy to tell him the darkest secret she had kept from him. The match was going to end, it was Sudan 2 and Nigeria 3 till now. Any strike of luck could change the game if Sudan equalled the score against Nigeria and make the teams both winners or both losers. It was just a matter of perspective that could be more explained with the old story of the glass being half full or empty.

She revised in her mind, all the possible dialogue she had prepared. Whilst on TV, things were going pretty smooth, the Nigerians had dominated the second half much better than they had the first one. Sudan was stuck at 2 and Nigeria won by one. Emanuel, the star quarterback was lifted on the shoulders of the rest of the team, the goalie was patted by all the team and the coach was running wild in the field. It was such glory, such emphatic triumph on ground, in the streets and every house of Nigeria. Hyder had developed interest in the sport when he had settled down. It was one of the traits of being Nigerian - loving football.

Vikki was waiting patiently for her turn. The game over, Hyder went over to the window as if in deep thought and stared sightlessly into it. He had been thinking about the information he had gotten about his girlfriend and had given it some time to seep in. After fifteen minutes that the game had given to him, he came to realise that the information had not really affected him at all. Being a Satanist, didn't change the fact that he loved her, his desire for her didn't cease to exist, her presence made him comfortable and every time he laid eyes on her, she managed to give him a spasm. She was looking at him, biting her lower lip, hands tucked securely beneath her bottom. He turned towards her and cleared his throat. She suddenly wished that this moment could be elongated, prolonged and put off until late. She couldn't bear it if he rejected her.

"What's this party you want me to go to?"

His response was still quizzical. Was he asking because he wanted to go to or was he asking because he needed more information before making his mind up?

"Umm, its Black Mass, like a gathering of local Satanists, happens once a year. It's nothing like the Christian mass, it's like a party," she tried to make it sound as interesting as possible.

"When?"

"Next week..." her voice was trembling a bit. He nearly meant yes.

"Okay," he shrugged and came away from the window.

Her eyes widened. "You mean okay, okay?"

He smiled, "Yeah, okay okay," he grinned.

Vikki sprang up from the couch and made a dash towards him. She clung to him like a paperclip had flown to go stick to a huge magnet with immense electromagnetic powers. She had put her hands on the sides of his neck and was pecking with the small pout of her lips on his face, anywhere she found space, she specked it with her kisses. He laughed.

"Hey, stop tickling," he laughed.

"You have no idea, how much this means to me, Harry, I can't thank you enough," she had misty eyes.

Harry bore his eyes into her face, his face wearing the same triumphant look that Emanuel had worn minutes ago. If he already had Vikki eating out of his palm, one would wonder, what his present escalation would mean to her. He was pleased with himself. Satanist or else, didn't really matter. The anticipation of going to the Black Mass was miniscule for him but it was his curiosity, his heart for adventure that he had taken the decision so quick, so easy. She had told him it was a party, he was a party animal alright, but the idea of observing kith of a cult was interesting as well as mysterious. And mystery, if anything, was his game.

The night Vikki had disclosed her belief system to Hyder, he had asked a few questions afterwards.

"Why would you worship Satan?"

"We believe Satan is not an entity who needs to be worshipped. Satan is an idea, a non physical being, just like the human mind – no one knows where it really exists in all the brain – the mind is a system, it is a cognitive entity and so is Satan. It is in each one of us. When we meet a person who uses his mind in every action he takes we call him calculative, practical. A person who uses his heart in situations is emotional. So a person who would listen to his id, his flesh and his Self, would be a Satanist."

Hyder had thought something quietly. The air between them was whispering what Vikki wasn't saying out loud – but neither of them said it.

Vikki had told him of the Gates of Hell and its comparative Paradise Lost. "It's your pick really, which version you choose to side with," she sounded very convinced, very relaxed in her expression. Hyder asked her if they were so convinced about their faith being the most logical one, why would they keep it hidden under sheaths socially. To which she had smiled and said, "I know what you are getting at, it took me a whole year to come out in front of you," she nodded her head, bent it to put her chin on her breast for a few seconds, then spoke, "Every time there has been a new religion introduced in the world, there has been chaos. There are myths of Gods fighting on Mount Olympus for power and reign, there are stories about Ram and Ravan showing their might and trying to show each other down, Prophets of Islam have suffered tortures of their own tribesmen when they declared the advent of Judaism with Joseph in Egypt, David, Solomon and Jesus in Bethlehem and Mohammad in Mecca. And the villain in all these theologies is Satan. Imagine what kind of reaction we could spur if we come out in the open. It's not for ourselves that we fear, it is not in favour of any body. Not everyone is like you, Hyder," she purred the last sentence.

"This is confusing," he said at last.

"I know, it is, it is opposite to everything we have been listening to ever since we grew up. Take me. My parents are Christians, Catholics, the Dark Lord have mercy on me. All my childhood I was woken up on Sundays, taken to the Church all washed up and dressed. Believe me, Hyder, I knew all the hymns by heart but to date, I do not know what most of them meant. I don't understand how we base our faith system on people and disciples we have never seen nor met, books of gospel we don't know whom they were written by," she was angrily speaking, her arms flailing, her eyes aghast.

Hyder had felt his heart do a few somersaults as she had talked but he was too proud to show any hurt that her words had caused to his faith system. He couldn't decide whether she was right or wrong, whether she convinced him or confused him. But one thing he could see, she was fixated to whatever she was following. Her dilated pupils as she spoke of her childhood and the hurt in her voice left room for some more questions.

"Where are your parents now? You go to see them often, you tell me when you go..."

She reclined back on the back of the sofa, threw her head back and shut her eyes. It was as if she didn't want to answer this question.

"Vikki?"

"They live in Zaria."

"I don't think you have ever been to Zaria in the past two years that I have known you," he said thoughtfully. Vikki shook her head. Zaria is another state in Nigeria, some 800 kilometres away from Lagos.

"So, they come to see you then," he prompted.

"They ABANdoned me, when I converted. What kind of parents do that, Harry? You ask me why I never trusted you with the truth, well here is your answer. I didn't want to lose you. But I couldn't keep things from you Harry, I have never done so. I couldn't keep what and who I was from you any more, I **love** you," she stressed so hard on the word that it brought tears to her eyes.

He pretended to not have seen the droplets that formed curves on the inner corner of her eyes, just above the tear duct. "So, when you told me you were busy on the weekends for a family dinner at your parents' house, you were..." she cut him off in mid sentence, "I was at the church in Lagoon," her voice was calm. Hyder nodded.

He had quietly gotten up and picked up the phone receiver that lay silently next to him on the coffee table near the sofa. He asked for the keys to be handy on the counter as he was coming downstairs in a couple of minutes. Vikki's heart dropped. Her worst fears had come true. "Where are you going, Harry?" she asked in a voice she had to tug at to bring it out of her throat.

"Taking you to dinner, where else? Come on, I am starving!"

A smile spread across her face, she sprang to her feet and asked excuse for a few minutes so she could freshen up and wipe the lines of distress that had formed on her face during the hectic talk. Later, as they shared a table-for-two at the most luxurious restaurant in Lagos, the Ocean Basket, their usual spot to have sushi and salmon, Hyder's favourite food, Vikki couldn't help beaming at the ambience which seemed livelier tonight, the usual red candles that glowered silently at their table flickered with excitement, the downplayed slow music sounded even more romantic to her and the delicacies on her plate more vibrant than before. Hyder although seemed to pick at his food. Moments later, he called out to the waiter, told him the food tasted like sawdust, wouldn't take an apology nor would he demand to see the chef and simply asked for a bottle of whiskey.

"Single malt or blend, sir?" the waiter had prompted.

"Whatever," he had waved his hand and scowled. Vikki felt uncomfortable. She put down her utensils and stared at him. he smiled, his eyes gentle on her face.

"It's my head, the migraine. Don't worry." He assured her.

That night, the scotch had him completely wasted, Vikki drove them back to the apartment, he asked leave to sleep as soon as they were there. Vikki undid his shoes, peeled off his socks, covered him in the duvet as soon as he was in bed, ruffled his hair with her fingers gently in a massage like motion and waited for him to fall asleep. When she thought he was almost there, with the featheriest of touches, she kissed his closed eyelids, ran her finger across his lips and put her finger to her lips. She stared at him as his breathing grew heavier. Hours passed, the object of her desire slept and she stared at him and the window that glazed with the nightlife of Lagos – a city that never seemed to sleep. The next day was a weekend and Hyder had decided to spend the entire day with Vikki in their apartment, to her delight. He thought of Maryam and Harris and realised he hadn't forgiven her disobedience and insubordination as yet. He wasn't ready to forget and he punished her by staying away, untold, unannounced. In any case, Vikki was clinging to him like a climber weed to a tree. He couldn't let go of her that day. In the evening, they went to their respective homes, to dress up for the Mass later that night.

Maryam, as usual had no questions to ask about his absence of the previous night. Harris had locked himself in the room as soon as he had heard the screeching tires of the Cadillac. Hyder spent half an hour preening his feathers in the room and then, as swiftly as he walked in, he walked out, no questions asked, no word spoken.

At night, he was dressed in khakis and a plain tee as per Victoria's instructions and had picked her up from outside of her apartment. She had been waiting at the step of the building where she lived and upon seeing his car, she had started walking towards it even before he had hit the brakes. He saw from a distance that a couple of yards away from where she stood, were two black boys, about her age who had been eyeing her with interest. She was wearing a sundress, mini sized with a middle parting that was buttoned up right from the neckline on top to the hemline on her thighs and held on with two thin spaghetti straps on her shoulders. The hem of the dress ended just in the middle of her femur bone. The boys had been enjoying the scene quite a lot and Hyder had felt a pang of jealousy. He had parked when she had reached closer, the guys were still following her path and when she got into the baturiya guy's car, they were sorely disappointed. Hyder smirked at their long faces. He looked at her before hitting the gears and told her, "You dressed up for the occasion," she smiled and replied, "I dressed up for you." She was not the least bashful in telling him how much he mattered to her. Hyder felt no compulsion to return back compliments, he enjoyed the hero worship. Still, he wasn't too stingy with words when he was in her company. "I like what you have done with your hair," he commented on the cloud of silk that sat comfortably on her head. It was a wig, a messed up French bob. She didn't tell him it was a late night spree at the local wiggery. "You look cute yourself," she had remarked. The cool blue shirt was becoming to him and his khakis showed off the perfect roundedness and shapeliness of his legs.

"So, where are we going," he had asked, knowing not where the Mass was being held.

"It's not very far off, in the middle of Lagoon Island."

"Lagoon? Is it a public thing?" he hadn't known Satanism could be blown-out common in Nigeria.

"Of course not, it's a small place around the coastal area, just a studio apartment kinda thing, only it's a single storey building with a compound. It's quite secluded and isolated," she informed him.

"Do the neighbours know about your," he paused. What was the word he was looking for? He couldn't say cult, it would be rude. Faith? Religion?

"Rituals?" she helped.

Yes, that was it. Rituals. She told him they didn't and even if they did, they had no reason to complain whatsoever about a group of twenty or so people gathering at a place once a month and party once a year. It made sense. That's why there had been no reports so far. They chatted through the hour long drive, taking instructions from Vikki, he finally came to a halt in front of a smallish bungalow sort of place.

"We are here," she chirped.

Hyder felt a knot tighten in his stomach.

CHAPTER 9

VIKKI

Vikki had been very graphic in her details about the house. It was a low roofed, one room house in an axis of 20'x30'. On the front was a compound with a bonfire spot laden with logs and crumpled sheets of newspaper on top. Close to the bonfire stood a humble looking tinned can of kerosene. A small flood light was lit up on the exterior of the door of the room which was the only source of light in their proximity. There were a couple of guys with three or four girls in the compound, standing and chatting when Hyder entered the compound with Vikki. He felt a little self conscious as the aluminates eyed him with interest. He was new. He was with Vikki and he was baturiya. The gang's interest was sparked on many levels.

Vikki clutched his hand, smiled broadly and tugged at his hand gently to signal him to walk with her. Hyder obeyed.

The small cluster of people welcomed Vikki with hugs and friendly kisses on the cheeks. He could see they were quite close to one another. Hyder extended out a hand to one of the guys who took it pleasantly and came forward for an embrace. Hyder hesitated.

"O take it easy, we cool man," the guy stepped back.

"Nothing personal," Hyder said.

"No, no, no, no, no," the black guy spoke. "Its okie dokie the first time, second time you will come hugging all of us," he joked and everyone laughed. The ladies all ogled at him and winked at Vikki. He was a good one. Vikki just beamed. People kept pouring in, all of them welcomed him, and Hyder got the feeling as if all of them knew about him already. He had an unpleasant queasy feeling about this. As far as he knew, Vikki and he were keeping their relationship secretive. There was neither space nor time to confront Vikki about it so he kept it for later and met new people until a familiar face appeared. He was jolted. Vikki might have done unexpected things to him but this was a bit too much. The familiar face was of a tall lanky man who wore a bandana round his head and as soon as he entered the limited premises, the ladies all whistled and clapped. Two of them started walking towards him to kiss him on the cheeks and embrace him. One of them started swaying from side to side as she clung to him. The alpha male Hyder had known from the University was standing right before his eyes. He took Vikki by the elbow and took her to a corner.

"Hey, what's wrong?" she asked.

"What is Nuoko doing here?"

"Nuoko is a member," she said matter of factly but then froze. "I didn't tell you, did I?" She looked anxious.

"Vikki, for the Devil's sake, how can you slip up such a detail from your date? He is my STUdent, for God's sakes!" his whispers were turning into hisses. Vikki looked around. A lot of people, around sixty had gathered in the compound and everyone seemed to be rubbing shoulders and arses with each other owing to the lack of space. A couple of heads turned towards their direction but Vikki was all smiles for them. She turned to Hyder, "Harry, Nuoko is the last of our concerns, don't worry about him. We are not backbiters," she insisted on the word We that made him feel left out a bit. He stood straight and thought of his options – to leave without being noticed which was somewhat not plausible. The other option was to trust Vikki. He thought for a second and took the latter.

He wondered how these people would carry out the rituals in such a closed and stuffy place. He realised, his temperament was also growing because of the flushing feeling he was having, with almost no oxygen to breathe and the one that was reaching to him was polluted with perfume scents, hair gel and tobacco smoke. There was no music but there was noise all around, people chatting, laughing, teasing. The scene was obnoxious. He also noted he was the only "grown up" there since all of them looked pretty young – doing college or university. Nuoko was busy with the ladies – chatting them all up, just being the gentleman that he was.

He had crowed his neck to check all around, his eyes had met Hyder's for the briefest fraction of a second but he had pretended not to see him. Hyder wasn't quite sure whether he had done that deliberately or was it coincidence that he hadn't noticed a white man in a swarm of black skinned youngsters? Vikki was looking at him, seeing his face turned red, deep in thought. Had he understood her point?

"Come with me," she pulled his arm and started moving.

He followed, bumping into a girl here and into a guy there.

She opened the bolt that would lead them to the room that was yet closed for everyone. Someone noticed but Vikki squeezed inside and he followed her too. The room was brightly lit up with black coloured candles. They were perched on a thin strip of wood that ran all around the four walls of the room. There was a familiar fragrance in there as well, he closed his eyes and worked his sensory nerves and was transformed back into Maryam's flower beds – the scent of tuberoses. He opened his eyes and looked at Vikki. She used her hands to point at different things in the room, she used no words at all. Right in the middle of the wall opposite to the door was the sculpture of Baphomet, the Satanic symbol of worship – a goat really but one that sent some shivers down his spine. He wondered if that was really the etching of Satan himself. That would mean today he stood face to face with the king of the underworld. The thought made him shudder. He diverted his gaze from the sculpture. From the ceiling there hung several five pointed stars, resembling those which he had seen at Vikki's house. The strange thing about them, which he hadn't figured out earlier, was that they all pointed downwards. In the middle of the room was an altar like structure with a black coloured metallic chalice and a small dagger.

"This is where I want you to join me, Harry, just for tonight," she came closer to him, his chest touching hers.

"Vikki, I came here to accompany you, but this Nuoko thing isn't fair," he complained.

"You have to trust me on this. Nuoko won't tell a soul. Just don't worry and enjoy this night. It's very very important to me. I will never ask you to come back here again but tonight, let it be for me." She was imploring.

Hyder looked at her and in a flash he considered himself lucky to have found love, in the most measliest of circumstances even, yet love. "The reason I have brought you here is that when you come inside, you should find this room familiar and not look like little red riding hood lost in the big bad jungle," she grinned as she straightened his collar. "Did I look like that out there?" his ego was kicked. "Well, a bit," she chuckled. He response was postponed by a loud cheer that came from outside. His facial expressions turned quizzical but Vikki smiled back at him.

"It's time," she whispered, gave him a peck on his pointed chin and walked out with Harry behind her.

In the compound, the crowd had divided into two groups. One was standing across the bonfire near the entrance gate. The other group was standing close to the main door of the room which Vikki and Hyder had to themselves for a while. Apparently, the group closer to the room was the one supposed to go in, take part in some rituals and the others were dates, on lookers, curious, the like. Hyder asked Vikki whether he should go stand with the "others" but she frowned and told him she had already explained the plan to him and so he stuck.

"I would rather go outside," he protested feebly. Vikki's pleading eyes made him change his preferences.

Once in the room, the Satanists all stood in a line across the circumference of the room. One of the guys who tore off his tee shirt once everyone had settled down, had lied down on the altar, face front. The sculpture of Baphomet was towering down upon him and the stars all hanging from the ceiling made it look like it was open air. The senior most member of the group, the same guy whose embrace Hyder had rejected half an hour ago, was performing the ritual. It was some sort of baptising the newbie into the cult. The guy on the altar was the infant Satanist and had to be properly christened. Hyder almost chuckled with the choice of words his mind was giving him. The priest chanted some Latin and called out for the forces of Darkness to help him with the chastising of the new paganist. The priest himself held the chalice and the dagger and pointed his face south as well as his both hands extended out far towards the same direction, "I call upon the power of Fire." Then he turned towards East in same movements and called upon the power of Air, to North for Earth and to West for Water to help him and combine the powers of nature to make this man capable of handling his infernal powers within and to wilfully follow the path of the Night Watchers – of logic, wisdom and satisfaction of human needs. When the ritual was done by the priest, the Satanists all started chanting the names of the Darkest among the Dark – Satan, Babalon, Lucifer, Belia, Laviathan. The guy on the altar closed his eyes as the moment drew nearer. The priest, as a conclusive act to the whole baptising, held the small dagger in his hand like a pen and drew a slit across the left side of the new guy's chest. A slit that was as clean as a line drawn by an artist. A couple of seconds later, a trickle of blood appeared across the line and the priest held his chalice close to the dripping end of the slit. The Satanists kept chanting the names of the Dark Lords as the blood dripped into the chalice. After five rounds of the name chanting was done, the chalice was lifted, the priest wiped the blood from the wound with a finger and swiped that finger across the rim of the vessel he held, so as to save that last bit of blood instead of letting it waste.

By that time, Hyder was getting dizzy. He was visibly disturbed by the noise, the gathering, the blood, the ritual, it had all gotten into him but Vikki, his sole support was engaged mentally in the task she had come to do. He looked at her and felt ditched. His mind started working up like the Hyder he was – he was hurt, he was harassed by the ogling, he was disturbed by the scene in front of his eyes and he was flustered with the images he would have to carry in his memory for God knew how many years. God, how do I escape, he found himself praying in the midst of the Satanists. The frustration was building up like a dust cloud inside of him. While Hyder was going through an inner commotion, the Priest had made way through the line of Satanists standing below Baphomet's sculpture and had offered the blood of the newest member of the cult to the statue by holding up the chalice to its mouth. Hyder was done, so were the rest, as the boy on the altar begun to rise, Hyder dashed towards the door, and ran out. Vikki whispered loud enough for the rest to hear, "Come back," but he didn't stop. He opened the door to get the air. Outside, the bon fire had been lit and the waiting group were dancing around it or standing aimlessly and waiting. Eyes had shot up as the door opened but people were disappointed and surprised to see just the baturiya rushing out with Vikki running after him.

"Harry," she called out, trying to grab his sleeve, his shoulder, his hand, anything.

"I am done with this bullshit, you can stay if you want but I won't be part of this anymore," he gritted his teeth to keep his voice as low as possible.

He kept walking and Vikki was left in the compound with others whispering. She felt stabbed. The others had come out of the room one after the other to join in the dancing and also to see where the blood had suddenly gone bad between the two lovers. Vikki standing alone with her eyes full of hurt told the story out loud. Others brushed past her, someone nudged and winked sympathetically, someone just smiled. She smiled back and felt a hand tapping her shoulder from behind. It was Nuoko.

"Care to dance?" he asked as if nothing had happened.

She smiled a slow smile, indicating yes and the party began. Booze and dance. It continued till the wee hours of the morning when most people were asleep under the starlight and Nuoko was sitting on the floor like an agile monkey. Vikki had put her head on his bicep and had fallen asleep.

The party had ended just a little later than the time when Hyder had reached home, had rung the door bell at a ratio of thirty five bells per minute for half a minute until Maryam, groggy from the sleep opened the door and had let him in, he had seen some freshly lacquered miniature figurines of the Greek goddess Psyche and her husband Cupid on the dining table, he had bubbled with anger and had thrown them on the ground, pounded on them with his feet, snarled at his wife calling her a good for nothing bitch who wasted time on objects of sin, stormed into his room and slammed the door shut, leaving Maryam in the sitting room wondering what wrong her new miniature statues had done to him.

CHAPTER 10

MARYAM

Next morning was a holiday. Hyder was still shut up in his room and Harris had, as on every weekend, woken up on his own at the crack of dawn and had sat by his mother who was sleeping on the couch in the sitting room. She woke up to find her little son staring at her.

"Hey, little angel," she smiled.

"Why are you sleeping here, Mum?" he asked, concerned.

"Um, I just came out for a drink of water, I guess and then must have fallen asleep," she lied. Harris kept looking at her as if he hadn't bought the story and expected her to try much better than that. He was going to prompt it.

"Mum why aren't you wearing makeup this morning?"

Maryam had told one lie and that was going to suffice for that morning so she changed the topic.

"What are the plans for today?"

It worked. He was super excited about something. "Today, I am going to Zainab's house with Obi," he screeched with excitement. "You know, Zainab's school is open on Saturday's but today they get off for some religious holiday, soooooo, we got a play date," he was jumping up and down on the couch.

Maryam laughed out at the monkey business going on. "Alright, then we shouldn't go empty handed. Let me bake a cake or pizza for you." She was being generous.

"Can we have both?" he asked and then added "Pleeeeaaase?"

She chuckled. "Okay sure, but it will take an hour."

"Great!" he jumped over the headrest of the couch and pranced towards the kitchen when he saw his mother's artwork in a complete shatter on the floor.

"Oh Jesus!" he bent down to pick the pieces that crumbled like fine grainy sand in his hands.

"What happened to these, Mum?"

"I am not sure, must have knocked over when I was getting water," she said thoughtlessly, holding her face up from the chin with both hands under her jawbone. She winced for not clearing up the clutter at night.

"That's such a pity! Mum I was going to ask you to lend me those two, I wanted to tell their story to Obi and Zainab," he was disappointed. She went up to him and cupped his face, giving him some comfort, "Well, the story is with you now, as I told you, you can always share that," she spoke in the gentlest of voices.

"Yeah, I guess, but it won't be same without the props," he pouted.

She laughed. "Don't worry, let us go through the story once again to see how much you remember. The story will allow them to imagine more and they will like it even more," she assured him.

"Will it? Then, let me tell you the story," he was all adrenaline today.

"Okay, and that will give me time to spruce up the bakery," she ruffled his hair with her hand and they both went into the kitchen where she began to take out pans and baking trays and ingredients while Harris settled on a counter that was usually used for the same purpose. She laid out a glass of milk and some homemade salty almond and cashew nut cookies for his breakfast. He didn't really have a big appetite, or at least not when he was home.

"So, once upon a time, there was a Goddess Venus. She was a goddess of....."

"Beauty."

"Yes, beauty and people worshipped her because she was the prettiest lady in town..."

"At mount Olympus."

"Yes, and she had a son Cupid who was the God of Love. The same Cupid you have on your dresser, Mum, the baby with wings and a bow to shoot arrows?"

"That's the one."

"Okay, then there was a princess called Psycho,"

"Not Psycho, her name was Psyche and she was a mortal, unlike the rest in the story."

"Psyche, Psyche, Psyche. Got it. She was even prettier than Venus and Venus got jealous. So she sent her son Cupid to shoot at her with one of his arrows and make her fall in love with a donkey. Mum, can a girl fall in love with a donkey?"

She paused, pursed her lips and said, "Yes, a girl can, unfortunately fall in love with someone as dumb as a donkey," she kept kneading the flour. "Continue," she prompted.

"When Cupid went to shoot her with a love arrow, he saw her beauty and fell in love with her himself. Bingo! Twist begins. He is afraid of his Mum so he goes to the king of all Gods," he was interrupted.

"GREEK gods, who exist in a mythology," she raised an eyebrow.

"Er, the king of all mythological gods helps him by telling a lie to Psycho's I means Psyche's father that she shall have to marry a serpent or else all his people will die. The king was very unhappy but Psyche decided to do it in any case. She was taken to the most beautiful palace ever and she was served by invisible servants. Her life was totally rocking. Her husband, the serpent only came to visit her at night in the dark so she couldn't see him. But one night she lit a lamp to see his face and he was angry and he went away, to not return."

"Hmmm, well you see, he did return," she felt sorry for not having told him the complete myth.

"He did? You didn't tell me," he complained.

"Should I tell you now?"

"Yup," his eyes grew bigger with anticipation.

"Okay, so she looked for her husband everywhere and then went to Venus herself to beg for a reunion with her husband. Now Venus had put her son in a cage since she too had found out about his secret marriage. Venus decided to put Psyche to such a task that she would die a horrible death and her son too, would forget about his mortal wife. She asked her to separate grains like millet, barley and poppy seeds from each other and to fetch water from the river Styx, the river that flows between the immortal world and the mortal world. Luckily, some ants helped her with the grains, an eagle helped her to fetch water."

"Wow, awesome ants and cool eagle," he was in awe.

"Yeah, you see, when the going gets tough, the tough get going and God sends help too," she was rolling out the dough with a rolling pin.

"But Mum, why was Venus so wicked?"

"Tch, tch, she wasn't wicked, she was just being protective and possessive for her son. Maybe she wanted him to marry an immortal instead of the human princess," she explained as much as she could.

"I still think she was wretched," he frowned.

"And you are entitled to have an opinion, so be it," she grinned.

"So what happened next?"

"The third task was to get some wool from the golden sheep and a reed helped her to do that," she was interrupted.

"Are there Golden sheep, Mum? Can I get their wool?"

"No, there is no such thing. It's a mythology, Harris, what did I tell you about mythologies?"

"That they could or could not be real. Darn," he wasn't happy with the definition.

"That's right."

The myth had to be left incomplete because at the far end of the sitting room, the lock of a door clicked and the door swayed open. Hyder emerged in his night suit, hair ruffled and a scowl on his face. He stood there for a while looking around the sofas, his eyes penetrating into the kitchen where the oven had just been stuffed with two baking trays – a cake mould and a pizza base. The air smelt of weekend baking. There was no newspaper on the dining table, where Maryam always placed them each morning. He felt listless and went back into his room. Harris jumped down from the counter top, asked his Mum how much time he needed to wait. She said fifteen minutes so he dashed to his room, to put on some clean clothes and fetch Obi on the way to Zainab's house.

When he came out he was wearing his school uniform – a grey shirt, grey trousers and black shoes with a black tie. He took after his father and would grow up to be really handsome. As much as she loved him in his formal attire, she couldn't understand why he would dress up in his uniform on a weekend. "Oh it's just to tease Binta, she makes a lot of noise when she thinks that I have run away from school just to play with Zainab," he smiled mischievously.

"Who is Binta?"

"Zainab's mother. She's jolly good," he said thoughtlessly tying up his loose shoelace.

"Have you been there more than once?" Maryam asked puzzled.

Uh-oh, Harris thought. That was not to be shared. Foolish mistake, he thought.

"Harris?" Maryam was firm but still soft.

"Mum I have been to her house only once after the donkey incident," he lied.

"You never told me, when was that?"

"Last Friday," he bleated like a lamb.

"Did you go from school?"

"Mum, it was only once," he insisted.

Maryam swooped her eyes downwards, in deep thought. If he was lying, she didn't want to confront him anymore.

"Okay," was the only thing she said. "But you need to tell me whenever you are going to visit Obi or Zainab. And as of today you will have to wait for half an hour or so until Garba gets here so he can accompany you to Zainab's home," her voice was calm but Harris knew she was upset. Did she buy his story? He was nervous so he flopped down on the sofa, praying hard his father would stay in his room until Garba got here. He was getting fidgety and sitting still was out of question. He counted his buttons, the holes in his shoes that threaded the shoe laces, looked at the lines on both his hands and spotted the differences between them and totalled them to seventeen. He could stay no more so he ran into the veranda to spot Garba from twenty yards away where the residential block started. Maryam had already placed the disposable plastic containers carrying slices of carrot cake and chunks of pepperoni pizza for him to carry comfortably in a polythene bag. She eyed him from the sitting room and thought hard on what she had just witnessed. She had seen genes. She had seen inheritance. She could take it from Hyder but Harris was something else to her. He was her centre of protectiveness, her object of possession, her baby Cupid, he was all she had. Moments later, he came running to her, panting with anticipation, "Garba is here, Mum, I will catch up with him, can I go now?" "Sure, baby," she handed him the bags and kissed the crown of his head when he jostled to run out of the door.

Today, Maryam had felt a sharp sting in her entire being. It made her restless, anxious and angry. Who was Binta whom her son was playing pranks at? He said she went all worked up if he had run away from school, it meant he had been there more than once. Zainab was a friend, she couldn't compete with that, she couldn't find fault with that. Binta made her curious and made her edgy. Her son had found a mother figure other than herself and it wasn't something she could live with. As usual, she hadn't said anything about it to Harris, she had asked him questions, he had answered them and she had taken them to be the truth, or the version of truth he wanted to give her. It wasn't Maryam's stride to confront. She thought about the things Harris had said the previous night when the two of them had been having dinner. He had wished for a sister. A sister like Zainab. Maryam realised, he felt lonely. He hadn't found a friend in Obi, he had rather found a brother – protective, caring, unyielding.

"Mum, I want to have a sister," he had said between mouthfuls. Maryam had almost choked on her morsel.

She took a few moments to reprieve herself and said very softly, "but I thought you found girls boring," she reminded him of how helpless and timid girls like Snow White and Aurora were. "The girls in your fairy tales are like that," he said with his mouthful again and Maryam had to reach out with a napkin to wipe his mouth. "And those in my school, maybe they are too, I don't know for sure but they don't like me at all. I mean AT ALL," he gave such facial expressions to her that she had to laugh. He was bruised a bit from the distance his skin colour created between him and the 'fairer' sex at school. "So, what changed your mind?" she asked him, interested in the metamorphosis going on in his character regarding women. "Zainab, she is super cool. She plays marbles better than Obi and his cousins. She can fly a kite and even make one, can you believe it? That's what we are going to do next time. I think I would like my sister to be like her," he sent shivers down her spine again. He was expecting her to bring him a baby sister. She would, if she could, bring him the water of the Styx and separate poppy seeds from millet if she had to, if that is what he desired. Her reason of putting up with a life she had neither planned nor wilfully desired was one – she didn't want Harris to grow up without a complete family. She had lost her mother at an early age and that had made her naive, she believed. She didn't have the wisdom of a mother's experience around her. She had made a wrong decision in her life but she couldn't amend it by making another similar decision. She thought very very guiltily each time she had asked Magana to bring her some of the magic potion from the witch doctor in her tribe to help her and not let Hyder's drunkard hormones affect the lonely ovules in her ovaries. She had given Magana her studs in exchange of the potion whose single gulp would be enough to erase any doubt from a woman's mind. That was her silent punishment to Hyder. That was her vengeance. That was how she spat back at his misadventures in the night in the bedroom. She had poured the contents from the coke bottle that Magana had produced into an empty perfume bottle and had put it on the dresser, right next to Hyder's cologne. And he never knew. She smiled inwardly, not the same girlish smile she had, but a smirk, a laugh lined with irony.

It wasn't till last night that she had been rethinking all her misdoings in a different light. She was denying Hyder something he would want but in doing so, she was also keeping Harris an only and lonely child.

She began to think on lines that she hadn't imagined before. Could another child bring Hyder back from the rose scented woman? It was a chance to be taken. The thought made her curse herself. Did she want him back even? Probably not. There had been too much distance, too many chasms to cover with another offspring. Had he been any better before his collars started to smell with that aroma of roses? Absolutely not. She had no problem with the other woman in her husband's life because she knew, that woman had nothing to do with the fissures and fractures in her domestic life. If Hyder took some pleasure from her, then be it. If that meant his hormones could go around a normal cycle if he kept his desire fulfilled by the other woman and not bother

her after downing a bottle of whiskey, she was okay with that. The thought pattern took her to revisit the year she was pregnant. She wasn't sure she hadn't forgotten the lack of sympathy from her husband during her first pregnancy. She hadn't obliterated from her heart the hurt the pain and the anger that those painful, cold and hurtful nine months had left her with. But still, she was thinking. Like a mother. Like a woman. She made a mental note to keep thinking and working on this issue until she reached a point. In the meanwhile, she had a garden to tend to. The courgettes had flowered and they needed some attention.

Outside in the garden, Maryam was entrapped in a capsule of her private world. This was where she kept her nourishing characteristics safe, amid the grassy patch of land she hid her love to tend and snuggle, her desire to protect and her need to caress. This garden was more than a patch of veggies and a bunch of flower beds. It was her private asylum. Her courgettes had flowered beautifully and the dark yellow shade of her gladioli-like flowers was contrasting beautifully with the dark green flowers of the climber plant that would soon give fruit and that is when she felt like a mother again. The cyclic procedure of creation and recreation satisfied her soul and heart like nothing else. The baby aubergines had been a bit of a surprise this year since she had planted seeds for the usual purple ones but the fruit had sprouted shiny white ones. She had hoped for them to turn a purple shade wholly when one of them had sprouted purple streaks on a white background, looking like a piece of art itself. But the colour had stayed the same and she found that she liked them for a change. She knew nature couldn't be controlled. Nature was wild as well as demure in various ways. There was the beauty of nature in flowers, motherhood and the cackle of an infant; then there was the coquettishness of it in a lover's glance, playfulness of water in a sea or spring alike; there was the wilderness of nature in powerful predatory jaws tearing into the flesh of weaker preys, the shrill sound of the shriek a mother gives when she forces out her blood bathed baby and in the snap felt inside when the heart breaks; there are depths in waters, valleys and emotions; there are heights in mountains, desert dunes and spirituality; there are numerous abysses of loneliness, despair, fickleness and faithlessness. Nature is beyond human control. The altitudes and vastness are all doings and musings of a greater being.

Maryam was lost in thoughts as she tweaked her plants, loosening the soil with a trowel, snipping the yellowing leaves with a pair of scissors, cleaning the dust covered vegetables with a spray of water from her spray bottle, trying not to touch the gentle buttercup-yellow flowers of the bitter gourds that hung silently facing downwards, getting ready to drop off as soon as the chameleon skinned vegetable would start sprouting from behind them.

She was planning on asking Garba to find her a felled tree log in the woods across the main road for she would, with his help, carve it hollow from inside and take out a chunk of its bark from one side, lay it flat on the ground and plant some herbs in it. "Would look beautiful," she congratulated herself on procuring such an aesthetic thought for her garden. Herbs would grow in days in the rich soil of Nigeria. The minerals were in abundance and the rain gods were being generous too.

She gave the vegetables one last hard look and noticed, they all grew in bunches, in twos or threes or in clusters. The vegetables that she spoke to, cuddled their seeds near her bosom before planting them made her understand what was going on in Harris's mind. She just couldn't make him understand how many rips her heart and soul had gone through and how much anymore rips would destroy her.

She could see Garba already returning from his earliest chore. He was quite a few yards away. She was still tending to her plants. Hyder was asleep inside and would not be disturbed. She decided on having Garba water her plants for her instead of doing the indoor chores while she would go pick up the broken ceramic figurines which had perturbed an already disturbed Hyder who had stood beneath the statue of the Baphomet the previous night, almost having sold his soul to the Devil.

CHAPTER 11

HARRIS

The plan for Harris had worked, Binta had screamed out at him for running from school. She had threatened to take him to the Headmaster's office herself. Harris had only grinned in response, knowing she wouldn't do that. The kids had all gathered in the compound. Mahmood the gardener was home today but he was about to leave for the school headmaster's home for whom he worked as a private gardener.

The cake Maryam had baked was downed by all as a welcome treat, Obi had enjoyed it the most.

"You lucky man," he had admired Harris's luck, "your Ma is super."

Zainab too had started fiddling with the English language and had remarked, "Very good," for which Harris had patted her on the back. The kids had stayed put until Mahmood finished his breakfast – porridge cooked with onions, tomatoes and chilli – a dish he had prepared himself. Binta had added some crunchy bits of fried yam on top of the savoury porridge to make it even tastier. The happy guy left for work and that was when it was time for some action. Obi produced some string and carefully tweaked strips of cane wood. Zainab produced some crepe paper. The stage was prepared in the middle of the compound for the compilation of a kite. Harris had never done it before, Obi had seen people do it and Zainab was an expert. The boys followed her guidelines and after a little more than half an hour, they were all looking happily at a diamond shaped piece of paper, about two feet in length and half the measurement in width, red coloured, it held up straight with help of the two strips of cane that had been tied across each other to give a spine to the bit of paper. String was tied in the middle of the two sticks where they crossed one another and the kite was ready to be flown!

Harris was bubbling with excitement. He wanted to have a go but Zainab told him she had to show him first. "I do it, then you do it," her language was simple, but correct, courtesy Harris. So the kids climbed a ladder that took them to the top of the roof and that's when they became oblivious of all that existed around them. Binta, who was peeling the green beans out of their shells, was looking at the small group of kids in front of her eyes and was transported back to a Nigeria that her mother had told her about. The colonial Nigeria when Lagos had belonged to the Europeans. Being the port city, the British settlers had found Lagos to be the hub of their transportation route. A harbour was built, the train and steamer had been introduced, the segregation of the port city where the white people had created a separate town for themselves on the east of the Lagos coast, near the Lagoon Island. Ikoyi, the place was called and was restricted to the baturiya people only and that too for their residential purposes. Blacks weren't allowed to trespass the area, except for those who worked as helpers or household servants. On the other side of the mainland Lagos was the place where the baturiya had their Golf course, the Tennis courts, their cricket pitch, their tea houses and clubs where they would mingle with the elite of the Lagos locales. It had been in 1960 when the baturiyas had decolonized Nigeria but a lot of them had not gone home. They had made Lagos their home. The Nigerians had not accepted them as one of their kind but had learnt to live with them. Binta's mother was a cook in one of the baturiya homes. She worked until her back gave out on her. By then, Binta was not able to find a similar job and had found a simpler way to earn – she bought a kerosene stove, a small wok and some ingredients to fry up kosay and yams to sell on the roadside and her small mobile kitchenette fed her and her mother for a couple of years until she was left to earn money for herself alone. She had seen the baturiyas look down upon the dark skinned, she had seen them smile at them. Sometimes their smiles oozed unneeded sympathy and sometimes it gave out pure genuine generosity.

She was listening to the shrieks and laughter of the kids playing up on her rooftop and let out a sigh of relief that they had not seen the segregated Nigeria, theirs was a more accepting, understanding Nigeria. The white boy was welcome to her house any time and so was his friend whom she was meeting for the first time. He was a good influence on her daughter, and he was an amusing friend to her. She smiled when one of them yelled at the others for letting the kite string slip away from his hands. It was Zainab, she was yelling in Hausa and Harris was calling Obi a dunce for ruining the day. When the poor boy had enough of their chiding she called them down to help her to cook lunch.

The climbed down the ladder very obediently, grumbling at the same time. Poor Obi looked embarrassed.

"What happen?" she asked as if the loud shouts hadn't reached her ears.

Zainab and Harris both complained at the same moment that Obi had let the kite slip away, they were throwing tantrums and making faces.

"So, it is done and it is over," she looked at her daughter, "daina gunaguni," she said.

"What did she say?" Haris whispered to Obi.

He replied, "She said, stop complaining."

"Come you boys, peel this masara," she handed them a basket full of fresh cobs of corn and gave them a bowl to put the separated kernels in. "You Zainab, wash the rice," and handed over a platter filled with white grains of rice to be washed and soaked before boiling. She herself went into the kitchen to carry on with her cooking. The kids had settled down on the compound, squatting on the ground, still teasing and upset. Harris would not have remembered his plan to tell them the story of Psyche and Cupid unless Obi's troll, the one he wore around his neck, didn't make a peek-a-boo glance at him through the space between two buttons on his shirt.

"Hey, would you like to hear a story?" he exclaimed, to which the kids looked up in eager response. And so the tale began. In the meanwhile, Binta had cubed some vegetables, carrots and onions, thrown in the beans she had peeled and waited patiently for the corn kernels. Zainab had handed her the rice and they were parboiled, cooked thoroughly in chicken stock and were placed in a serving dish to be stir fried with the rest of the vegetables.

Outside, when the story was finished, the boys were done with their job too. The kids had enjoyed the story and Obi had proposed he too should be given a chance to relate a religious story of his faith.

"I belong to Ibo tribe, my ancestors have given me that religion. There are many gods in our faith but the one my family worships the most is Ala. She is the mother of all Gods, and of all humans. She is the goddess of Earth and of humanity. So, when a mother has a child, it is because Ala gave the child to the mother, when a person dies, we bury him in the soil and he goes to the womb of Ala, back where he came from. We do not have statues of Ala at our home but there are huge ones at the Mbari near my home," he was interrupted.

"What's a Mbari?" Harris was the curious one.

"It's a place of worship. Just that it does not have walls, just a square ground. My mother told me that when she was married to my Dad, she went there every day to ask for a son and I was born. She stills says thank you to Ala every time we are there."

Harris yawned. "That wasn't a story," he looked at Obi who was obviously hurt by his discouragement.

"I think it was a nice story," Zainab said softly and that put a smile back on Obi's face. Harris was offended. He made another try. "Do you know the names of the days of the weeks, Zainab?" she nodded and counted all seven in front of the boys, "Monday, Tuesday, Wednesday..."

"Do you know why Tuesday is called Tuesday? Well, it's because there was an Anglo Saxon god named Tiv and he was worshipped on the same day of the week so the day was named Tiv's Day," he was beaming on his disclosure.

"So Wednesday also has a God?" Obi drawled, knowing what Harris was doing – trying to impress the girl.

"Yes, sir, its Wodin the warrior god, Thor the god of thunder on Thursday, Frigga the goddess of marriage for Friday, Saturn the king of them all for Saturday and Moon for Monday and Sun for Sunday," Harris had some pride in his voice.

"Who told you?" Zainab had a question.

"My mum," but then he added, "I also read it somewhere."

"My Ma says, there is only one God," Zainab said plainly.

"My Mum says that too," he said quietly.

"You go to mosque?" she asked Harris.

"No, do you?"

"Yes, on Friday after lunch. After you go."

"Really? Next time I will go with you," he jumped with excitement.

"Okay," Zainab beamed.

The kids played, talked, ate their fried rice and it was around three in the afternoon when someone knocked at the door and the faces turned to see Garba standing there.

"Harris," Garba spoke out loud, "Madam sends me to bring you home."

"That's not fair," Harris wasn't prepared for a pick up.

"We go now, Sister," he addressed Binta, perceiving that he would have trouble trying to convince Harris. She smiled and said "Sai Anjima," pleasantly. Obi and Zainab too waved a cheerful Sai Anjima – bye - and Harris walked along Garba.

They had walked the distance silently. Harris was obviously not happy. Once home, Garba said cheerfully to Maryam, "Madam, Harris no happy, you bring him home quick, he want to play more," Maryam had smiled, given him some leftover bread and some jam. "For dinner," she said, Garba thanked her, blessed her with a prayer and left.

"Mum, it's not fair," he sulked.

"You still have homework to do, sonny," she said as lovingly as possible.

He grunted.

"Have you eaten?"

"Yes." Sullen as ever.

"What?"

"Fried rice, can I go to my room now?"

She sighed inwardly. He disappeared into his room. She could hear the wood of his chair screech on the floor, which meant he really had sat down to work. Maryam looked at the other door which had been shut since last night. Hyder could not be sleeping for so long. She had gone to check up on him and he was lying flat on his face on the bed. "Are you okay?" she had barely asked to which he had replied in a sleepy voice, "Leave me alone." Maryam hadn't bothered him since. She switched on the TV, the national channel was running The Bold and the Beautiful. She settled down on the couch, legs folded and head thrown back. She didn't realise when the hypnotizing rays of the screen lulled her to a sleep.

CHAPTER 12

HYDER

If anyone had told a growing up Hyder that he would be a rich successful person living in a colonial bungalow in some North African country he would have either laughed or sorely wept. His early years and his adolescence were not promising. They didn't veneer him to his destination, he had managed to climb out of the well of poverty slowly but with obstinacy. He had learned the ways of how a "sahib" behaves and had put them to practice. And he had perfected them.

Hyder's origins took him back to Lahore in Pakistan where his father had been dead since he was a toddler and his mother a housemaid. The house was located in a dinghy residential area in one of the ignored neighbourhoods of Shahdara, a town located on the outskirts of Lahore. There was always a serene calmness in the house. The mud walls surrounding a small 12 x 16 room stood like half melted wax candles, aged and stoic. If one looked closely, they all seemed to have faces etched into them: wry, sunken, baggy near the eyes and droopy around the mouth. They were smothered in mud and a special clay called multani mitti – sand from Multan, a city within a desert. The person, who had done so, although, was either bothered by her children and had completed a hurried task or had gone asleep with boredom with the tedious undertaking of applying a layer of pasty mud all over her house because the coating had lumps and holes, thus giving character and features to the walls. One of his favorite memories was of his mother, Nisreen. He could think about her and smile – a rarity in his nostalgic moments. Of all the other mental pictures that went on reeling inside the cog works of his brain, he could play, rewind and watch over and over a particular character from his childhood, his niece Falak was the favorite.

Falak, literally meant the sky. Hyder had named her and to him she was the prettiest doll he had ever seen. He picked her up gingerly in his arms and kissed her forehead every day before going to school.

The chance that Nisreen had taken at sending her only boy at school had worked well in her favor. The boy had turned out to be solid gold. He worked hard and being an only son, and brother of five sisters he understood his sisters had been deprived of education just to let him be the 'chosen seed'. The school Nisreen had decided to send him to, was around five kilometers away from her home. Since they lived in a rural countryside, the only option Hyder was left with was to walk all the way down and back every day without fail. Sometimes Nisreen would accompany him in the afternoons. The track that he followed daily was an interesting one. It had a graveyard, a lake and an area that was in ruins. Rumor was, the dead rose from their graves at night and haunted the place and thus the residents had deserted the place and the ghosts had turned them into ruins. It was also claimed by a few that the evil spirits could be heard or seen at night.

Hyder, for one, was the Wordsworthian boy who felt immense joy in prancing these paths every day. Sometimes he would venture to go into the ruins and find an object of interest. It could an abandoned loop of thread or a bottle top with RC written on it (RC was the local version of cola) or if he got really lucky, a dead baby bird that could be picked up, dressed and washed and then buried. Heat of the sun would perturb him as much as it could a boy out on a solitary adventure. He considered his little excursions as practice for the real big plan he had laid out for his future. Hyder secretly wished to be a pirate.

He wanted to get loads of money in a jiffy and mend all his mother's problems. Then she won't have to work as a housemaid. To be a pirate he would need a ship and he had it all sorted out. During the summer holidays of his tenth year at school, he had discovered a secret place for himself. Amongst the ruins, was a small shelter, a cabin really with bits and odds and signs of being some sort of a shed. It had a few planks of wood and a couple of logs too. Between his school and his apprenticeship at the workshop he didn't have too much spare time but there was just enough to start collecting wood for the ship. So from broken down branches and loose firewood to small shrubbery stems, all was kept safe at the shed. Every day, he added to that pile and went home, quietly pondering on the fact, how much he still needed and then there was the question of buying tacks too. "But that can wait till summer," would be his solace. Right after his Noah's task would be done, the ship would be put in the lake and as his geography teacher had explained several times in class, the lake would finally drop into the big sea and that would be the end of all his misery. Once at sea, he would be a pirate. Easy money, no hassle, what a bloody life. For a teenager, he was still pretty simple, innocent and naïve. The reason could probably be his absolute absence of social life.

He studied at school in the morning and went out to work as an apprentice at the motorbike repair station commonly called the 'workshop'. It helped him pay his school fee. He spent his day doing jobs no one else wanted to do – wash and wipe the motorbikes that had been worked upon and were to be returned to their owners the subsequent day, fetch cold drinks for the loyal clientele and simmering cups of tea for everyone thrice a day from the teashop across the main road. The owner of the workshop was a skinny man of around 45 who had a habit of smoking cigarettes all day long. His business had been going on well for the past many years so his main job was just to sit and supervise. Three other older boys did the work and Hyder was the odd-job-boy.

When there would be nothing to do, Hyder was summoned to stand behind the owner postured in the "sitting Buddha" position and give the older guy a shoulder massage.

"What, didn't your mother give you breakfast today?"

This question wasn't asked out of concern but was a loaded force to make the boy scrunch his palms with more pressure to ease his muscles. Sometimes he would get a smack on his face as a reinforcement to do better. The other three boys treated him like an assistant too. So he was the one no one could seem to do without but he was the most ill-treated too.

Hyder didn't enjoy his job. While scrubbing dirty tires and washing the upholstery that had been pulled off the seats of the bikes, his imagination would take him far off in the land of ruins and the precious collection of wood to build a ship or at least a boat big enough to carry him and his belongings along with Falak and Nisreen. The rest didn't matter at all.

His childish dreams were put to a halt when his precious collection of wood started to get stolen. Someone had discovered the secret place! The first time only the firewood and branches had disappeared and Hyder had remained stoic. It must be some poor wanderer who would have taken it as firewood. It wasn't such a big jolt because there were still a lot of trees near the ruins and he could easily get more of them. The next day, (although it was summer and the vacation had begun after his high school examination and there was no need to cover five kilometers in the blazing heat to go check upon some planks of wood), he was heartbroken and devastated when to the soreness of his eyes, the planks and logs were missing too.

That day Hyder wept. He wailed like a baby, crying out and spitting abuse at the thief. He walked through the ruins, every broken door was crossed, every window was peeped through, every wall was punched and fisted, he poured down tears of rage, sat down when the excursion around the ruins became too tiring, put his knees up close to his chest, fitted his head between his knees like a ball stuck in two entwined branches, folded his hands over his head and went to sleep in one of the houses. They were all the same to look at – mud plastered walls, doors standing without walls and windows popped out of their hinges and lying flat faced on the ground. There must have been a neighborhood here a long time ago since the streets were also visible quite easily, without having any digging to do. The boy was forlorn and heartbroken. His dreams shattered, he slept a dreamless sleep for over an hour. Soon it was dusk. The birds flitting around screeched as if calling out to kin and mates to join them for a flight back home. The sun turned a hazy purple from the beautiful orange that it had been a few moments ago. At dawn the earth is stretching out its arms like a bloomed young woman, exposing and flaunting every tiny detail of her profile, fruits heavily laden with nectar and glistening with dew drops from the night gone by, the folds of flesh straightening out bit by bit until its vales and mounts become visible to the naked eye.

Now, as the day had come to an end and the sun had to go, the earth was going back to bed like a baby: crying out a crescendo with all the energy it had left – crickets, owls, wild pigeons and crows, rustling trees as the settlers snuggled in their nests, squirrels and stray dogs all finding a refuge- the baby earth was trying to deny the empowering stillness of sleep and kicking about in all directions with loud noises, nestlings crying out for the last bit of supper before going to a furry bed and flowers discreetly turning back into buds as if they were holding tiny Thumbelinas in each one of them to cuddle and snuggle all night long while a cool bluish night Lamp kept burning faraway.

Hyder awoke. It was past sunset. Heck, it was dark. He lifted his head from his knees and looked around. At first he thought something was wrong with his eyes and he rubbed them with his fingers. Nothing changed. For the first few micro fractions of a moment, he couldn't remember where he was. Night time at home wouldn't be so dark, there would be the firefly sized blinking lights of the traffic far on the main road, the loud horns of a truck and some lantern burning nearby around which mosquitoes and moths would be dancing an apache-like dance. Most comforting was the hard fact that whenever he would stretch out his right arm outwards from his jute bed, it would always touch his eldest sister's charpoy. He waved his hands frantically around him and felt nothing but the air. Sightlessness was being equal to breathlessness. He stood up and tried to run in search of light and air and after taking a few lunges forthrightly, banged into a wall. He knew there would be a sore there but the hurt was nothing compared to the suffocation he was feeling. He was inhaling heavily but it felt as if someone was in between his air passage and the air around him, as if someone was sucking the air that he wanted to breathe. He moved in another direction and bumped into a wall again, the third time he started feeling the wall with his hands and moved gently like a blind man. This time, after a few footsteps, his hands fell into a hole in the darkness. It was an opening! He felt it with his feet and it transpired it was a door. He dashed through it and it took him into a narrow corridor where he could place both his hands on each side against the two walls and walk in between. The corridor ended and as he took the last step, he stumbled as

the floor had ended and his feet touched ground about half
a foot below. The step led to another and to another. Finally
he could feel the air around him different. It was fresh. The
moonlight was dim but it made him see a little. The eerie
silence prevailed. The benefit he had had of being a regular
visitor to the place was that he knew the houses all stood
facing one another in two straight lines and on either side
of the neighborhood was open land that could take him on
his route to the lake and the graveyard and from there to
home. The thin sheath of clouds that had been enveloping
the moon till now parted ways and the moonlight made his
eyes start working again. He started running as fast as his
legs could. The silence around was broken by the clattering
sound his rubber slippers made when they made contact
with the dusty path. The houses kept standing exactly as
they were, seemingly watching the boy run past each one
of them and the sounds he made with his running grew
fainter and fainter.

Hyder had reached home where Nisreen had already begun
the search for him. His sisters, his neighbors, they were
all looking for him and Nisreen herself had gone to the
workshop to see why the boy hadn't returned. There she
was told he never came to work that day. Nisreen had been
sobbing all the way back home and had pressed him close
to herself, kissed his face a hundred times when she saw him
sitting on his charpoy all wet with perspiration, cuddling
Falak in his arms.

The ship of being a pirate had sailed too soon for Hyder
but the experience of the grave-like environs made him
stop going there anymore. Nisreen had him admitted to a
college in the city and booked a room for him at the hostel.

She sat with him outside the hostel for a couple of hours. Asking him to study well. Making him promise he will not go wandering around anywhere and keep himself put. She wiped droplets of sweat forming on his forehead with the edge of her scarf. She left, saying 'God be with you,' and smiled. Hyder knew she would cry in private. He geared up his courage and walked to enter the hostel, a big block of building from the outside really. He had never seen a red brick building before except maybe on TV. He touched the bricks and ran his hand across the roughness of the brick tile. It transferred some bolts of lightning excitement in him. He was free. He was alone. He had finally attained his goal. He had sailed out of Shahdara into the big city, into a sea of people. A people of all kinds and all sizes and shapes, all sorts of excitement was going on inside the hostel. Just before he stepped into the entrance gate, he saw a roadside barber – his only equipment being a worn out chair whose leather was missing in several parts of the seat and it exposed yellow colored foam from beneath. Next to the chair was a small stool on which the barber sat himself waiting for the next customer and under the stool, in a smallish drawer, he kept his utensils – razors, shaving foam, scissors, combs and a compact mirror. Business was good, for the boys needed a shave and a haircut regularly.

Hyder walked past all of them. There were boys of all types around him sitting, strolling, gossiping, fighting, yelling, cheering, smoking, sipping tea and standing in solo or in groups. The level of activity was out of control. The freshmen could be spotted easily, they were all wearing untrendy clothes, were carrying knapsacks on their backs and wore a nervous look on their faces. Most of them sported a moustache and a beard. The sophomores and seniors were also easily recognizable – they wore more hip clothes in accordance to their environment in Lahore – denims, tee shirts and shirts. They were loud and confident, they seemed to know everyone around them - Feeka the tea stall owner, Raja the barber, Bhai Niaz the laundry guy and Sheeda the shoe shiner. The businessmen were also part of the conversation going on. They would also pipe in their smartass comments with the guys and keep working too. They all had lists of boys who owed them money for weeks and months but there was no bad blood. It was all cheerful and gay.

As he gingerly approached the flight of stairs that would take him to the dorms as per the signboard, he saw a few eyes turn towards him. A couple started laughing out loud for apparently no reason, a few stuffed their fists into their mouths, some high-fived one another. Hyder saw all this from the corner of his eye for he was not bold enough to meet them eyeball to eyeball. He kept climbing and climbing but the stairs didn't seem to end. If he would have to climb this many stairs every day, he would have to grow a new pair of legs every week. He had taken about forty steps till now but the winding staircase kept growing, it seemed. Finally it came to a door after about sixty steps. The door was closed but not fastened. It was an iron door, painted black. He gave it a gentle shove and it creaked open. He stepped into it, with a smile on his face considering it his new home when he saw the strangest scene ever.

This was no dorm. It was the rooftop. He was standing atop three floors of dormitories and in front of him, the freshmen were all getting a shave from the senior boys. They had perched the newbies on chairs and they all sat there with looks as if they had been strapped on to the electric chair.

"You will thank us for this later," the senior boys were sounding as if they were giving them a favor.

"The girls in the city, tut, tut, very demanding! They don't like boys with moustaches, do they?" they were nudging each other.

On the other end of the roof top, those who had already been clean shaved were giving the senior boys a foot and leg massage. The older ones lay flat on their stomachs grinning to each other, winking and the victims of this ragging were doing their jobs with serious faces grim with displeasure. The pranksters had marked the narrow staircase that led to the rooftop as DORMS and had waited for the preys to land silently in their trap. After all the boys were shaven and stood looking cleaner than before and all the older boys had gotten their massages as a 'payback', the older ones demanded a mujra dance, which could only be understood as the dance of a courtesan at an emperor's court in the past and a prostitute's den at present. Hyder was not just the only one to be picked since all the pretty boys were assembled, cruelly discarding the less than average looking boy, and there was held a competition for the best dance. The losers would be all made to stand on the water tank installed on the rooftop all night.

The freshmen danced, one after the other, they were booed at, hooted at and ridiculed. It was a scene worth enjoyment if one would be the audience, the ones dancing were at their wits end. Hyder's turn was last. He had no idea what dance to perform but he knew one thing – he had no intention of spending the lonely night in a strange unfamiliar place alone on the rooftop so he danced all the moves he could remember from the stolen glances he had had at an Indian film star Rekha and Helen at the neighbor's TV screen back home. He was having jolts of embarrassment but his experience at the ruins had gripped his heart with fear once again as he imagined whatnot could be done to him alone on the rooftop. Turned out, Hyder was the winner. The boys whistled, they clapped, they jiggled their own shoulders when he danced and there were a lot of cat calls.

Resultantly, Hyder was named Anarkali – the latter being the most popular courtesan of the mogul courts in the subcontinent. So at the hostel, among all the boys' names that were heard calling out to each other, Anarkali too was one of them. That afternoon, when the platoon came down and was shown the real passage to the dorms, the ragger boys introduced Anarkali to the rest of the boys at the mess. They laughed, they hooted. It angered him, stabbed his plump male-ego but it couldn't be undone. Anarkali he was to the end of the session.

At college he studied Sociology and Anthropology along with Oriental-African History. He had opted for the subjects because he liked the sound of them, they were different and no one was really looking at them with interest. They seemed challenging and also, he had hoped, would keep him out of trouble. The more popular the subject, the more mingling he would have to do and the older boys scared him enough at the hostel. He didn't want to bear a crowd at college calling him Anarkali in front of the girls and the professors.

Hyder majored in Anthropology with only twelve batch mates – ten of them girls. He was a good student. Studious and hardworking since, he didn't really have anything else to do on campus. He wasn't one of those lucky ones who had money in their pockets to go hangout or eat out of campus. His day began with breakfast at the hostel cafeteria, for which the money was already paid along with the college fee. He went to class after that and returned for lunch, went up to his room and studied. The rooftop where he had seen the massacre of his moustache and had won his first accolade, had become his favorite places of all. His college, the Government College for Boys was located in the oldest vicinity of the historical city of Lahore. There was a museum nearby, three or four historical monuments, an age old library, a public park and the Urdu Bazaar – a heaven for book lovers where books can be bought from the shops or the footpath. All of this helped him with his course of study. His environs, more than the people in it, became his friends and he found comfort in them.

Hyder had found comfort in Lahore. He never ached to go back home. His bouts of nostalgia and homesickness were befitting enough for a letter he would write back home once or twice a month. And it seemed to suffice. He wrote simple sentences, knowing the postman would have to read the letter out to the recipient. Nisreen went around her small locality, trying to find anyone who could reread the letter to him as many times as she wanted and also be kind enough to jot down a few sentences in reply. In one of such letters, Nisreen had asked an innocent question: Who is Anarkali since all his letters were signed by some Anarkali at the back of the envelope. Hyder was dumbfounded. He exactly knew he wrote Hyder on his envelopes. This mystery was solved pretty quickly by him as he realized he gave the sealed envelope to the warden each time to dunk it in the mailbox. The warden, who shared a special friendship with the senior boys, couldn't be trusted any more. He was careful the next time onwards to go across the road and slid the envelope marked "From Hyder Khan" into the mailbox near the museum.

He completed his graduation degree after four years and passed with honors. Nisreen came to attend his ceremony as per his wish and couldn't stop crying. She sat amongst the other parents in the jam-packed auditorium while Hyder and his other fellow batch mates stood on the stage, having received their medals and rolls of honor. He could see his mother easily from where he stood, the woman with a white chador wrapped around herself and her head, her white hair that had never been accustomed to hair dye shone on her forehead and she was wiping her tears from the corner of that chador. He had seen her wear that chador ever since he was a little boy. He was having his pictures taken with the Chancellor and the chief guest who had handed him over his roll of honor. It was Nisreen's dream come true. She had succeeded. She had no idea what her son had studied all these years, what he was capable of and what not but he was standing amongst the cream of the educational sector and her dream had been fulfilled. She was on cloud nine.

All these four years, Hyder had spent no more than a fortnight per year at home. He would see his sisters, all of them married by now, Falak had started to go to school and still loved her precious uncle more than anyone else. Nisreen had stopped working as a housemaid but still had to earn the dry bread for herself and her granddaughter. So she embroidered and sew whatever she could for the ladies she had earlier worked for and tried to make a living. She coughed a lot. Everyone thought it was old age. But one day, a month before Hyder's graduation ceremony, she spat blood and when she saw it, she smiled and thanked God.

Nisreen was an old woman, her hands all wrinkly and skeletal from the hard work she had been doing since her childhood. She had no parents to eat off from. Her father had married again after her mother died during childbirth, leaving a two year old Nisreen motherless. Her father's second wife bore him six sons and that left Nisreen a lonely daughter who was to be rid off as soon as possible and the day Nisreen hit puberty, her step mother went to her dad and spoke secretively.

"Your daughter is a big girl now. I cannot protect her from the roaming wolves any more. Get her married off as soon as you can, I have young boys in the house and cannot explain to them why she is crying out in pain."

"She is still a little girl. How can I give her away to someone already? She is just a child, look at her!"

"Don't blame me when some day she makes love with some village idiot and comes home with her belly full. I am telling you, I cannot guard her anymore."

Nisreen's father hung his head in shame. Having a daughter had never been such a load on his head or his bosom. One daughter was burden enough. And it had to be removed. So Nisreen was married off to a man of forty five who could offer her nothing but an acre of fertile land. Ten years later,

Nisreen had given birth to three daughters Misbah, Samia and Saba and a son whom she named Hyder. Hyder's father was elated upon his son's arrival. However, he had died a few months later, at the age of fifty five and Nisreen a young widow of just twenty two. He left her nothing but the acre of land. She sold it and rented a small house in one of the poorer countryside on the outskirts of Lahore. She didn't want a fate for her daughters like hers. She couldn't rely on the norms of the village. Her education was zilch and the only way to feed her kids was through hard work so she became a housemaid. She paid her rent and bought them food and paid Hyder's fee with her hard work.

But now she was done. The blood in her mouth was news for a long holiday she needed. Her daughters were with their husbands, her son had graduated and would do all he could for himself and his sisters. There would be no better time to die.

And she did. Hyder was there. He had taken off from the city life for a couple of months waiting for his travel documents to arrive. The Sociology Department had noticed the flying colours with which he had graduated and had offered him a scholarship abroad. He had a choice to either go to Canada or America. He had opted the former and had applied for his documents. In the meanwhile he had gone home for a couple of months to relax and enjoy his summer with Falak who had started writing letters to him when he was away. She was extremely shy, though. Whenever she would see him, she would hide her face in her hands and then glance at him shyly. He would signal her to come and her footsteps were taken so gingerly, so coyly that it made him laugh. She was fond of birds but Nisreen wouldn't let her keep one. "How can you love a bird when you put it in the cage?" Falak was too small to understand her grandmother's philosophy of love but she complied. When Hyder got to know about the dilemma, he made a birdhouse for her and perched it on top of the wall. Then he bought her a big dish made of clay to use as a bird bath. The local sparrows and larks became regular visitors to the house and Falak was told that they were all her pets.

Her eyes had shone and she hugged her uncle. He was Hyder Saab now to the people around him, for his appearance had changed and his way of talking, walking, sitting, standing, it had all changed. He didn't look like one of them. He was a mama's boy and these two months, he had been fed like a baby bird, from bhagar daal to dahi khichdi, everything was shared between the mother-son duo.

Nisreen hadn't told him or anyone else for that matter about her illness. She spat in the toilet when she wanted to so no one could see what she spat.

"It's just age coming on to me, don't worry," she would remark when Hyder would show concern about her regular coughing.

"I will bring some pure honey from the spiritual healer in the neighbouring village. They say he is a great man of God," her convincing tone hushed him up.

The day she had to go forever, she had swept the hearth and wanted to cook kadhi for Hyder. For reference, kadhi is a dish made with chickpea flour fritters dipped in a sauce made with sour curd and lots of turmeric. People enjoy it with flat bread, rice or just like that. Hyder preferred rice. He had gone to the post office to see whether any mail had arrived when terror gripped his household. Misbah had gone to work at the begum's house, Falak was sitting talking to the birds that flew around and Nisreen vomited blood near the stove.

Falak didn't know what to do so she started crying, the neighbours came to help but Nisreen's time to go had arrived. She was made to lie down on a charpoy and someone was sent off to the post office to fetch Hyder. She died before he could arrive. There was mourning and ceremonies. Hyder took part in nothing. He just went to the ruins that had scared him four years ago and wept. He wiped his tears with the sleeve of his shirt and sat on the ground to be covered in dust. He couldn't see his mother dead so he hid from it all. It was too much to bear.

CHAPTER 13

MALAM YAKUBU

The school was nearly empty now as it was almost a quarter of an hour later than home time. Malam Yakubu had asked him to wait for a small conversation after home time. Harris had dreaded the meeting all day. He had not yet forgotten how his creative writing assignment had been treated last term – Malam had given him an F and had also later given the composition to Mum. He didn't know but she had read it many times over and wept for his ignorance, his lack of information and experience. This was the final term now, in December, the assignment Malam had given to the class was to write a poem.

"What about, Malam?" someone had asked.

"Anything, anything at all. It can be the cup from which you drink your water, the weather that makes you happy, the person that matters the most," Malam had been very unhelpful. 'Anything' was a very looming topic.

"That confuses us, Malam," Obi had stood up and confessed.

Malam had walked towards his desk, made him sit down on his chair and had replied very gently, "The easy way is this, Obiyara. Sit down in a quiet place and empty your mind of all thoughts., now this is easier said than done. It might take you hours, but once you do, you need to be very tactful – you need to grip with both hands the thought that keeps coming back to you again and again. You will shun your head, stuff cotton wool in your ears, close your eyes, switch off the lights but one thought, one person, one feeling, will keep coming back to you. What is that feeling? Locate it, and then write about it."

It did sound convincing. So the class tried to do the exercise there and then. Harris had been unsuccessful at emptying his mind for it wandered to what Obi was thinking, did Malam's formula ever work for him et cetra. Malam had not been hard on the students. He had given them a week to write the poem, it could be of five lines or five pages, he had said, but it should be poetic.

"I don't want you to write a poem with rhyming words, it's not twinkle twinkle little star for you anymore," the class had laughed. "But your words should be gelled with one another, each line should be balanced with the other and when I read that poem, it should give me a look into your heart." Malam Yakubu was being tough. Teachers of other forms had just given book reviews to write or enactments to prepare.

Harris had spent the weekend trying out Malam's poetic meditation and for him, it had not seemed to work for him at all. The day he was summoned home from Zainab's place, he had locked himself up in the room, put out the lights, sat down at his study desk and put his head on the desk. He was thinking alright. He was thinking why his mum had been so cruel as to pull him out of his play date, knowing how important it was for him to get Zainab and Obi together, he was thinking why he hadn't seen his Dad, and he was thinking how to get rid of these thoughts. He sat up, heard a familiar lady's voice coming from outside. Mum was trying to convince her that she wasn't asleep at all, the familiar voice was being apologetic to call at such an odd hour. He tried to block out the voices and tried to focus, he couldn't. He gave up trying and left the desk to go see who the person with that voice was – he had heard it a lot many times before but he just couldn't place it.

"Auntie Needi," he almost exclaimed when he saw the lady sitting with her mum alongside the sofa.

"Say Namaste," Mum prompted.

"Namaste," he said and his aunt put out both arms, demanding a bear hug. She got one and she pulled him to make him sit on her legs. "How's my baby boy?" Harris glanced at his mother, he didn't like it when she treated him like a baby. "I am okay," he said meekly. "He was at a friend's, just came home to do homework. How far have you reached, Harris?" Maryam asked lovingly. "No where at all, I can't focus," he complained agitatedly, almost springing up from Mrs Needi's cuddle.

"What are you focusing at?" she asked puzzled, homework was never a problem for Harris, he was usually good at everything. "I have to write a poem and Malam Yakubu says empty your mind of all thoughts and the only thought that keeps coming back again and again should be the topic of your poem. Now I can't focus and I don't have a topic and I don't have a poem ready for him tomorrow," he painted a picture of doom. Mrs Needi intervened.

"Harris beta, you would like me to help?"

He was taken aback. "Yeah, I guess," his voice quavered.

"Okay, let's sit down on the mat first and relax. Cross your legs like I have, good boy. Aray Maryam, why are you not joining us, come, it's good for the body and the soul too. Come come, good girl. Now, first forget about the assignment, and forget about the teacher. Just sit with me as if you are giving a break to that brain of yours that keeps thinking so much, also to your heart that races and paces with all your naughtiness. Maryam, try too. Now let's close our eyes. No, Harris, don't slouch, sit up straight. Like this, shoulders straight, every muscle of your neck straight, every chip of your backbone in place. Put your wrists on your knees and your fingers curled like mine, not this finger, the other one, right, and now close your eyes and say with me... OM... OM... OM." Mrs Needi kept on with the japa for several minutes. During that time, Harris had opened his eyes many times and looked at the ladies, shook his head in disbelief, was it working for them? He was staring open eyed at them, watching Auntie's mouth round up to a circle when she recited the mantra. He observed the two ladies. Auntie was fat, wore a sari, always wore a mala made of 108 beads of the tulsi wood, she was wheatish skinned, had curly hair, her eyes were round and had a sliver of kindness in them. She was a government servant in the electricity department. Her son used to live with her till a few years ago but now he had gone to the United States for advanced studies. Mum was slimmer, she looked like auntie's daughter when he juxtaposed their countenances so closely. She was pretty, fair skinned, pink cheeked and her silky hair flew in strands in the lightest breezes. He was lost in his scientific readings when Auntie stopped the mantra and opened her eyes.

"You naughty boy, how can I help you if you won't listen to me," she faked a frown. She was smiling.

Maryam smiled too. "Now you know the exercise, you can do it yourself," she suggested. "That would give me a chance to make a cup of tea for us to share," she continued. "Aray nahi, Maryam, don't bother," auntie protested. "Its jasmine tea deedee, it's very soothing," she assured already sailing into the kitchen. Auntie didn't say more. Harris too went into the room to meditate some more.

It didn't work, he wasn't following instructions. Later that evening, Maryam popped her head in his room through the door and asked him how well it was going and she was greeted by a long face. There were sheets of paper scattered around in the room. She gave out a laugh at her tiny Shakespeare. She disappeared and came back moments later with a diary in her hands. It was a small leather covered diary, it looked pretty old.

"See if this helps you," she patted his head and he took the book, with a grimace. She left him with her treasure and he started to flip the pages. It was filled with poems. Some of them were difficult to understand – there were odes and dedications to people like Apollo, Aphrodite and Julius, there were religious poems – Prayer on the deathbed, Vision of Heaven, Lines of Scripture. He was confused. Who had written these poems? The handwriting was his mum's but there was no poet's name at the end of any poem. He kept turning pages until he arrived at simpler themes – the Sphere of the Night, Autumn Tree, Darkness. He read a few of those and liked them. He read another one and read it again. He went through that poem thrice. It intrigued him. The style was simple. It was like conversation, not very difficult to read or write.

He closed his eyes. His mind was still not empty. He was thinking, had Mum written all these poems? He couldn't rid himself of the thought. He opened his eyes, and blinked them again and again. His topic was his mother. How plain and simple. He punched a fist in the air, read his favourite poem again and sat down to write.

"Did it help?" she asked about an hour ago when she brought him his dinner in the room.

"You bet, thanks Mum," he gave her a big hug.

"Oh, you are welcome. Here's your burger, no slaw, just cheese and patty," she smiled.

"Thanks."

She turned to leave.

"Hey, Mum, did you write these poems?"

"Why?"

"Just asking."

"I will tell you some other time. Did you manage to write your poem?"

"Yeah, about half of it," he said counting the pages he had scribbled on.

"Can I see?" she came forward with expectation and curiosity.

"No, not yet. When it's done, I will show you," he grabbed the sheets and held them close to his chest as if she would snatch them from him.

Now after two days of his submission, Malam Yakubu had summoned him for a private meeting and he was dreading to face him. Was he going to get an F again this term? Why does Malam make assignments so tough? Can't he just score him on his class performance? He is exceptional. At the sixteenth minute, the door to the classroom opened and Malam appeared, signalled him to come in and closed the door behind him. He asked him to sit on his seat and himself, Malam took the seat next to him. "So, Haris, how are you?" Harris blinked. "I am fine, thank you Malam."

It was apparent that Malam was having difficulty in choosing his words. He was hesitant to talk.

"Haris, I read your poem," he said, with his eyes stuck on the wall opposite to them both.

"I understand," Harris bleated, fock, he thought, it IS about the damned poem.

"Is there something you want to tell me about your poem?"

"There is nothing to tell, Malam, I wrote it yesterday," he said quickly. "I did have a lot of problems trying to think of a topic but in the end the other poem helped me."

"Yes, the other poem, your Ma wrote that?"

"Well, she wouldn't say, but I believe it's something she wrote."

"And what would make you say that?"

"She... she... I am not sure. It sounded like her words when I read them again and again."

"I want to see your parents, can I?"

"My Dad's pretty busy these days," he gulped in his heart that had come to his throat. Would Malam not promote him to next form just because of a stupid poem? Why Mum and Dad?

"Okay, then your Ma, she should come. I want to talk to her," Malam said firmly.

"I will tell her," he promised helplessly.

"Okay sonny, see you tomorrow, have a good day," Malam showed him out of the room with these words and he ran like there were hounds chasing him. He didn't stop until he reached home. Maryam was waiting with a dining table laden with lunch, he told her in the same breathless countenance that Malam wanted to see her. "What about?" she had asked. "Dunno," he spoke between two gulps of water.

All Harris did till the next day was fidget and worry. The next morning, Maryam told Hyder at the breakfast table about Malam's request. Hyder had emerged bluer from the room this morning. Bluer than yesterday when he had locked himself up in the room all weekend and had not even come out to see Daas when Maryam had knocked on his door to tell him he was waiting in the sitting room. He didn't acknowledge Maryam's query. That meant, she would have to go alone. Like always.

"So, I will go today," she informed him, in a manner of asking. He still pretended not to hear. Maryam handed Harris his snack for school and fussed around to put Hyder's car keys handy to him. Hyder had been staring at the newspaper. He had neither turned the pages nor unfolded the fold for the past fifteen minutes. He was wearing a scowl on his face and Harris wanted to run to school although he still had a good forty minutes before the assembly started.

"Okay, got to go," he called out as happily as possible while trying to wear his backpack. Maryam went forward to help but he ran off, letting the backpack hang from one shoulder. She dashed to the veranda to call out "Slow down!" to him. Maryam glanced at Hyder from the corner of her eye, he was still reading the same page of the paper. He hadn't made eye contact with either Harris or her since Saturday. "I wonder what's going on with him," she thought. She thought of bringing up school again but thought better of it. She had found it funny, because a couple of days ago, she had gone to the school and Hyder had acted as if some natural disaster had occurred, his honour had been ripped or the world had turned upside down. But today, he had been so aloof and detached that he hadn't even bothered to know why a teacher would like to see the parents of a brilliant student just before the scholastic year ended. She had walked with Harris to the school, asked him to show where the staffroom was. She went into the staffroom, leaving Harris to wait in the playground. He had plucked a few blades of grass and had looked at the closed door again and again. Inside the conversation was nothing either Maryam or Harris had expected. Malam had been very courteous and stood up for the lady, waited until she made herself comfortable in the chair right across his.

"Mrs. Khan, Haris has recently stepped into the world of poetry, you must know?" he commented causally.

"Oh yes, he told me. He has been quite occupied with the assignment I must tell you, all through the weekend, actually," she smiled and spoke demurely.

"Did you read the poem he submitted?"

"Err, no, actually he said it wasn't complete until his bedtime and Monday morning he left for school early," she said thoughtfully, her brows in a frown. "Is all okay?"

"Yes, for me all is okay. The poem itself was disturbing, it reads as if it has come from a disturbed mind," Malam looked straight into her eyes.

"I don't understand," she was confused.

"You see, Mrs Khan, Nigeria has advanced and progressed on many levels. We still cling to our culture with fierce passion and emotion but the social order has changed. Women are quite, let's say emancipated, for the lack of a better word." Malam Yakubu noticed Maryam was looking confused with his words. He kept going on, "There are many organizations that help women in trouble... of any kind."

"I apologize for being so dumb, Mr Yakubu, but how does that connect with Harris, or for that matter, me?"

"Mrs. Khan, is there an environment of violence at your home?"

She had shuffled in her seat. Seeing her discomfort, he had handed her the two pages Hyder had given to him as an assignment. One was his poem, the other was hers, the one he had read over and over. He had titled his work, MARYAM. The other poem had a scribbled handwriting that said, "Poem by Maryam Khan, my Mum but she won't tell."

"I have to tell you Mrs. Khan, you have a brilliant boy there. He takes after you, I believe."

She looked up at him.

"I read the poem you wrote. It was very touching and it spoke to me. Harris is lucky to have educated parents like you, but I have felt he is losing his focus, especially during this term. You need to pull him back"

"Do you think his selection of poems has anything to do with my being a mother or a wife?"

"What I want to tell you is, that he knows whatever is happening at your home. If you know that he knows, then it's none of my business, however, it is of concern to me that the same treatment must be or could be meted out to the boy. But if you don't know that he knows your ordeal, then there's news for you."

She felt she couldn't lie any more to deny his words. She just fumbled the sheets of paper in her hands.

"You must remember it's not the first time we are having a chat about Harris's writings. The previous term had given me some idea about him being an unhappy child, but I coaxed myself to not be presumptuous." Maryam listened.

"Also Mrs Khan, I have been noticing a strange pattern for a couple of months. Haris comes to school on Fridays but only until recess. After that, he vanishes. Do you know where he goes?"

Maryam sucked in her breath. Her questions and doubts had found their answer. She explained about Zainab.

"I see, but that's not a good thing."

"I will talk to him," she promised.

"Alright then, we are done here," he said cheerfully. Maryam handed back his son's assignment. Just when Maryam got up to leave, he stood up and said, "If you ever need help, this is my number," he shoved a paper into her hand. "I have many lawyer friends and some friends in social security too. If you ever need help..." Tears sprang to her eyes, she hadn't wanted the melodrama. The woman just shook her head, her face turned puffy from holding back tears. Malam began, "I am sorry madam, I didn't mean to..." she just looked at him and mouthed a thank you before exiting the door. When she was out there, Harris advanced towards her.

Her eyes were all red and puffy as if she had been crying. He was worried. Had Malam kicked him out? Was it something else? Had Malam noticed his weekly school bunks on Fridays and told on him? He only dared to ask, "What's wrong, Mum?" to which she had not replied, she was still sniffing back tears, biting her lower lip. She only cupped his face with her hands and whispered, "I am sorry," and told him to go to class while she, clutching at her coat and woollen scarf with one hands for support and the folded bit of paper Malam had handed to her in the other, walked towards the gate that would lead her home.

Harris Khan

Fourth form

English Assignment

MARYAM

She is not a flower...
Do not pluck her
As if it won't hurt her.
Do not pick her up
Just to colour up your collar
Why do you think,
All she is, is colour and form?

She is not a doll
Do not toy with her
Do not think
Her feelings are the key
You can wind up as you please.
She has her own songs
Why do you want her to sing yours?
Why do you think
All she is, is smiles and songs?

She is not that dog,
Sleeping on your porch
She needs more than scraps
She needs more than a bed
Stop kicking her!
Why do you want her,
To wag to welcome always?

Why do you think
All she is, is alive?

She is not a thing
She isn't a corpse
Just like you
She wants to live!
Don't make her choke
Every time she breathes.
She is a woman
Let her be.

Harris Khan to Malam Yakubu

Poet: Maryam Khan – my mum but she won't tell

I just took help from this poem, I copied its style

> *Darkness …*
> *Shrouds the sky,*
> *It*
> *Envelopes my sight,*
> *Erases the sun*
> *And eradicates life.*
> *I live as a dead corpse*
> *I am dead.*
> *My soul was snatched long before*
> *Thrust in a pit….*
> *Is it a cauldron?*
> *I have along with me*
> *Coals, Ashes, Smoke.*
> *I choke.*
> *I hear*
> *At a small distance*
> *A voice like my own*
> *The rhythm, like the beat of a drum*
> *Goes on….*

CHAPTER 14

HYDER

"Are you out of your freaking mind?" Daas had exclaimed in amazement and anguish when Hyder had told him about his misadventure into the church of Satan.

"I didn't expect any of the things that happened," he defended himself, "she said it would be like a party."

"Are you going to tell me you have become a wuss and she takes your decisions for you?" Daas was prancing in the small 6x8 cubicle that gave privacy to each staff member with a small personal desk, a computer system and a small extra chair. Daas had been putting that extra chair into use until Hyder had dropped the bomb on him, telling him why he hadn't seen him last weekend for their weekly booze night.

"Do you have any idea how much damage this whimsical trip of yours can cost you? For heaven's sake, you are a baturiya, an expatriate, you do not AFFORD to get into such sticky situations," Daas was lecturing.

"Tell me something I already don't know, dammit!" Hyder pounded his fist on the table.

"Oh, now you are going to go all scary bear on me? I told you, I told you from the beginning, these hippie style girls are not good for us. We are used to women who kowtow to us," Daas was slapping his forehead with the palm of his right hand again and again.

Hyder was only listening. His hands were fumbling with an unopened envelope that had arrived for him from the ministry.

"Did you tell anyone else?"

"Of course not. What's there to tell? A bunch of bored college students gathered to create a new religion because the faith mummy daddy taught them is boring and obsolete?"

"Shhh," Daas quietened him down whispering, "don't say all these things, you never know, you could be under observation."

"I am going to leave her," Hyder's voice had dropped to the lowest fathoms even with the mere idea of a life without her.

"You will just enrage her to expose you to the college fraternity, the board of governors. She will get to finish this last term and pass out of college and you will lose everything you have created for yourself," Daas had made use of the chair once again. He was sober now, but equally sombre.

"I don't care," Hyder said in the same tone. It seemed he was pulling his voice out of his gut and even then it didn't help him much.

Daas sighed outwardly. It was useless talking to him at the moment. He picked up his briefcase and left the cubicle, only to enter his own and feel sorry for his friend.

Hyder stayed where he was. Facing Nuoko and Vikki wasn't going to be easy and he had taken the coward's way out. He had not gone to class all day. All he had done was summon Mustapha to his cubicle and had handed him over the topics for research papers that the students of anthropology were supposed to write.

"Sir, do you have any particular student in mind for each of these topics or should I just randomly distribute these?" Mustapha, the perfect assistant for him asked.

"Just randomly give these to all of them, of course you can pick the one you like," Hyder had drawled.

"Are you alright Sir?"

"Yes," he spoke thoughtlessly but after a pause he asked, "Why?"

"It's just that you have never missed a class and we all know the research papers are not to be submitted until a fortnight ahead. And we don't really need to cut class for them," Mustapha was concerned.

"We are done with the curriculum and there's nothing more to teach you," Hyder said, "it's all over," he said in a voice that had come from a broken heart. He had, in an agitated motion, ripped open the envelope he had been toying with.

Mustapha stared at his teacher for a few moments. "Is there anything else I could do?"

Hyder didn't reply for a couple of minutes since he was going through the contents of the letter. The sudden arrival of a tiny spark in his eyes told Mustapha that he was reading some good news. Finally when he was done, he looked up above the rim of his spectacles and saw Mustapha still there.

"Eh, what was that?"

"Anything else I could do, Sir?" he repeated.

He looked at Mustapha and then at the letter and then again at the letter. A small smile appeared around the corners of his mouth and he said, "Yes, Mustapha, I think there is," and he started describing to his student his next assignment.

The day seemed to be the longest in his twelve year old career in Lagos University, it wouldn't come to an end. Just half an hour before it was time to go off, Hyder collected all his things lying uselessly on the desk and started for the parking lot where his beloved Cadillac was waiting for him. He had wanted to escape the premises without being approached by a colleague or any students he could bump into at the parking lot. He had been a mess mentally and psychologically and the tremors in his heart caused by the thought of having to leave Vikki were showing lines of distress on his face. He didn't want to be asked questions. Hurriedly, he brisk walked to his usual spot on the parking space, hit the accelerator and sped off. Just at the corner of the lot, at THEIR usual spot, he saw Vikki and Nuoko sharing a smoke. He had seen them together many times in the same situation, Nuoko bent on the bonnet of a car and Vikki standing close by or sitting atop the bonnet, inhaling or exhaling smoke. He had heard of the rumour around campus – of Vikki and Nuoko being secretly involved and had never given a damn about it. He had actually taken it with a grain of salt, pleased, that at least the rumour, as long as it kept afloat, would keep him out of the sequence. Luck had always been on his side.

Today however, the same scene which he had seen so many times before, set him on fire. The entire day that he had spent in the room, using his mental juices trying to block away people's faces had gone down the drain in a jiffy. He had always been blind? Are they really a couple? Vikki could hide things from him quite well, that was established. Why can't Vikki smoke with some other guy? Or a girl? What did they talk about? Were they discussing him? How much did Nuoko know about Vikki and his affair? Questions of the sort bombarded his mind and he felt sick. He drove past them, pretending he hadn't noticed. Vikki, who had been sitting on the bonnet of the Charade, had hopped down and come a couple of steps forward, hoping he would see her and stop his car. She was left standing there, hurt and deprived like the day he had left her at the church of Satan, in the middle of the ritual. She watched him whizz past her and followed his dusty trail with her eyes. She knew he would be looking at her in the rear mirror. She knew he was burning to talk to her, just as she was. She was right. But with Hyder, hearts weren't really taken care of.

He had not wanted to go home. Vikki was his escape from the loneliness and apathy he felt at home. His wife had dedicated her life to everything around her – her plants, her son, her sculptures, her need to keep things spotless, her desire to be a loner. Everything that breathed or didn't, mattered to her but he didn't. She was anything but a wife. A cook he could hire, a housekeeper he already had. Surely she knew that. She didn't realise her presence in the house was a source of discomfort to him, and yet he had never interfered in her personal space. All he wanted from her, was to be obedient and subservient. And minding her own business, and smile like she used to in the early days of their marriage. And wait up for him when he was late. And make him the center of her attention instead of Harris. And hug him and kiss him even after he had hurled out fireballs of abuse at her for something as stupid as having put out mismatched socks. Why couldn't she love him as much as Vikki? She used to do it all, for the first couple of years but then she had changed. She had pushed him out of her life and he had tried to work it out. He had tried to establish a writ in the domestic setting by imposing who the boss was and his needs were primary and far more superior to hers. He had tried to keep the flame in the bedroom burning, in any way possible. He did become a little... he looked for a word... harsh... that's a good word... he realised he did become a little harsh sometimes when the whiskey had blown out his brains and was tormenting his manhood. Why, oh why did she put up a fight? Why couldn't she just comply? Why couldn't she agree? If she wouldn't push him back and cross her arms over her chest, it wouldn't really go as bad. The posture, the curled up, shielded pose she made when he approached her, it drove him absolutely mental. Her eyes that gave him the coldest, most hateful looks the next day didn't escape his sight... he just chose to ignore them.

It was all Maryam's fault. He wouldn't have to seek solace in another woman if his wife had been giving him what he wanted and what he wanted was pretty simple – he wanted to be loved, unconditionally. Women are supposed to do that, aren't they, he had questioned himself. Vikki did it to him. Any woman would. Why not Maryam? Having driven out of the university, Hyder was now on the main road, taking the turn to a popular cafe where he was to meet Mustapha. The thoughts about his bad luck with a sour marriage had been tormenting him and he had been empathizing with his id and his ego for having to bear so much. Vikki made him forget all the sores of his heart and now Vikki, she too, was away. He had reached the Cafe Vanessa, handed over his key to the valet and had chosen a table for two. It was still five minutes to two, five minutes before Mustapha was supposed to be there. He was brought the complimentary flute of champagne, which he readily accepted.

He ordered lunch for them both, even before Mustapha had arrived – some sandwiches and a share plate for a salad. Mustapha reached on time. He spotted his teacher and got seated. He too, was offered the complimentary flute of bubbly which he politely refused.

"The portion is too small to get you drunk," Hyder tried to encourage him.

"Sir, it's not that. I just don't drink," he replied, without a trace of apology in his voice.

Hider cleared his throat, tried to make a comment, thought the better of it and started on the new 'project' he had assigned to his student.

"We leave at five in the evening. Should be a good time for you, I suppose?" he wasn't asking, just making sure.

"Yeah, I will come around to your place," he replied obediently.

"Good, that settles it then. We would rather stay at a hotel nearer to the canyons instead of having to commute every day."

"The university, Sir, must have been taken care of?"

"Oh don't worry, I have informed the Dean and also about you, you get to write your final paper with actual research work on the field, so that's what's in there for you," he had taken a mouthful of the sandwich in front of him.

Mustapha nodded, also beginning to eat.

Hyder had gone home, packed himself a small bag with tees and jeans and his daily supplicants like toiletries and had told Garba to tell Madam he would be away for a week. He had had his houseboy tow his bag to the trunk of the car and had his gear oil, brake oil, water tanker and gas tank checked. In the meanwhile, Mustapha had reached there and Hyder had set off on his expedition, something he would have refused to do if the ministry had approached him in usual circumstances but these, weren't normal circumstances. These were disturbing, annihilating, tearing situations and he wanted an escape pad. The research work the Ministry of Environmentalism, which worked in tandem to the ministry of Petroleum, had assigned to him, of looking for anthropological loopholes in the underwater canyons that lay just East of the Lagos Lagoon was something that could give him a shell like that of a snail. He needed to hide. Lagoon was the perfect place to be.

Mustapha as usual was his chauffeur that evening. They both stayed quiet during the drive. Hyder seemed lost in thoughts and Mustapha didn't really want to disturb him. The silence between them prevailed for the entire week.

The ministry of environmentalism had asked for the assistance of some marine biologists, some geologists and a couple of shining anthropologists for their assessment on a proposal of building a city near the underwater canyons of Lagos, adjacent to the Victoria Island. The claim, was that the Atlantic had gobbled up so much land from Lagos, in particular and Nigeria in general, that it was time to get even with the ocean, deal with the erosion the Atlantic had done to the country by taking back the land, filling it with rock and sand and build an entirely new city in the middle of the ocean.

Ever since the arrival of British settlers, who eventually got to become the colonists of Nigeria in the early nineteenth century, they had given the original topography of Lagos as it was to-date – heterogeneous, socially stratified and one with contrasting cultures. The city that once had been the capital of a United Nigeria for the British colonists who had found themselves more at home in Lagos than in any other state or city of the country, was now densely populated, unplanned housing had affected the natural beauty of the city and its islands – the Lagoon, the Mainland and Victoria. Though all three of these were connected with each other with a network of bridges, the demographics of the people who resided in these islands differed from each other at many levels – education, social status, monetary position to name a few. In spite of all that, Lagos was the richest state of Nigeria. The governor of the state had some plans of building a new city – for attracting tourists as well as taking the lavish lifestyle of the Lagos resident to an entirely higher level.

Something that could leave Ikoyi miles behind. Ikoyi, the suburban area of Lagos, the eastern part of the city that had been populated by the European settlers in the early twentieth century. It would even leave VI behind for it would emerge as the newest hub for covetable property. Hyder had teamed up with the biologists and geologists to study the inference of the canyons and how greatly they could affect the new city. The Avon canyon, a submarine canyon really, could only be observed underwater for that is where it existed. He had dived under water to study the soil erosion, the impact of the surges of the ocean and how old the canyons could be. He also needed to study how much the canyons were still being carved by the water so as to establish how well or otherwise the idea of building a new city from reclaimed land would be. Hyder was loyal to his work. He dug in, he dived in, he compared ideas and notes, he scribbled on his note pad, and he gave instructions to Mustapha regarding how to tackle the same issue for his final research paper. The week went really busy. The Atlantic was blue, luring and coquettish. The beach reminded him often of Vikki but he would shun his thoughts and distract them by asking Mustapha how well his paper was forming.

At nights Hyder took it easy. He shun all thoughts of Vikki and Maryam, he became once again the teenage boy from Shahdara trying to build a pirate ship to escape into land unknowns. Escape he did, each night during the week, the beach was enticing, it had loads of welcoming condiments to drench his heart into – liquor, drugs, girls and the beach itself. He would get drunk at the bars and then go to the sea to wash it off. Then he would smoke for ecstasy and then again go dive in the coastal waters where a couple of girls would be showing off their swimming gear.

By the end of the week, when all research had been completed and the others had voiced their opinion of the project being a viable one, Hyder had submitted his advisory to the ministry. He had suggested the government should not underestimate the strength of the ocean surges. Investments in properties, lives and governmental resources could sink to the bottom of the Atlantic in one powerful oceanic surge. The dam, as promised by the government to hold back the surges would do no good to the very idea of constructing a city at the footrest of the sea. He had seen people eye him suspiciously as he trashed the entire project.

"Bloody baturiya," someone whispered. "Can't see us grow, can they," someone had mumbled.

Hyder had only chosen to ignore just as he had always done, picked his briefcase and smiled a goodbye to the team members sitting around a table at the bar beach, sharing a celebratory drink as the week was over.

Despite the coral reefs, multi coloured and airy which had waved at him and danced in joy when he was underwater, despite the cooling breeze that had hit him in the face and had made him smile each time, despite the coffee coloured girl who had wooed him at the dance floor of the nightclub adjacent to his hotel with her beauty and flirtation and had stayed with him overnight, despite the fact that Mustapha had been the best companion ever, despite all of this, Hyder had missed home. He wanted to go home, spend some time there, and not alone. He wanted to see Harris, his prankster smile and his fidgety prance. Hyder packed up after the week finished and set off for home with a smiling Mustapha who had probably the best paper under his arm and had already submitted it with his professor.

CHAPTER 15

MARYAM

Maryam had gone through Malam Yakubu's note thrice and she hadn't still understood why her boy's teacher would take so much interest in Harris's psychological well being. She was worried about her son but not to the extent of considering therapy. In her opinion, if anyone needed therapy in the Khan's house, it was Hyder, for anger management issues, for being a disloyal spouse and severe symptoms of disrespect, misogyny and distrust.

She had felt quite affronted when Garba had informed her of Hyder's absence for a week. Where was he going, she had asked to which Garba had merely shrugged. Was it a weeklong vacation with the rose scented woman? She hadn't asked the question out loud but the sharp sting she had felt when her own thought had hit her head, was unbearable. She had been seeing the change in him for almost two years now. His indifference wasn't new to her, it had been there ever since she had gotten pregnant. But this strange aloofness, callousness for days at a stretch, which was something the rose scented girl had done to him. He pretended as if Maryam didn't exist anymore. Maryam had tried to do the same, but she couldn't act as if she hadn't heard the car screeching, or that it was his time to leave for university or what his favourite kind of flowers were to be arranged in the vase near his study table. However, she had been quite unsuccessful.

She had, till now, kept her domestic business very personal, very secretive. Garba was witness to some of it but he never said a word. Malam Yakubu was a first. He had sensed something had been wrong with Harris's life from a couple of creative writing assignments. Since her meeting with Malam Yakubu, she had been quite perplexed about the state of mind Harris had been in. Did he know? All the while that she had been protecting him from the darkest and ugliest shadows of her life, he had actually been there, watching, tolerating, and squirming like he did in her womb when Hyder had pushed her to the ground? She wept bitterly. Her heart filled with guilt, remorse and pain for her child. He was her Hercules. Indeed, he had great powers, he was stronger than she had thought him to be. She had been giving him an incomplete life, without any filial harmony, taking beatings from her husband, thinking her endurance would ensure a happy and normal life for her son but what good had it brought? Ten years of secluded imprisoned tortuous life, her fortitude and stoicism which she had considered her assets and points of strength had actually been translated as spiritless by her son. Ten years of a barren, loveless life! She had thought she was the one shielding him while in real, it had all been the opposite. He had been shielding her from embarrassment. He had never spoken of it.

Then why shouldn't he wish for a new family? Why shouldn't he let Binta scold him, love him, feed him. Why shouldn't he let Zainab bully him, tutor him and mentor him? Why shouldn't he consider Obi his family? Why shouldn't he write a hundred words about Obi when his teacher asks him to write about his family?

She shed silent tears as these questions tormented her mind. Malam Yakubu's letter soaked in her tears. She saw the blue ink of his letter get blurry and dissipate into blobs of blue. She looked at the tiny puddles that had washed away the concern of a stranger who cared. The drops that carried a lot of her in their miniscule being – there was some salt, some water, the whole of her torn heart, the pain, the strain, the maximum loss, the minimum gain of these ten years. She tried to suck in her tears, held her breath, knew the place of these drops was not on her cheeks but in her heart – a vessel that had been broken and cracked. She tried to hide them but they were not listening to her. He kept dropping until the letter was all washed away.

Harris had come home earlier that afternoon and had gone to his bedroom, saying he had a headache, throwing a sealed envelope on the table for her to see. It was a letter from Malam Yakubu. After that, she had been waiting for him to emerge so she could talk to him. Early evening, Hyder too had left for a week. She wanted to talk to her son, but what was there to say? He must have sensed something was wrong, that's why he had chosen to avoid seeing his mother. Or maybe Malam Yakubu had spoken to him. She had to take the initiative maybe, go up to him, tell him how much she loved him.

After the hard first step of walking up to his bedroom, rapping on the door, sitting beside a wakeful ten year old, telling him how much the loved him, wiping away his tears when he confessed having peeped through the keyhole each time he heard noises from her bedroom. It ripped her. Yet she knew if anything, it was her son who needed her comforting.

"I thought you were too young to understand, son," she whispered.

"I am sorry Mum, for the way he treats you, it makes me sad," he said without looking at her.

She cupped his face in her hands, "It doesn't matter anymore. You are what matters, my love."

He looked up at her face, "I love you, Mum."

"I love you too, Harris."

She picked him up like a baby and made him sit in her lap.

"My boy is a big man now," she teased as his weight put a strain on her muscles.

"Mum, let's run away from here. Let's go to live somewhere else."

"There's no running from home, Sonny, we stay, we fight, we try to change things," she spoke very lovingly.

"It won't work, mother, we will never change anything," the loss of faith and hope in her son broke her heart.

"It will be," she said in a very hopeful tone, "You will see, it will be fine."

The rest of the week went pretty smooth. Harris was home each evening. They cuddled, snuggled and talked about a lot of things – she told him of his grandfather Dr Ahmar, the botanical garden back at her home, the reason why she had turned the dust rough patch outside their home into a vegetable garden, how much she had wanted a friend in him and not just a son. To Maryam as well as to Harris, it was a strange connection... to be able to connect to each other's heart strings and not just go through the daily duties they owed to each other as a family. Maryam had been doing her duties as a mother to perfection but she hadn't trusted him, and he in return hadn't trusted her. It was the beginning of a beautiful relationship, she thought as he had put his head in her lap on the sitting room sofa while she read another of Malam Yakubu's letters brought home by Harris, this time unsealed. She had to write a reply, but only when Harris would awaken from his afternoon nap. That day, she ran her fingers through his hair and smiled - A warm genuine smile that she had forgotten about since the earliest days of her marriage. All this while, her fear had been hurting Harris. Constant fear had weakened her. She believed Harris was her weakness. Undoubtedly, Hyder thought the same. She was elated to have found her strength in Harris. He was, on the contrary, her sturdiest rock of strength. She felt comforted, in a very very long time. She let her mind transport her back to the cane woven swing in her father's garden and closed her eyes. The smile wouldn't leave her lips. She felt as if some missing pieces of the jigsaw puzzle had been inserted and her tattered body had become a complete whole again.

Dear Mrs. Khan,

I hope this finds you well. Allow me to begin by apologizing for my sudden interference in your personal life. Of course, it was meant to be a gesture of goodwill and concern for my pupil. I admire you for having brought up Harris to be such a well mannered, intelligent and obedient boy, I do not have many like him under my supervision. Please let me know if I can do anything to talk to Harris regarding the disturbed behaviour he has reflected in his poetry. He will be moving to the middle school next year and we would not like him to carry some burden on his psyche till then too. Do you believe in therapy?

Sincerely,

Yakubu Usman

*

Mr. Yakubu Usman,

Please do not apologize for anything. I am glad we got a chance to share some notes related to Harris. It has helped me know how much and why my son had been drifting apart from me. If anything, I owe gratitude to you. For better or for worse, Harris is in a state of mind where he needs to be trusted rather than protected. He has probably taken my Hercules story too much to his heart. Please feel free to contact me if you think something needs to be discussed.

Regards

Mrs. Hyder Khan

*

Dear Mrs. Khan,

Do you like reading? I am sending you a copy of one of my favourite writers – my favourite line is quoted:

"God surely did not create us, and cause us to live, with the sole end of wishing always to die. I believe, in my heart, we were intended to prize life and enjoy it, so long as we retain it. Existence never was originally meant to be that useless, blank, pale, slow-trailing thing it often becomes to many, and is becoming to me, among the rest."

Charlotte Bronte, is a delight to read, I hope you will agree. Shirley, the book, taught me to keep going but also, my favourite belief is to have faith. One must not give an extension to pain by not looking for a way out just because the unknown scares one. Faith, is important. Faith, is more than believing – it is a strength to be able to let go without fear or remorse, to look forward and expect the unexpected and have the courage to accept it, endure it and go through it to yet another phase wholeheartedly.

Yakubu Usman

p.s.: Harris doesn't enjoy fairytales as he told me today, I am giving him a collection of Rudyard Kipling books, which I hope you shall kindly accept.

*

Dear Mr. Yakubu,

Many thanks for the books. Shirley was a treat to read. I had forgotten a lot about the sweet taste classical literature can leave on your mind imprinted forever, it can be savoured for a long time after unlike no other taste in the world, it can be imagined like no other scene in the world. I remember having felt this way when

I read Emily Bronte many years back in my father's library. Speaking of whom, I have an heirloom paper weight, carved out of marble, engraved with Sanai Ghaznavi's quote – "This too, shall pass." It belonged to my father. One of my most prized possessions. I wonder if it could mean as much to you as it did to me.

Regards and prayers,

Maryam.

*

Dear Mrs Khan,

Many thanks for your gift of kindness, it shall always stay at my desk. Little communication that has been between us, I have been wondering, if you would have time to write? I am member of a literary magazine. It is not your regular mainstream media, it is just a small portion of the alternate media as you get it, an Islamic magazine, we welcome small contributions from people who can write based on a monthly theme. Next up is women's rights. Do you think you could write something? I am sending you a guideline to see if it helps you make up your mind.

Regards,

Yakubu.

- Chapter 2, Verse 187, Koran: Your wives are a covering for you and you for them.
- Chapter 4, Verse 4, Koran: If you dislike one thing about your wives, you have many things to like about them too.
- Chapter 30, Verse 21, Koran: And among His Signs is this that He created for you wives (spouses) from among yourselves, that you may find repose in them, and He has put between you affection and mercy.

*

Dear Brother Yakubu,

I think I can do what you have asked of me. But I cannot promise on its standard. That is what I trust you with. Also I don't think I could write a totally objective write up since I do not have an ideal situation domestically, you already know. I wouldn't have the courage to lecture others about what I personally live with.

Regards,

Maryam.

*

Dear Mrs. Khan,

I know what you mean. But that is the whole point of it. If you write something about which you strongly feel, its impact is going to be immense. It would be heartfelt and maybe, you may derive some strength out of it. If you don't mind my saying so, I had this in mind for you ever since I last saw you. And if you need a reassurance, as an English teacher and a student of Literature, I can assure you, you can do it.

Awaiting,

Yakubu

p.s.: Sometimes a bully has to be slapped back to be told that the absence of a violent reaction is not a weakness, it is a choice. And a mighty brave one at that.

*

Chapter 16

MALAM YAKUBU

Just outside the window, he could see the dawn break the sky into two equally proportioned halves – the sharp red line that was cracking up the horizon above the sugarcane field, was giving off sparks of crimson, yellow, orange and the shades in between these colours. The image in front of him was one of solitude and serenity. Nature seemed to be getting up from a slumber, cracking up in the middle, faintest sounds emerging from the silently standing trees in forms of chirps and tweets, colours coming forth from the darkness of the night. Among the silence breakers was the call of prayer entering his room through the open window and Malam Yakubu, as every morning, rolled out his prayer mat, a meter's length of raffia really, nothing fancy or opulent.

Yakubu had been giving a lot of thought to Maryam lately. A young man himself, had felt sympathy for the woman when he had understood her situation but with the little exchange of notes and her manner of conversing had arisen something more potent and richer in quality in his heart. He found himself peering through books of literature, psychology and religion to find tidbits that could inspire her. He thought of letting her take out her pain through writing for his academic magazine, he wanted her to strengthen her relationship with Harris so that both of them would not have to look around for support but be each other's strength against the enemy within the four walls of their house. Malam Yakubu pictured that delicate face of hers being slapped and punched and couldn't quite bring to his comprehension how anyone could bear to hit that face – the face so radiant with innocence and honesty. He had hardly had a chance to speak to her again in person, however, her image was one that had stuck in his mind.

The night before, Maryam was the last thought on his conscious mind. He remembered that much but couldn't really pick up the strand of thought which had left him at the threshold of sleep. It could be the image of her eyelids, drooping down with shame as he had confronted her with the meanest truth of her life or it could have been the paperweight that sat comfortably on his study desk just two steps away from his bed.

"This too, shall pass," he had muttered many times while tossing in bed.

Malam Yakubu was a man who lived his life in poetry – the youthful poems of Blake and the philosophical odes of Wordsworth, the classical tales of Chaucer and the poetic verses of the Koran. Just like every morning, Malam Yakubu said his prayer and sat there, kneeling for a while longer, his hands on knees, praying and having his daily conversation with Divinity:

> *"Give that woman Maryam peace of mind and heart. If this ordeal is a test, help her go through it. If the discomfort in her life is incurable, help her to rid herself of this disease. I have not yet understood, what is this feeling I have inside of me? I feel sorry for her but at the same time, I feel she is wasting her life and her son's. She needs courage, she needs faith. Her broken heart needs to believe. I don't know why destiny has brought me in her path, what purpose I am to serve in this whole design of Yours but in the meanwhile, my heart is filled with a strange sense of responsibility. I feel I have been somehow chosen to help this woman out. My heart has a surging feeling every time I think of her. I wonder what this surge is telling me. I wonder what this upheaval of feelings is? Disclose to me the twisted ways of the human heart. Aameen."*

He got his books, the lecture notes for the last voyage of Gulliver's Travels, loose sheets of the student's class test he was supposed to return that day ready and arranged on the desk and cast a glance on his white riga, only garment he wore on special occasions. He also perched atop his head, his white cotton cap, embroidered with white silk thread, sitting like a white dome on his head. He looked handsome. He was a young man and currently had his heart blazing with an emotion yet unknown to him. The emotion did not feel like love, at least not how they described it in verse. It didn't vex him or irritate him. It made him feel he could be more than what he has been all his life. He was more than what the children back at school knew him for, or better than the amount of love he received when he went to his village every last Sunday of each month to his aging mother who sat on a mound of clay, wearing a cotton robe and smoking tobacco from a hookah, grinning a toothless smile upon seeing her older son. His younger brother had not really taken to the village school and had rather taken up his father's land and worked happily as a farmer. He had abundance of corn every season, at least enough to send his six kids to schools and bring his wife a new bit of cloth for a robe every month.

"When will you give me my grandchildren, Yakubu?" his mother would always ask. "Look at Ahmad, your younger brother, he has everything." To this Yakubu would smile and say, "The time has not yet come, but it will, soon." He would tell his nephews and nieces stories from his school's textbooks and the kids loved their uncle for his long beautifully spun tales. Every afternoon, after their communal family lunch, the kids would huddle around him, the youngest girl of three would climb her way from his knees to his shoulders and sit up, holding his hair in tiny fists for support. The story time would take an hour, sometimes two and the older people, although pretending to be busy at cleaning or sewing or simply lazing in the sun, would too cock their ears and listen to every word Yakubu would speak of the land of the dead, the fairies or foreign lands where only the imagination of a common villager could take him.

Other Sundays, Malam Yakubu had other business to take care of – he taught English to the Nigerian kids who could not go to school. Street children, running after cars, flying kites made out of polythene bags, tying an empty soft drink can to a rope and tugging it along like a toy car. Those kids Malam gathered every Sunday on a footpath or along the woods and taught them to count till ten, to say hi, how are you, please, thank you. The kids laughed as they heard the sounds of the funny words but each of them grabbed knowingly or unknowingly, a pearl from the open chest of Yakubu's heart.

So, mercy was well known to Malam. So was love. What encompassed his heart therein, those days was something different. And he was eager to find out, what it was.

Chapter 17

HYDER

The first thing Hyder had done upon his return home from his research trip, was to propose an evening out to his son.

"Where do you want to go, the Polo Club or the Kemari Lake?"

Harris had hesitated but had finally opted for the Polo Club.

The same evening, it was a Saturday, a day that often Uncle Daas met up with Dad at the club. Today, Harris had been assured it was just a day between Hyder and him.

They first went out to the Pool room, cluttered with men and women alike, each trying to get a chance to have a go at the cue sticks and score a point. At the far end of the room was the executive table, reserved for the creamiest of the members at the club. Some men in suits were having a go at their game with assistants at their sides holding their glasses of liquor to present at the slightest indication.

Harris stayed close to his Dad, trying to make his way through the crowded room to the Foosball room, hoping to find an empty counter. Once they were there, a little swarm of kids appeared before their eyes. The stalls had all been taken.

"So, you want to wait for a turn or go play golf with me at the rear of the club?" Hyder asked him.

Harris wanted to go see the match that was about to start in half an hour.

"We will be there, in the meanwhile, what do you have in mind?"

Minutes later, Hyder found himself squealing like a kid with his son at the prospects of winning a racing game in the gaming arcade located next to the foosball stalls. He had not known the pleasures of the joystick until Harris had taught him moments ago. The father-son duo was getting stares at the level of excitement being poured out of their gaming zone. The match had been on for the past ten minutes but they were having far too much adrenaline pumped into their systems with that game of racing some death-row cars in the midst of heavy traffic.

"You still wanna go out there?" Hyder had asked his son in between gaming lapses.

"Yeah, let's go," he ran ahead of his dad.

Hyder always had a VIP enclosure booked with four seats. Most of the times it was with friends but today it was only his son and they had the tiny cubic enclosure to themselves. Hyder bought him some edibles and they settled down to see the Lagos Lions get beat up by the Victoria Victors. Harris cheered, pumped his fists, spilled his popcorn and thoroughly enjoyed the game. He had been on a lucky spree. The past week had been heaven at home, alone with his mother, reconnecting the dots of his relationship with the person that most mattered to him -

Maryam. He had been out to Zainab's on Friday and they had tried their hand at kite flying again, had succeeded and had lost interest in it as soon as they had conquered the art. Obi had come to visit him at home and for the first time, he had let him inside, taken him to his room, played netball in the rusty net hanging out in the veranda. He had preferred to stay home throughout the week, trying to get as much time to spend with Maryam as possible. With Hyder's shadow looming around, he found it difficult to move around in the house, fearing his hoarse voice would go booming in the house if something went wrong.

The evening in the club was different. Hyder was being nice. He was always nice to him when he took him out. The last time was about a year ago when Uncle Das had gone back home in Calcutta for his Christmas holiday. Hyder had been sulking around home the whole week until Harris had shown up on his plans. This week was no different. Saturdays were spent with Vikki. And Vikki he had been avoiding.

The thought of her had been pestering him all weekend. Mustapha had helped deal with the disturbance of his thoughts and now, Harris was doing pretty well too. The match had entered its last fifteen minutes when the tactical leader of Lagos Lions hit a strike, almost went past the defence player of the Victoria Victors to score a goal when the leader of the Victors backed by his defence hit the ball to a different direction, tossing away the game for the Lions for good. The ball went through the first and second players aimlessly for the next few minutes until the game was declared to be officially over, the ball was declared dead, the Victors had won with a ratio of 7:5. The Victorians celebrated, especially those who had betted money on the game. There were tables of refreshments for the guests. The teams were both patted, their hands shaken by fans and their charm ogled at by the ladies.

"Can I have an ice before we leave?" Harris had asked his father to which he had reluctantly agreed. Hyder didn't really like going to the refreshment tables. They both sat at one and ordered ice cream for Harris. He had wanted a grape flavoured ice cream with raisins – his favourite but had readily settled on a mint and lime one when the waiter told him they didn't have it in the menu. Hyder enjoyed his dessert with a lemon flavoured wafer when he saw a girl approaching their table. Hyder was too busy fiddling with his digital diary that he hadn't noticed. She girl came nearer until she reached the edge of the table and Hyder had to look up.

"Hello," she said.

Hyder's face turned white. He looked at his son who was looking at the girl talking to his dad with interest.

"Hello," he chose to say.

"Can we talk?" she tried to sound casual.

Hyder stood up and told Harris to wait for him. he walked a few steps away from the table, faced the pool and the girl joined him. From the distance, Harris could not hear what they said, but he was sure his father was upset. A couple of minutes later, Hyder retraced his steps back to his seat and the girl followed. She had tears in her eyes. Anyone could see she was making an effort to keep them in her eyes and not let them drop on her chocolate brown cheeks. She wore a sundress with spaghetti straps on her shoulders. Her hair was combed but still in an Afro that had been tamed by keeping it short. The ends of her hair shone in the dimming sunlight.

"Hyder, don't do this to me," she started.

Hyder shot her a bloody glance and spoke through his teeth, "I said I need some time," he looked with the same glare at Harris and stood up.

"Are you going to get up or not?" he snarled at Harris who hadn't known he was supposed to leave his dessert unfinished and walk with his father. He got up immediately and gave a forlorn look to his dessert. They both left the premises in a jiffy. The car was sped up like the racing car in the gaming zone. Only it didn't give either Harris or Hyder the same pleasure.

Back home, Harris had once again run into his room. Maryam had believed they would have had a blast like they usually did. Strangely, Harris hadn't come to her tonight, with his eyes all starry with the adventures he had been through with his Dad. She set a dish of oven roasted chicken on the table with the condiments to go with it. Hyder saw the table but just went to his room.

Maryam went to see if her doubts were true and entered Harris's room to find him flopped on his bed.

"Everything okay, child?" she asked concerned.

"Mum, I am scared of Dad," he said feverishly, sitting up.

"Why, what's wrong?"

"He had a fight and got all red and angry like he does," he blurted out.

"Fight? With whom?" she asked quizzically, hoping it was one of his meaningless fights with the fellow drivers on the main roads.

"A girl, she came to see him at the club." He related the complete story which Maryam listened to with interest. She closed her eyes when Harris stopped. So she had been right all along. As much pleasure the news of a fight gave to her, as much a winner she had felt for not doubting her husband for nothing, she felt crumbling inside at the thought of

Hyder going through a lover's tiff especially when the tiff wasn't with her, she trembled slightly at the thought of that girl having influenced Hyder's temperament so much that he forgot all about himself being a father and a husband in her presence. She opened her eyes and looked at Harris who was already trying to block out the scenes from his visit to the club by hooking up to the game boy in his hands.

She had stayed in his room for almost half an hour, clearing up his study desk, sorting out done and undone laundry, piling out unironed clothes for Garba and making his bed as comfortable as possible. She had wanted Hyder to be done with dinner when she went out. Harris obviously didn't want to join him and she didn't want to force him.

When she went out, the chicken lay untouched and cold on the table, Hyder was watching news in the sitting room and wore a calm but thoughtful look on his face. She sat down on the arm chair away from the couch.

"How long have you been sleeping with him?" he asked her in a cool tone.

Her eyes shot amazement and disbelief. Was that question meant for her?

"Who are you talking to?" she managed to choke out.

Hyder jumped up on his feet and slapped her on the face. It was not just a slap, it was a mighty blow that his hand came down with, her head yanked to one side, stars danced in front of her eyes.

"Hyder, what are you saying?" she had screamed out, for the slap was nothing new but his accusation was.

"This, this fucking piece of shit, this is your standard? This is what you desire, you whoring bitch?" he yelled at her, threw a piece of paper at her, it hit her on the face. She bent down to retrieve it when he kicked her head and she tumbled down to a side.

"You need proof? You bloody bastard!" he spit out abuse at her that made her ears burn. She was still unable to understand what had gotten into him.

"You need a man so desperately that you jumped at his invitation? I leave you at home for a week and you start screwing around every man you see?" he was either a lunatic or heartless or maybe both. Maryam had picked herself up with effort, straightened the hair that had scattered on her face in the event of a broken clip at the back of her head due to the fall and looked up at him. He pulled at her hair and made her stand up, the folded piece of paper still lying helplessly on the ground.

"What have I not given you? WHAT?!" he roared so hard that the walls could have shaken. "If THIS is what you wanted, shouldn't you have come to me?!" he was yelling on the top of his voice. Maryam was still in awe. She didn't understand what he was talking about. He brought her up to his eye level, still pulling at her hair, and let loose a series of face slaps, he slapped her, punched her nape, her back, he used his foot to kick her shins, her thighs but suddenly he stopped. She felt his grip on her neck tighten, he was strangling her, she lost her breath, her face turned as white as a sheet, his rough heavy hands wrapped around her neck made her eyes bulge out, she couldn't even gasp when his grip loosened for a second and then he let go of her all of a sudden. She stumbled on her feet, sucked in air in long wheezing sounds and a moment later saw what had happened. Harris had shot at his father's head with a slingshot and rubber bullet he had made with the ooze of a gum tree. Hyder's face turned as dark as thunder. He ran towards the boy in a fit of rage that he was, Harris ran into his room and locked the door from inside. Hyder banged on the door, hurled abuse at his son, threatened to fry his guts when he knocked down the door. The few seconds when his focus had shifted to Harris had given her enough time to look at the crumpled piece of paper that had made him accuse her of committing adultery. She looked at it, her eyes widened in disbelief and her blood began to boil. Maryam limped up to him as fast as she could and pulled at his arm

"Stop scaring him, you brute, stop harassing him," she had lost every bit of her patience.

He turned round and slapped her once more. Maryam was tired of being bounced around. She had taken a lot of his temper and had not complained about it. She had not climbed into bed and mopped about being beaten up. She had always stood up straight, telling him he couldn't hurt her, he couldn't break her. But this moment when he was threatening to hurt the source of her strength, her beloved son, she was no longer the wife who was giving in to everything her husband had piled on her, she became a mother. She had to protect her son. She had to stop this from happening. She couldn't let him touch him. Some sane man's words rang in her head, "it doesn't take much", she took the advice from the only counsel she had had in the past decade, and she gathered her crumbling guts and slapped him back. Had it been her alone as always, she would have taken the beating but she wasn't going to get her son get hurt by this man.

It was the most unbelievable moment in Hyder's life. His empire had fallen. His son and his wife whom he had so kept in place, had defected. He wasn't one to stay put after the assault. He shoved her to the wall, banged her head against it, at the same time using his knees to kick at her underbelly, her upper legs. Harris unlocked his door when he heard his mother yelp. The click of the lock was audible despite the painful shrieks escaping Maryam's mouth, Harris shouted at his father to stop, he surrendered himself to be beaten instead of his mother, a plea Hyder listened to. He held his son by the nape of his neck and grabbed a handful of Maryam's hair, dragged them both through the dining room and threw them out on the porch, spitting abuse at them all the while and locked the door. Maryam banged at the wooden plank for a little while but Harris stopped her. She took him in her arms and kept murmuring, "Sorry, sorry, sorry, sorry," Harris didn't know what she was apologizing for.

Night had fallen and in Lagos, in the residential areas, people put out their lights early. Maryam knew she couldn't spend the cold night of December out in his porch and neither did she have the courage to stay in the house. Not for the time being at least. Her best shot was Mrs Needi. She picked up a weakened Harris in her arms like a baby and started walking across the street towards Mrs Needi's house when Harris who could barely open his eyes due to the sudden nerve wrecking experience he had been through, managed to open his eyes and spoke very feebly, "No, Mum, he will find us there. Don't go there," he implored.

"I have no where else to go, my child," she whimpered.

"There is a place, Mum, come with me," he said with a little more energy, as if the prospect of a better haven had infused some energy in his body. She decided to trust her son and asked him to give her the directions. She complied.

CHAPTER 18

BINTA

Mahmood had opened the door when he had heard someone pound at it with gentle fists. He had recognised the boy from school but he was puzzled why the mother was carrying him in her arms. The lights outside the house and in the compound had been put out already and Mahmood had been carrying a kerosene lantern in his hands. Mosy had stood up in surprise too. His feeble bray and ruffling of his hoofs could tell the poor jaki was asleep when the visitors had arrived.

"I am very sorry to come to your house like this," Maryam stuttered each word. She didn't know whether she would be welcomed or turned away.

"No, eets okay Madam, come in," Mahmood who had been gaping at the boy and his parent for a few seconds made way by inching away from the doorway and let Maryam pass.

"Is Binta home?" Harris asked.

"Yes, I call her," Mahmood rushed past the compound to climb the steps on which Harris played marbles with Zainab and also had his meals at Binta's on Fridays. He went inside and moments later, Binta's face appeared peeping through the door to see if her husband was really correct – the boy was here in the night with his mother?

"Wayo, wallahe tallahe," she was laughing as she came down the steps, round as she was, she was ten times slower than Mahmood with those steps.

"You Harris bring you Ma this time, poor woman she," she was complaining lovingly as she always did.

Maryam had never interacted with Binta and neither had she ever been in a similar situation – pale faced, her lip torn, her hair scattered like a bush in the wind, her eyes bloody from crying, streaks of tears and blood on her chin and her cheeks flaming red from the slaps, she was thrown out by her husband with nowhere to go, asking refuge from someone she barely knew.

"Salam," Maryam could say no more. Binta had finally sailed like a ship through the compound and had reached at a whisper-able distance from Maryam. She held a lantern close to her face and gasped.

"Abin da ya faru, ya?" she asked what was wrong with sympathy in her eyes. She had called her sister.

Maryam thanked Magna for having taught her enough Hausa. But when she opened her mouth to reply to that innocent yet heart breaking question, she only found her lips quavering, her eyes shedding silent tears.

"Zo ciki," Binta put a hand on her shoulder and signalled to come inside.

"Binta?" Harris spoke up.

"Yes, Haareez," Binta looked at him.

"Can we stay at your place, tonight?"

"Sure, tabatta, my son," she said putting her hand on his forehead. "What happened, Harreez?"

He looked at his mother, asking her silently whether he should give away their secret story. She just dropped down her eye lashes to close her eyes. She was feeling guilty. She was responsible.

"You done nothing bad, have you?" it was Binta's right to be a little sceptic. She was just some gardener's wife and couldn't get involved in some criminality.

"No," Harris said and struggled to stand on his feet now. "My father hit us both. He kicked us out on the porch and we need to hide from him."

That wasn't the real objective, Maryam had silently thought. Of course she will have to go back some day, if not today, but she wasn't hiding from him, was she?

Binta was kind. She took the injured pair inside and brought a warm bucket of water mixed with some herbs and a bit of cloth which she wound up as a soft cushion. She wiped Maryam's face and her neck, dabbed an orange tinted antiseptic on her lip from where the blood was dripping. Once or twice Mahmood had come to see what was going on. He asked a couple of questions to his wife to which she replied very briefly. He went away while Binta was done with Maryam and had moved on to Harris. The boy had no wounds as such but the nape of his neck had the imprints of Hyder's fingers. Binta could count all four fingers on the right side and the mark of a thumb on the left.

"Ayi, ayi," she mourned in pain. "Animal," Maryam heard her mutter under her breath.

"You eat?" she asked them both, who had sloppy eyelids. The both shook their heads. Binta called out Zainab who had been standing there for as long as Harris had arrived in the room.

"Zainab, sa da gadaje," she told them to make some beds for them.

Whilst the fat lady herself walked out of the room, Zainab spread out a raffia mat and laid an old flowered sheet of cloth over it. She brought a pillow and a cushion from the room next door and sat down near Harris.

"What happened?"

Harris gave her a sad, tired smile. "Nothing," he said. She sat silently, didn't ask any more questions but she would look at Harris every now and then, if he were looking, she would smile gently, if not she would stare for a brief moment and then swoop down her eye lashes. Quarter of an hour passed just like that, Maryam watched the little pair of children in front of her. She admired Zainab and understood why Harris wanted a sister like her. Binta came into the room with her hands full. She held a cassava bowl in each hand and some steam was rising out of them.

"Now, in my house, when I cook, people eat. Nobody say no," she said authoritatively. Harris knew what she meant. Maryam felt uncomfortable.

"Look," she put a hand on Binta's arm when the black woman sat down beside her, "I don't want to trouble you anymore. You have already done so much," Maryam began but she was made quiet by a single signal of hush from Binta.

"You look your face, woman? You look sick from years. And this boy, look at him. I saw him yesterday. He was red in the cheeks. What you done to him today?" Binta had a way of showing her love. It wasn't the motherly cuddly style Maryam had. It was rough, tough and straightforward. Yet it was warm and genuine.

"Now you eat, I help Harris. And why you sit on floor? You don't like the bed my Zainab make for you?"

Maryam complied obediently and took Harris with her to sit on the sheet of cloth. She held the hot bowl in her hands and waited to be given a spoon but when she saw Binta was urging Harris to take 'small sip' from the rim of the bowl, she did the same. It was some sort of cereal. There was milk and sugar and some grains, only it was difficult to decipher. Millet or pearl barley?

It was hurtful to curl her lips into a pout to sip at the ingredients of the bowl since her lip was torn and it bled when she tried to work it. She managed somehow. Her heart felt a pang of pain when she saw how comfortable Harris was around Binta and Zainab. He had chosen to sit closer to Binta than to her and she was encouraging him, in words of Hausa and English to drink up the whole thing. Her hand sometimes patted his head and sometimes she put a motherly reassuring hand on his shoulders. Maryam cast down her glance. She had been wrong. She had thought keeping her pain away from Harris would protect him when all it had done was separate them, introduced a fissure of estrangement between them. She had taken Hyder's beatings silently, without putting up a fight to shield Harris when in actual, the spiteful angst of her husband had grown in size and had enveloped her son into its might as well. She asked herself, Could she really cure Hyder with endurance? Had she been able to cause a dent in his volatile personality?

"Maryam?"

She looked up startled, "Yes," she managed to choke.

"Eets okay I call you Maryam?"

"Oh yeah," she smiled.

"Okay so Maryam and Haareez, you say your prayers and go to sleep. God will help you," she said with so much authority that no one could protest. They lay down although her back was stiff from Hyder's kicks, she managed to turn to one side but her ribs hurt. "Must be a bruise," she whispered to herself and the corners of her eyes filled with water. She gulped them in lest Harris would see them. She turned to the other side and faced Harris who had both his hands behind his head, he lay flat and stared at the ceiling. She wanted to comfort him, but feelings of guilt, remorse and helplessness sucked her tongue dry, immovable.

Sleep overcame her, to her surprise. Harris looked at her mother as her breathing grew deeper, signifying she had gone to sleep. He pulled the blanket over himself and Maryam, curled up like a furry kitten and closed his eyes. He couldn't sleep for hours but he thought as hard as he could and couldn't come up with a plan to keep them away from Hyder for as long as possible.

Maryam and Harris stayed with Binta for three days. Harris had to skip school but Obi had managed to slip Maryam's note into Malam Yakubu's hand and he had taken care of things. Harris helped around the house, Maryam tried to but Binta wouldn't let her.

"You my guest, sister, you talk to me. You no talking too much? I talking too much..." she would make a conversation out of nothing. She was, as talkative as one can be yet she hadn't pinched at her heartache. She knew Maryam had to be snapped out of the trauma. The second day, at evening, Harris and Obi were at the rooftop, going through schoolwork through Obi's textbooks and notebooks, Zainab was weaving some raffia and the two ladies were in the compound squatting on the ground, Binta separating corn kernels from the cobs and Maryam peeling off the chaff and hairy beards of the corns for her newly acquired friend.

"So you tell me, when you come to Nigeria?"

"Ten years ago, when I got married," she answered with a faint smile.

"You happy in Nigeria?"

"Nigeria is great. It's like living in a vast landscape of nature. Colours, sounds, sights..." her voice trailed off when she realised her fancy language might be out of Binta's league.

"Yes, I love Nigeria too," Binta replied quietly. It was as if she was eating her words, which was not an easy task for her. Maryam watched her intently, waiting for her to say something.

"Binta," she herself spoke finally, "I am very grateful to you for letting me in your house. I had nowhere else to go."

"No, no, no say that, no need to thank me. But what you do now?"

"I will go back as soon as Harris wants to."

"Harris never want to go back, Maryam." Binta spoke matter of factly and it jilted Maryam's heart.

"He is a child..." she protested feebly.

"No," Binta looked straight into her eyes, "he not child. You foolish. You go back to him who treat you like animal?"

"I have no choice," Maryam spoke with her head thrown down like a criminal found guilty of charge.

"Why you no have faith in God? In yourself? Why so empty is your heart? You have choice. You have choice to live, to smile, to give your son his innocence back. You go there to get beat up again?" Binta had stopped peeling the cobs and was waving her arms around her head as she spoke in a typical Binta-ish manner.

"Binta, I cannot let Harris spend a fatherless life."

"Wayo, Allah ya ba ta kwakwalwa! Where is your brain woman? You give him father like this? Look at my jaki, my donkey not beaten by me or Mahmood like you and Harris beaten by your husband. My child get hurt I cannot sleep that night. How he hit Hareez? How he throw him out in cold?" her eyes were pouring down tears. "You think you are giving him father? Hmph," she stood up and walked away.

Maryam sat still. She looked up towards the rooftop, two heads were bobbing up and down. Harris had hollered half an hour ago that Obi was teaching him the statistics' sums they had done at school. She knew Harris was far more comfortable here than he ever was at home. He wasn't rushing to hide in his bedroom or run out of home into the woods across the road. He was happy. But she couldn't stay here. She didn't have money to pay the poor gardener's wife for her hospitality, her room, her food. She would have to leave soon but where would she go? She wrapped her arms around her legs and sank her heads between the nest she had formed in her lap. What? Where? How? Her senses were bombarded by these questions, to which there was no answer, not even a foolish one.

As night fell, everyone sat on the floor in the kitchen waiting to be served fufu for their night meal, Maryam couldn't help noticing how smilingly Mahmood received his bowl of okra soup from his wife and how she preferred to serve the guests first, her husband second and her daughter last. The platter filled with fluffy balls of rice was put in the middle, for everyone to reach easily. After a day's work of digging the cold soil, watering the grassy playgrounds back at school, tending the broken plants wounded by the boys' mischief and gently spraying water on the miniature plants in the principal's office, Mahmood had had a day and the meal placed in front of him was a reward for all that toil. The man was happy. He asked for a bit more a little while later and Binta stood up from the circle of diners and happily served him more. Maryam saw, as she turned to hand the bowl over to her husband, she thought the better of it, dipped the ladle back in the pot and added just a little more.

Maryam closed her eyes as if it was a scene she couldn't watch any more. It gave her shingles of despair. Binta sensed her discomfort and tried to make conversation.

"Hareez, did you tell your ma Malam Yakubu might visit us tomorrow?"

Maryam's head shot right up and she looked at her boy questioningly who had shrunken his shoulders and thrown his head just two inches above his bowl of okra soup.

"Why is he coming here?" she looked at Binta.

"I dun know. Hareez told me he will come," Binta replied shrugging her round shoulders.

"Harris, what's going on?"

"Nothing mum, Obi gave him the note you wrote yesterday and today he told him that he might visit Mahmood's house tomorrow evening."

"I don't want to see him, Binta," Maryam said flatly. "I don't want to involve anyone else," she was firm.

"Eets not my plan, sister," Binta said equally firmly. "He like your son, he is teacher, what is wrong to see him? You must see him, he educated, he might put some kwakwalwa in your head," Binta spoke in her peculiar style and stood up from the floor, urged Zainab to finish her soup by drinking direct from the bowl and got ready to tidy up the kitchen.

Maryam followed her, grabbed her arm and said, "let me clean up, Binta," she almost implored.

"No no, you guest, you not well," Binta replied.

"No, I am alright. I am feeling useless and ungrateful, eating your food and using your things. But I have nothing on me," her voice quavered.

"Wayo, wallah, look Maryam, if eet makes you happy, you clean kitchen, I go, no problem but you no say nothing about money to me, okay? Hareez my son, you my sister, Mahmood your brother, okay? And this," she pulled Zainab who was watching them both with her mouth open, "this your daughter, okay?"

Maryam had to smile. She waited until everyone was done with their dinner, washed the dishes, dug out ashes from the clay stove, added fresh firewood in its pit for breakfast, swept the hearth, tied up the garbage and started picking slivers of chaff from the porridge Binta would cook early in the morning for breakfast. She washed the grains and soaked them in tap water until tomorrow when they would be fluffy and plump, ready to be boiled with milk and sugar until the three ingredients became a grainy yet homogenous mixture. She thought about Malam Yakubu, what he would have to say to her and why? He shouldn't get involved, he shouldn't come here. That's all her brain cells shouted into her ears until she fell asleep beside Harris who was asleep before she came in. She stared at her son, sleeping with both lips slightly parted and snoring gently. She chuckled. He took it from his father, the snores.

What to do?

When to go back?

Should I go back?

Where else to go?

The questions kept ringing bells in her ears until sleep overcame her heavy eyelids. Sleep came silently, kissed her eyelashes and soothed her nervous brain into a deep slumber that erased away all pain, all misery, all queries for a long part of the dark night. She dreamt of a botanical garden, a swing that floated gently with the breeze, awaiting someone to sit and rock it. She dreamt of a steaming cup of tea lying silently in the corner of the garden, with an empty bamboo chair and a glossy illustrated book about orchids flapping its pages in the gentle breeze. She dreamt on walking through the garden and reaching a stone figure – a man with his hand on his chin, delved deep in thought. The Thinker. She dreamt staring at it and felt his hands move, reach out for her. She dreamt running away from the statue, aghast, afraid, horrified, but it ran after her, tugging at her clothes, her neckline, her shoulders. The statue was trying to grab her but she ran and ran and the moment she stumbled on the ground and fell, Maryam sprang open her eyes and found no air in her lungs or her air-passage. She gasped to find her breath, her heart raced violently and she looked around her to be sure it was a dream. Harris's hand was the closest thing to her so she held it, kissed it and softly put her hand over his. She shook her head once again to shun the image, lay it flat on the pillow and thought of the garden she had just visualised.

"If I ever could..." she breathed and spent the rest of the night trying to restart the dream which brought her tears of nostalgia that fell one after the other from the outer corners of her eyes and gathered in the cups of her ears.

CHAPTER 19

GARBA

Upon Binta's insistence, Maryam had baked a cake. For Malam Yakubu.

"I poor woman, Maryam, what can I offer to the Malam? He man of knowledge, respected. He teach English to baturiya children and I no speak good English. I get you flour from market and you bake the cake."

Maryam had tried to protest, saying she would serve him fried yams and kosay even if he came to visit her at Hyder's home.

"I will bake a cake for Zainab when I am leaving," Maryam promised.

Binta gave her a stern look, "No, you bake cake now, for Malam. Zainab no eat your cake if you no bake cake for Malam," she folded her arms in defiance.

Maryam chuckled. She was the boss.

So the cake was baked on the clay stove. The baker had invented a new way of turning the clay stove into an oven by placing the cake mould in the pit of the stove where Binta lit her firewood and red hot coals instead of flaming firewood was shoved under the mould. Binta covered the top with an earthen dish and the cake turned from a doughy batter into a cotton-wool soft bun.

It was hard trying to keep Obi, Zainab and Harris away from the cake after lunch since they had been giving the round eatable stealthy looks all afternoon. They had to be pushed on the rooftop to study. Just before sunset, the wooden door knocked and Mosy brayed a little as if asking the inhabitants of the house to attend to the caller. Binta was sure it must be Malam and she took one last look at the arrangements – the bamboo came stools were arranged in the compound in a cubicle manner perfectly, the small stool she used to climb on to reach the higher shelves of her almirah was dusted and covered with an embroidered table cloth, set in the middle of the stools and the cake Maryam had baked was cut into slices and waited on the kitchen shelf in her yellow and red serving dish to be served to the honourable guest once everyone was seated.

Binta walked to the door and without bellowing out to ask who it was as she generally would, silently opened the door and saw a black guy standing with his arms hanging loose on both sides.

She was startled for the briefest of moments for this was not who she had imagined to turn up on the doorstep. The visitor had a small beard on his thin face, his cheeks sunken and hollow, wearing a tee shirt that was a little oversized and a pair of pants that had been jagged mercilessly from the hem to shorten its length. Binta took this all in a couple of seconds, overcame her astonishment and managed to say, "Salam alekum!"

"Walikum assalam," the meek little fellow said.

The guy looked very familiar but she couldn't place him at the moment. Her brain had taken a huge shock for not having seen Malam Yakubu at the threshold. "Why you come here?"

"Sister, is Madam Maryam here?"

Binta got a flash of memory. Garba, the houseboy Harris talked about. What should she do? Maryam was her guest, her house was Maryam's asylum.

"No, Maryam not here," she choked out. The blunt loud mouthed Binta had her tongue rolling when she told a lie.

"Are you sure?" a gruffer voice spoke, Garba glanced to his left, the source of the voice, bent his head in submission and stepped back a little. The space was filled by a baturiya, white skinned, eyes covered with sunglasses, an overcoat covering him from neck to knees and his patent leather boots shining spotless.

Binta breathed in deeply. So *this* is the monster. She folded her arms on her chest.

"Because if you aren't, I might have the police raid this house and if my wife is found by the police, I will make sure you get a good worthy sentence for kidnapping a baturiya woman and her child," he continued in a flat tone, neck stiff and hands in the pockets of his trousers.

"You not scare me," Binta said with her chin high. "Go send police. I will tell how ugly your polished baturiya face is. You hit woman? You hit child? You shameless!"

"Shut up! And tell me where my wife is, you worthless wimp!"

"She not here. Go send the police!" Binta moved back to shut the door when Hyder intervened with his foot and shoved in into the threshold thus blocking the door.

"Maryam! Harris!" he yelled with all his might. So loud that even the neighbours peeked out of their homes to see what was wrong.

"Maryam!" he tried louder.

Maryam, who had been standing over a pot of tea in the kitchen, expecting nonetheless Malam Yakubu was stunned upon hearing the familiar voice. She turned to stone. Fear gripped her heart with a cold hand. She couldn't move. Then she heard Binta screaming, "Get out! Get out!" and then she heard Hyder let out a spurt of abuse at Binta. That was unacceptable. Binta shouldn't see or hear anymore of Hyder so she ran across the kitchen door and appeared in the courtyard where Hyder could see her.

"Maryam," he lowered his voice upon seeing her.

"Yes, don't say anything to Binta. She has been a friend," she spoke.

Hyder's face just glowered in response. "Where's Harris?" he uttered through gritted teeth.

"I will bring him. You can go start the car," she tried to sound calm although her soul was shaking and her heart was working like a mortar and pestle thudding hard, hard, hard.

Hyder eyed her suspiciously, threw a dirty, scornful look at Binta and went out of the door. Maryam ran to embrace Binta and sob 'sorry, sorry' in her neck.

"You no worry, Maryam, but why you come out? I not giving you up. That man is a brute!"

"No, it's alright. I had to go. Better be today. Just help me into coaxing Harris," she said.

"Hareez no go. I not send him, Maryam you crazy to go back? Go back to *him*? You see how he look at woman? How he speak to woman? He thinks we are shit. He thinks he God. Wallah, God no like men who treat their women badly. Why you stay with him? Why you care?" Binta had placed both her heavyset hands on Maryam's shoulders and was shaking her, asking her questions, not being able to figure out what metal Maryam's heart was made of, how could she go back? Maryam however, had thrown her head down. She had lost voice and had nothing to say to Binta.

"Bring Harris, please Binta," was all she could mutter.

A little while later, Harris and Maryam were sitting in the backseat of the car with looks of criminals being caught red handed in an act while Hyder drove silently, his sunglasses covering his eyes and bloodiness in them. Garba had been told to walk back home since he wasn't appropriate enough to sit in the precious Cadillac. It was a ten minute drive till home and in those ten minutes, Harris hadn't let go of his mother's hand. He could sense the moment they stepped out of the car his father would kill them both.

"Why is he quiet?" he thought over and over, "Why isn't he storming?" the silence was perturbing Harris more than the boisterous noise Hyder's abuse had agitated him back at Binta's house. Maryam was stone-faced. She neither responded to her son's fear nor her husband's muteness.

Binta had shrunken in size since Maryam had left. She sat on one of the stools arranged in a geometric fashion in the compound for her guest, her head in both her hands and despair written all over her face. Moments went by and Zainab came to her a little later, ushering a gentleman wearing a white riga and an embroidered cap on his head.

"Yana da Malam," the girl said to her mother who looked up at her guest and while keeping her seat, politely told him that Maryam and Harris had just been fetched by Hyder.

"Za ka iya zuwa, Malam," she said staring at the ground, asking him to leave.

"Da bangaskiya," he replied briefly, telling her to have faith, turned and left. Binta was trying to make a telepathy contact with Maryam. She wanted to know all was well. She wanted to know there was no more violence.

Maryam had tightened her grip on Harris's hand as they approached the house, Hyder parked the car in front of the vegetable garden, only, the garden was there no more. Maryam wanted to rub her eyes but she blinked them instead – the climbers were all gone, the plants had disappeared, the flowers no where to be seen, the garden she had tended to all these years like a baby was giving a forlorn look of a recently dug up construction site. There was no speck of green anywhere, the brown soil sat on the piece of land. The gardener got out of the car, not noticing how insecure and frightened Harris had been the moment she let go of his hand and slipped out of the car to have a better view. She looked quizzically at Hyder who was looking straight at her but had neatly concealed his gaze beneath the dark glasses. She tried to understand what, why and who had done it but deep inside she knew her answers were quite obvious. She managed to put on a brave face and signalled Harris to come out of the car. Hyder got out of his Cadillac too, a satisfied smug smirk on his face. Maryam went in and along with her Harris did too. She wasn't sure whether she should expect some surprises inside as well.

Nervous, she looked around and didn't find any. Hyder took off his business jacket and wore a windbreaker lying on the sofa and left again.

That was it? She thought. No exchange of words?

Harris dashed into his room. The housekeeper in Maryam awoke in an instant and she went to the kitchen to fix something for Harris's tea. She turned on the deep fryer to make some quick snacks from the freezer. While she was engrossed in the activity to make Harris feel as comfortable as possible, she heard the main door click softly. Her body tingled. Was he back already? She heard footsteps but she could tell they were not his. They were small, quieter and sounded like rubber slippers flip flopping. She turned to see from the kitchen door and found Garba standing in the doorway.

"Oh Garba," she was relieved, "you almost scared me," she smiled.

"Madam, please forgive me!" Garba spoke with his head thrown down in agony, "I did not know you were hiding."

"Garba, what are you talking about? I was at a friend's..." she wasn't going to let out her shameful secret.

"Master asked me, your friends, I said there were none. Then master asked about Harris's friends, I told him about Obi and then I remembered Zainab so I took him. I am sorry, Madam," Garba was in tears. Maryam walked up to him and put her hand on his shoulder, "You don't need to apologize, Garba," she waited for him to look up.

He didn't.

"Your face, it is coloured up again, Madam. It is blue and red."

"I fell down," she said.

"I will never forgive myself for bringing you back here Madam," he wiped his eyes with his wrists, the elf of a man, Maryam almost smiled looking at him, acting like a child.

"It is not your fault," she reassured him, "You were only helping Master."

"Let me hide you somewhere Madam, you and Harris, far away. I have family in Sokoto..." his eyes shot up with eureka.

"Garba, keep quiet. If Hyder listens to you he will..." she stopped in mid sentence.

"I am sorry about the garden Madam, Master made me do it," he was back to his submissive position again.

"It's no big deal," Maryam shrugged casually. "We will restart. It's a good thing actually, we will plant new seeds," she smiled at him but he was looking at the floor.

"Master threw all the tools. We can't start again," he said sombrely.

Maryam swallowed the lump in her throat. She turned to fiddle with the deep fryer.

"Also Madam, you should not try to find your things with which you made those statues," he continued giving the news of Hyder's deeds.

"My tools?" she turned around, eyes opened wide.

"Master threw them too. I took the garbage myself," he was apologetic.

Maryam needed support to keep standing so she spread her hands on the kitchen counter, realised she couldn't breathe. What was he doing? Was this some new strategy to engulf her with loneliness or was it a new attempt to isolate her?

"Something burning Madam," Garba's alarmed voice brought her back. The fry ups in the fryer were burnt to a charcoal. "Garba, please, make some new crackers for Harris. I need a moment," she could barely talk.

"Yes, Madam," the poor houseboy who felt responsible for Maryam's return to her doom was elated by the fact that Madam didn't hate him.

CHAPTER 20

HYDER

Hyder was at the Polo Club. Three days and nights he had spent in remorse. When he had thrown them out, he had never expected them to vanish. He was doubly assured Maryam would beg to be let in, even if not for her sake, at least for Harris's. He had hunted up and down the neighbourhood, without as little as hinting towards the missing family. He had socialized, with every neighbour, visited them, taken them small gifts – pre-Christmas he called it. He did what he was best at – being charming. All of them had received him with kindness, accepted his small presents – a bag of almonds, a box of chocolates, a fake Christmas tree and the like. Yet, none of them had mentioned anything about either his wife or his child.

He was still cutting class at the university. He was still indecisive about what to do with Vikki and looking at her being, full of enticement for his manhood was only going to tilt the scales, if anything. He had missed her, indeed. He had missed his being able to let all worries, all cares in the world go to Hell when she was around. She let him think he was some kind of king. As if the world rotated around him. As if he was god. Nowhere, could he get that solace, that feeling of being worshipped like he did in her presence. But she could be a risk now. The adventurist in him was coaxing him to take the risky path but his cautious mind was warning him against it. He needed time to think. He needed to explore his head and his heart. Most of all, with all set in paradise, he could finally eke out some time alone for himself.

He made himself comfortable at one of the lounging chairs in the deck of the club, the spot that watched over the pool. It was evening and the crowd was thinning. The waiter brought his favourite scotch and let him sip as he quietly waited for Daas. It had been days and they needed to catch up on a lot. Hyder considered Daas his rational mind. They thought alike, had the same lifestyles and could absorb all kinds of negativity from each other without being judgmental about it.

Once he arrived, Hyder had already downed half the bottle.

"Have you told her?" Daas was referring to Vikki.

"No," he drawled.

"You are going to repent this, Khan, you listen to me or you repent it," Das warned him, sitting on the edge of his seat, pouring himself a glass.

"She said Satanism is not about Satan," he spoke slowly – an affect of the drink in his hand and his drunken thoughtfulness.

"I don't damn care what it is about. The very name of it sends shivers down my spine," Daas reclined with glass in hand.

"That's it, that's the thing," Hyder retorted, "its fear of the unknown."

"It's none of my business what faith you follow or what creed your girlfriend belongs to. What I know is that this cult you are getting involved with is gonna get you in trouble," Daas was being sincere. "Take the easy way and find someone new. Believe me, you will feel better."

Hyder chose not to respond. Daas was right. It *was* no one's business to interfere in his religious life – he hardly had any – but that too wasn't anyone's business at all.

"When Vikki told me about it all, the words I could gather was manipulation, self-centrism, vengeance, egoism. That's the capsule of her creed. Every person, Daas, every person, I have known in this life is a manipulator, selfish, indulgent, revengeful, egoistic, hypocritical. Friends, foes, myself, all,"

Hyder spoke slowly, stressing on every syllable, pausing after every word.

"It is the only way to go buddy," Daas drawled casually.

"So that would make everyone a Satanist," Hyder found his conclusion.

Daas sprang up from his chair and threw his glass on the deck, smashing it to a hundred pieces. "You are impossible to talk to! Go to Hell and get in bed with Satan for all I care. You are damned to be ruined." Daas walked away. In his fit of rage he even forgot his jacket hanging around the chair.

Hyder finished his drink solemnly and asked the waiter to call him a cab.

CHAPTER 21

MARYAM

Maryam lay in her bed wide awake. No one could sleep next to Hyder when he was snoring.

He had come home just at dinner time. Harris was in bed, upset from the day's outcome and Maryam was in the lounge, in solitude, having a conversation with God. She remembered Binta's many advices. One of them was to talk it out. Since the walls and the TV set didn't look like much of listeners, she closed her eyes to connect somewhere far. Her monologue would have continued longer provided the cab driver hadn't rung the doorbell. She let Hyder in, his windbreaker hanging on his shoulder, his eye glasses missing. His breath stank so she didn't have to ask where the Cadillac was. She expected to get the whiff of roses from his collar, his shirt, his hands, anywhere but he just carried his own cologne tonight.

Hyder looked around to see where his boy was.

"Harris? He's sleeping," she answered without being questioned.

"Alright, I am asking nicely. Let's restart. I want to restart."

His words were coming out with great effort. She had dreaded this moment. She closed her eyes for a brief moment.

"I want to restart," he fumbled with his words again, "did you hear me?"

Maryam nodded. She had given up on that word – Restart. She had restarted on this relationship every day, every time they had crossed each other in the doorway, every time she had covered her bruised up face with makeup, every time she had smelt roses on his collar.

"Maryam," he was getting impatient.

It was too much too soon. How could he think she could bare her heart, her womanhood just after what had happened. She knew she didn't have time to think. Her brain was bombarded with thoughts of Harris sleeping in his room, the turmoil he had been through and deserved at least tonight's sleep peacefully in his bed, Binta saying if she couldn't normalise her relationship she should rather end it, the fact that his tipsy movements made her grimace, the truth that saying no to him now would be indeed taking a step back, she gulped the ball forming in her throat, blinked her eyes hard to stop any water droplets forming inside them, looked at him to find out that he had moved very close to her.

If only he could show some affection, Maryam hoped in her nerviness. An embrace, maybe a snuggle. He was devoid of any such expression. It was an ordeal for her. She closed her eyes and let the moments roll on. While Hyder breathed heavy and bent his torso on hers she thought of a botanical garden with a swing dancing in the gentle breeze, she imagined an empty barebones apartment in the midst of the walled city of Lahore with a window hanging loose out of its hinges swinging with the wind and letting in the soft music the neighbour was playing on his radio, she felt a sharp persistent pain in her groin and moved her imagination to a vegetable garden with fresh crimson radishes sprouting their leaves, long French beans hanging slyly around the canes standing firm in the soil, she imagined rubbing her hand on the skin of the sparkling red cherry tomatoes as soft as a baby's skin, she felt a lot of weight on her lower body and she shifted her thoughts to the figurine of the Thinker, she mentally sifted through the process of turning her favourite sculpture into a figurine by mixing the ceramic cement in her cassava bowl, forming the structure with her bare hands, poking her tiny chisel and needle to carve a statue out of a lump of a handful of cement mixture into one of the greatest remains of ancient art. She kept going in her imagination, creating frowns on his forehead, making sure the eyelids were droopy. She didn't know her fingers were making gentle movements as she moved them in her imagination and the imagery went on until she heard snores in her right ear. That's when she heaved out, opened her eyes and stared at the ceiling.

CHAPTER 22

MARYAM

Hyder had been worrying about Harris for days now. It had almost been a week since his family had returned home but he had hardly seen his boy. He had not forgotten how he had been the aim of his boy's catapult but he had also learnt during the three days, Harris meant a lot to him. Ever since he had come back, Harris would be cooped up in bed taking an afternoon nap after lunch or gone to the woods with Obiyara. At evening, Hyder went out to the Polo Club or the Ministry's office and at night Harris was tucked in bed fast asleep. Hyder had been waiting for the weekend to spend some time with the boy.

Maryam had an inkling of what was going on. She knew Harris was not one for afternoon naps. He was avoiding both his parents. He was annoyed with Maryam for having returned home. At school Malam Yakubu had warned him against trying to run from school.

"I know where Zainab lives. If I find you missing from any class, I shall come to get you," he had chided in a fatherly manner. He didn't want Maryam or Harris to get into any more trouble. Harris missed seeing Zainab and Binta, he didn't want his father to come near him for the bruises on his neck had yet not healed. Maryam understood and just tried to give as much space and time as possible to both the men in her life. She now knew, Harris was brainy enough to come out of this situation himself. She had also been wondering how to fill her empty days. Her fingers twitched with uselessness. She ached to mould some ceramic cement into miniature figurines. She looked at the empty plot filled with soil. There was not a blade of grass left, not a weed.

What did the garden ever do to him?

There was no answer. She looked towards the kitchen and it seemed uninviting. For the first time, she felt listless. She opened the fridge then the larder, she explored every cabinet as if there would be something tempting in there, jumping out at her, ready to be mixed, whisked, baked, and presented. But there was nothing.

She had asked Garba to go on leave so that she would have something to do around the house. The poor man had wept in distress. "Madam, you are firing me? I am sorry, please forgive me."

"No, Garba, I am not firing you. Only Master can do that."

"No, you are angry with me?"

"I am not," she sighed, "I am not angry with you. I just need to keep busy or else I will go crazy," she admitted.

"Okay, then I will help you."

She shook her head. It was no use.

"Alright, you help me."

Garba's face lit up.

When Saturday arrived, Harris waited for his father to go somewhere before he left the vicinity of his room. It was almost midday when Hyder entered his room.

"Say, Harris, let's go fishing today?"

"Dad, I've got tonnes of homework," he tried to make an excuse.

"We will be back in three hours."

Harris wasn't convinced.

"Is there some place you would like to go?" Hyder gave it another try.

"Well," he said thoughtfully, "I love the woods. There's always so much to explore." The idea behind the proposal was the fact that Hyder didn't like the idea of marching through swamps and getting his shoes soiled and his clothes dirty. He would definitely say no to the proposal and would be out of the boy's hair in no time.

"Okay then, the woods today," Hyder said much to the dismay of Harris.

"Get dressed. We will grab a bite at a cafe first," Hyder instructed before leaving the room.

Harris muttered curses to his luck while combing his hair and freshening up.

As soon as the boys had left, Maryam had the whole house to herself. Garba had washed the Cadillac, he had saw Master and little Master off to their expedition and now stood uselessly in the veranda, waiting for Madam's next instruction.

"Garba, do you know how to raffia?"

"Just a little," he grinned his mischievous smile, revealing a set of crooked teeth.

"Okay, then you teach me from tomorrow, alright?"

"As you wish, Madam."

"I am going to change the bedcovers in all bedrooms. You can sit in the sunshine if you like," she told him. Minutes later, she heard the doorbell. She expected Garba to answer it but hearing it twice made her go out to the door. On her way she saw Garba lying in a knot on the veranda's floor, fast asleep. She opened to see a young girl, wearing shorts and a tee, her hair an afro with the peaks shining like golden tips. The cold breeze that gushed in as soon as she had opened the door brought in a whiff of her perfume. It was roses.

"Hello, Mrs Hyder Khan?" the girl had a voice like silk.

Maryam came out of her trance, she nodded and gulped at the same moment, realising, she had finally met her.

"Is Dr Khan in?" she continued to speak.

Maryam's tongue was sealed. She just shook her head.

"Oh," the girl was clearly disappointed. Maryam noticed, she too was taking her countenance in with interest. There wasn't much to take in though, she was in her pyjamas.

"Could you tell him that Vikki came to see him? I am a student of his," she purred demurely.

Maryam choked out an OK and forced a smile. The girl smiled back and turned to leave. Maryam closed the door and gathered her nerves after flopping down on the couch.

"She is a beauty," she admitted.

CHAPTER 23

VIKKI

Vikki called a cab as soon as she had hit the main road. She was angry and frustrated.

"This is why he doesn't leave her, that bastard of a man," she thought to herself.

Hyder's wife was dumb enough to be wearing pyjamas in the middle of the afternoon, she was dumb enough to not receive or respond to a guest with proper eloquence, she was dumb enough to take his irrational nonsense without responding to it and she was dumb enough to not know her husband was sleeping with another woman. That is why he couldn't leave her. Because she was dumb and suited his needs. And to top it, she was beautiful.

Her fair skin, her silky hair, the truthful eyes she had that spoke for her before she could curl up those lips of hers, they all haunted Vikki and she felt out of place, a misfit and an oddball. Of course standing next to him, she would look better. With me, she thought, it would be an ethnic cross.

Vikki had asked the cab driver to take her to VI. She wanted to go to their love nest. Hyder had been avoiding her for almost a fortnight now. It was the longest they had ever stayed apart. She ached for him, her heart pained for him. Was it all over? Was she a fling? Her study course was almost over, with the final exam about to begin in a week's time. Was he going to replace her with a new freshman student? Was her job done here? Anger made her blood boil inside her.

She paid the cab driver with a fist full of naira notes, not counting them and dashed to the elevator to get to their suite. It was exactly as they had left it. The night they had spent together on the couch in front of the TV watching a foot ball match, baring their souls to each other. The beds were made, the fridge was stocked. She went into every nook and ever corner, just to feel his presence everywhere around her. The silken sheets looked inviting and the feel of them stung at her heart. She felt crumbling to bits thinking it could be possible she would never see him, touch him, and speak to him ever.

What had gotten into him? He had taken the ceremony too seriously.

She had beaten herself up enough times for not telling him the psychodrama going on at the church of Satan was just that. A psychodrama. The burning of holy artefacts on the bonfire, the blood offer, the rituals, were all part of an enticements for the newbie. She had wanted him to experience it so that he would maybe demand his own ceremony. But his gall had given out on him. He hadn't given her a chance to explain.

"Nuoko was right," she thought to herself. He had always warned her against his fickle nature.

"He has a wife back home, you know," that's all he would say.

She was at the precipice of tearing the hair out of her head. Despite Nuoko being right, despite knowing Hyder was a hypocrite who wanted the best of both worlds, the man who had so conveniently discarded her, she couldn't think of letting him go.

Vikki knew she wouldn't find him home but had still gone. Part of their deal was that she should never ever visit his home. She had broken the deal for she knew in his anguish, he would hunt her, come to her. Vikki was fatigued with all the psychological turmoil she had been through. She stretched herself on the silken sheets and waited for any intimation from Hyder. The stress had traveled from her nerves to her entire frame and as she made contact with the bed which she shared so lovingly with her lover, the coolness of the sheets comforted her. She lay there silently, waiting for Hyder to turn up at their apartment. It was, after all, Saturday night and they had spent every Saturday night together. He would find her, she hoped and waited.

CHAPTER 24

HYDER

Harris and Hyder had returned from their expedition. Vikki's visit was mentioned casually. Maryam had just seemingly tossed words into the air. She had noticed Hyder's face turn dark but she had acted as if it didn't matter at all. He stayed mum through lunch but the vacuum his silence created in the room was filled with Harris's voice – "We collected gum from the gum trees", it pained Maryam to think nother tree had been wounded and bled but she kept mum, "Dad told me he would teach me how to hunt birds... with a GUN!" her brows shot up as she glnced at Hyder who proudly smiled at his son, "Obi will be so jealous if I told him I went to the swamp outside Lagos. He was *dying* to go there!"

Maryam looked at her little boy, smiled and nodded at everything he said, while inside of her, she thought how innocent a child's heart is. How easily conquerable his mind is. A moment of love, a day of attention can bring utter happiness to a broken child. How flexible a child's psyche is. She thanked god for having put a smile on her precious boy's face. She wished it was as easy to mend broken fences in adulthood. She thought how idiotic she had been that night, complying with Hyder just because for once, she had not smelt roses on him! Just a fortnight ago he had tried to strangle her, left his hand prints on her neck, accusing her of having a love affair with Malam Yakubu. That woman, the other woman, she was not the reason for that throttling. She had no hard feelings for Vikki. Her desire for Hyder's love had squeezed out of her heart when he had hit her the first time. After that, it had been a mere project for her – heal him, normalise him, ease him of all violence that had seeped in him during his childhood, chisel off some of the inferiority complex the name Anarkali had given to him at college. But she had failed. She had spent her youth, her prime, her emotional being on a man who was never hers to claim. She started to feel sorry for him, for having made the mistake of marrying her instead of waiting for someone like Vikki to turn up.

Until the end of lunch, Hyder was quiet. He left silently as soon as he was done.

Maryam didn't ask him about his departure. She never did because she didn't care. Today, she didn't ask because she knew where he was headed.

And she was right. Hyder had gone straight to Vikki's apartment and had found it locked. It was just before dusk. He heaved exasperatedly, knowing where he could find her and drove off to Victoria Island.

The route was long and Hyder was deeply immersed in thoughts of Vikki. He had given her the harshest treatment there was – pretended that she didn't exist. His disturbed mind had found peace with Harris in the woods but he wasn't ready for yet another monster in the dark. He feared, why Vikki had been so desperate that she had traced his footsteps back to his house. She wouldn't want to break up, would she? She wouldn't make a public affair of his secret affair with her, would she? He didn't want to let go of her, she knew of his love for her, didn't she?

Bombarded with all these questions, Hyder made his way into the building that encapsulated his love nest. Hyder had crept into the apartment he shared with Vikki. He knew she was in there, but was she alone? Was she making use of his apartment without him? With another man maybe? He tiptoed from the lounge into the bedroom to find it empty. He was puzzled. He peeped into the other room and found what he had been looking for. Vikki. She was asleep beneath the sheets. Her face was buried in the pillow and her head shone in the light that the setting sun threw on the bed from the window. Her form was so perfect visible even from beneath the silk duvet. The curves and arches of her figure lit a fire in him. He had been punishing her, he had thought of leaving her but no reason in the world had seemed strong enough to let the woman of his dreams go. With her, he didn't have to prove what a man he was. He was worshipped by her like a deity, she was ready to eat out of his palm. That assurance was enough to push all his buttons that led him to stretch his tired muscles and gently sink in the soft mattress, right beside his beloved.

Vikki awoke, startled, looked into his eyes, stroked his cheek to make sure she wasn't dreaming, heavy lidded and puff lipped, she smiled and lay her cheek against his for a brief moment. She knew he would come and her eyes spoke volumes of her love, her heartache. Her eyes could have kept talking but they were closed as he smothered them with the faintest of kisses. Vikki's heart received the comfort it had been running after for so many days now and she held him close, closed her eyes and went to sleep.

No words in any language could be spoken. No excuses were needed, no explanations were made. Love had found its place to nestle between the entwined arms of the lovers.

Hyder had decided to stay for a while, but not stay the night.

"You can stay here for as long as you want Vikki, but tonight I need to be home," he had asked her when she woke up, still clinging to his arm.

"You came back, Harry," she purred, clearly not yet out of the trance his presence had left her in.

"I never left, dearest," he murmured back.

"Go then," she spoke lovingly.

"Just take your exams this coming week and then I am going to ask you to bring all your belongings here. This would be our home," he ran his fingers gently across her cheekbone and her jawbone.

"You mean..." she sat up.

"We deserve more than a stolen weekend together, Vikki."

"But your family?"

"They needn't know."

"So..."

"You will just have to send me home sometimes," he grinned.

She smiled, a half sad smile, "Whatever."

"It might mean they get to be watched by a day watchman and a night watchman" he thoughtfully added as if talking to himself and remained lost in the thought for a few moments.

"Okay then," he shot up from the bed, "I will see you tomorrow."

"Night night," she whispered.

"You too," he mouthed and exit the building a couple of minutes later.

CHAPTER 24

MARYAM

As soon as Hyder had left, Maryam had gone in his bedroom with a heavyset carving knife. There was some noise like someone trying to put metal through wood in the room while Harris looked puzzled and Garba didn't know whether to go help or stand still. Later she emerged with a paper bag. Garba had been there all day. His slumber in the veranda had been disturbed with Hyder's car screeching in the driveway.

"You need to tell me, what's going on Mum?"

"I have told you, just as much as you need to know now, Harris," she whispered, teary eyed.

"You have to trust me," she implored and let go of his hands. Harris was standing all dressed up in the winter jacket Hyder had brought for him and boots as if he were going on a long hike. Garba was there too, grabbing a small satchel with some important papers, ready to leave the moment the mother-son were done saying goodbye.

"Will he hurt you?" he asked, his eyes as sad as a puppy's.

"He won't," she tried to sound as convincing as possible, "I won't let him."

He embraced his mother and took Garba's hand extended in the air. The doorway was jammed with the three of them. The anticipation of the horror about to come had made the air denser and heavier around them. Maryam knew she had to put on a brave face. She cheerfully said goodbye to Harris and gave Garba a wistful look that asked him to take care of him.

"God be with you, Madam," he said in a very quiet voice and then led his little master to their destination.

Binta was right, Maryam had come to the conclusion. Harris was burdened with the idea of having a father instead of having the solace to depend on his old man. He wasn't safe with him, she wasn't safe with him. Maryam repented upon the years she had thrown away to the winds, the pain she had caused to her son... herself didn't count as much.

As soon as Hyder had left, Maryam had no qualms about his whereabouts. She knew he had gone to the rose scented girl but tonight she had run out of forgiveness. Her vessel of pain had burst. It had spilt out the patience that kept it intact. Her heart had hardened with his accusations. A bloody note to the teacher had made him throw her out of the house – the house she had considered home through all misery. He had the authority to throw her out of the house that she kept like a loyal slave. The house that was her asylum. The barren patch of land and the absence of her decade old sculpting tools had taken away all source of comfort from her. How could he do it, she kept asking herself. And why?

All these ten years of forbearance and endurance had meant nothing to him. He hadn't learnt to trust her but had expected her to trust even his lamest of lies. He hadn't known how hard she had often prayed for him to tell a lie about spending his weekends way so convincingly, that she would have no other option but to trust him.

"Make him lie to me, make me believe him," her heart called out to the Omnipotence above each time.

Each time.

She couldn't deal with the sickeningly familiar scent anymore. Harris had been sent to Malam Yakubu, to be safe and hidden until she spoke to Hyder, told him he was free to be with the one he loved without any baggage tied to his sides. She didn't want to sneak, she wasn't one to be stealthy. She was done with hiding and she was ready to face him. Maryam, took the hunting dagger from the tools cabinet – the same that she once wanted to slit her throat with – hid it in the back of her denims, wore a jacket over her shirt and waited for his return in the corridor.

She wasn't sure whether he would return tonight or the next day, as was usual, but still she had to be prepared. And she had to be brave. The sight of him could weaken her heart, she doubted herself. The reason she had sent off her boy was the very fact that he, his presence was a weakness to her. She didn't want him to get hurt in Hyder's last violent attack.

Hyder would normally have not rushed back home the way he did that night. Ever since he had brought Maryam back from Binta's house, he had noticed a change in her. The sadness in her eyes, the sad frown that turned her mouth downwards all the time had vanished. Her lips were tightly pursed all the time. He hadn't known she had the courage to go find refuge in a stranger's house. She would bang the door, implore, beg to be let in, that's what he had had in mind. He was afraid, she would disappear anytime and had to be kept under lock and key. And under the watchful guard of a watchman. Or two.

As he parked his Cadillac in the compound, Maryam felt a bout of nerves travel from the pit of her stomach to her groin and from there to her legs that shook a little but she gathered all the courage in her heart to gain composure. She hadn't bothered to lock the door and when he came closer to the entrance, he swung it open.

"What the hell?" he stormed upon entering. "why is the door open at this hour?"

"Hyder, I am going to have to leave you," she spoke as softly as if pouring down honey glazed words in his ears.

He stood there for a moment, the colour drained from his face, his eyes aghast with astonishment.

"I understand I am no more than a liability," she kept talking.

He fetched some of his spirit back, gritted his teeth and came forward with his fingers curled into a ball.

"Don't," she stepped back and glared at him.

"Have you gone mad, woman?" he spoke at the highest intonation.

"Maybe I have. But I am leaving you, right now," she stressed on every word. "And you need to behave," she added.

"Shut up! You thankless whore, who the hell are you screwing with? Tell me now!"

Then he answered his question himself, "Is it that bloody *teacher*?"

That was the last button he could have pushed. She had wanted to end it amiably but he was not worth the A of that word.

"Go to Hell," she hissed, "the devil in you has finally gotten the better of you, Hyder," she spoke with her jaws firmly tightened on each other. "You tell Vikki, she has finally gotten the biggest prize of her life and you Hyder," she paused briefly, "you have lost yours."

He sucked in his breath and stared at his wife in amazement, the woman who stared at the ground as he hit her, punched her, kicked her, and was looking right into his eyes, stripping him of his lies with just the name of his lover.

"Harris will stay," he choked out glancing towards the door of his son's bedroom. He knew this tactic would bring her crumbling down from the high horse she was riding.

"Harris is nothing to you. And believe me, you are no one to him," she spelt it out both ways for him to comprehend it better.

"He is my son!" he yelled.

She drew a deep breath. It was not how she had planned it but the mention of a kind benefactor in the most impish way by her husband had flipped her brain and she didn't care what would happen next. She flopped down on the couch near her and he moved away from the door towards the veranda to face her, thinking he had won the argument by striking at the weakest joint.

"He is not your son," she whispered, her eyes fixed on the carpet's pattern that lay under her feet.

"He is my son more than he is yours," he growled.

"How do you know?" she lifted her gaze to meet his. He looked puzzled.

"How can you be so sure, Hyder," she stood up, her eyes ablaze, she wore her fiercest face ever, "How do you *know* that he is *your* son?"

Hyder took a step back. His face showed disbelief, dismay, distress and disappointment – in all the colours his face changed.

She almost felt sympathetic but hardened herself. It was not the time to be Maryam again, she had to fight for her son, whatever it might take.

"What..." his words were lost.

As much elated she felt on her success to finally exploit his misogyny to her only advantage, she felt disappointed at how easily he had taken a seedling of an idea of mistrust and accepted it in a wasted moment. She hadn't admitted to anything, she had merely asked a question. But to Hyder, it was enough.

Just wind, most words are. He breathed in the wind and let it nestle inside him in a jiffy.

She gulped down the disappointment and wore her brave expression, stared him down and walked down the door as he turned around, grabbed the curtains on the Italian window that opened into the veranda.

In the middle of the night Maryam walked down a solitary path that took her to her son. While Hyder stood in the window for a long time, wondering why she didn't take her son with her. He, however, did not bother to look inside the boy's room.

Maryam looked straight at the path, the cold biting breeze dried up the tears that fell. The moonbeams were milky coloured and the halo around the moon was a deep purple. Every now and then a piece of floating cloud would cover the moon and then drift way. It seemed as if the clouds were thatching together for some grand conference. She looked at the glowing sphere in the sky and thanked the Heavens for lighting up her path in the middle of the night. She slid her hand under her jacket and pulled out the last bit of Hyder from inside her clothes– the dagger. It shone like some precious metal in her hands and she flung it on the soft Nigerian soil, kicking some of the sand over it lest someone should make some ill use of it.

CHAPTER 25

THE SATANIST

Hyder had never felt so vulnerable or as exposed to pain as he was feeling at present. The woman whom he had considered his honour and his pride had actually been unfaithful to him. She had owned up, without any shame that she had cheated on him. The boy whom he was bringing up, clothing, feeding and loving, was not his son. Behind that innocent face of hers, the sad eyes and the melancholic expression lurked a whore who had been cheating on him for he wondered how long. Whose son was Harris? He sifted through all possible candidates she could have met ten years ago. No one fit at first but as his brain started churning out ideas, it seemed to him that everyone fit. It could be anyone, his friends, his colleagues, the Indian neighbour who lived down the street, the Bengali doctor who she insisted upon taking Harris to when he was sick. His mind flooded and as much as he tried to shun his thoughts they kept banging on his psyche. It would be a couple of days later when he would go to his room to find that the stealthy woman had found the guts to break open his cupboard and take her traveling documents as well as her son's.

Presently, he looked at the closed door of Harris's room. He wanted to pull that boy out of his bed and throw him in his mother's way. She should have to deal with her filth, not him, he thought silently. He thought of going after her in the middle of the night and piercing that slut with a knife but he remembered in time he was not going to get anywhere with the word 'honour killing' in Nigeria. Hyder leapt towards the door that was making faces at him. He flung it open to find it empty. He checked the bathroom, the cupboards, everything was just as it should be, except for the boy. He had vanished. Hyder was feeling a strange ripping feeling in his insides. He was crumbling down to bits like a demolishing building. He felt his soul inside had turned to rubble and there was literally nothing he could do to build it back. He sat with a thump on the boy's bed. The computer on the study table was still on and was letting out sounds of wheezing and churning in the silence of the room.

With an aghast look on his face he had been sitting there for not more than fifteen minutes but the look on his face was centuries old. It seemed as if he had seen and foreseen immense moments of pain. Thus he looked like one of the computing gadgets he sat amongst: as mechanical, still and lifeless.

Desolately, he reached over and switched on the light bulb –
his only source of light. He sank back into the crater of the
mattress with a huge thump as if he had gone through a
tedious exercise. "Maybe a deep breath would do good,"
a voice from within said. Maybe it was Nisreen, an active
cell of his brain signaled to him. But at that moment he
was ignoring all of such voices and sounds including the
persistent beep from the computer, the churning of cogs
inside the computer and the voices from inside.

Amid all of this commotion, most disturbing to him was the
silence. It was hammering on his audibility: the silence of
his heartbeat, the disturbing hush-up between his two ears
and the deafening silence of the six walls around him. The
silence was like a splash of color or a tearing flood that was
slowly covering all the objects within the reach of his sight.

Time had come to a halt.

He wanted to come out of this ennui. He wanted to move or
just let out a shriek. He tried to open his pale dry lips to suck
in a gasp of breath or even a sigh, to blink his eyes but his
body was not under his control. He felt like an outer being
had held the reigns of his reflexes and his brain had cut off
all wires and connection with the rest of the body. It held
him hard. He felt like his astral body had moved out of the
clay sculpture God had created and had left behind a lifeless
dummy that had begun to crumble from inside.

He was thinking about nothing, it was as if his cognition
had frozen completely. His eyes were as stony as studs in the
blank walls of his face. He was cold and isolated. He felt as
lost as a child in a labyrinth and he was too grown up to shed

a tear of fear. He was longing for a hand to clutch, a bosom to rest his head upon and benign fingers to soothe him to sleep. But more than all of that, he desired a deep inhalation. A dog howled somewhere in the woods across the road and two or three more howls were heard coming from different directions of the dark abyss around his house. He breathed. A deep and long breath and blinked. He thought he was losing his mind.

"Vikki," he thought of the only person who would take him in during this spiritual demolition.

"Yes, Vikki," he said aloud and dashed outside to the car, fastened his seatbelt in so much haste as if the car would leave him behind. He geared up the engine and sped towards VI to his apartment, their apartment. As he drove, he had to struggle to keep his focus. He parked outside the building and raced up to the room, clicked it open and had found it empty. His heart sank. Not Vikki, not her, he wished. Where could she have gone at this hour? And with whom?

Something struck him and he ran downstairs, not waiting for the elevator to come up. As he stepped out, it had begun to drizzle. The sprinkle of cold water on a cold night was not very common in the Nigerian weather charts. His brain had fizzled out with the apprehension and awe. He forgot his car and ran on the pavement, he ran until he could run no more and he realized he had hardly reached the bridge that connected the two islands together. From there, he could only walk for the next one hour.

An hour later, his feet seemed to drag him as he approached the muted grey building that stood just five steps ahead.

He was like an etching of ennui himself – his time seemed stopped long ago. The Nigerian rain had been heavy on him. Drenched right from the top – the lanky hair down to the black ratty pullover soaked and clinging to his wafer thin body and from there to his bare feet that were no longer under his command, were carrying him to a destination whose destructive effects were known to him but he was most eager to go there and find what he needed most.

The Church of Satan was not a picture of fiendish architecture - there were no skulls hanging or vile looking birds perched upon arches, there were no arches actually. It was a regular looking house with a regular compound and a huge door. The greyness of the architecture made it look sombre, ignorable and daft in the same glance. As he jerked forth after stumbling upon a stone lying in peaceful slumber in the middle of the road, he almost thought he heard it groan like an old man who had been awaken from his sleep with a startle. As he turned around to spot the stone which had made him jump and lunge forth instead of walking the zombie-like walk he was walking, it was the first time for these deadly couple of hours that he had moved his head in some direction other than the pose of utter submission to whatever had taken the place of almightiness in his faith system. His head had been bowed for the longest hours ever since he had been treading on this wet road cold as ice, under the fearful shower of a chilled November night, his hands were tucked securely in the puddles forming in the hip pockets of his jeans and as he walked his desolate walk with chin on his chest, he looked like a prisoner being taken to the gallows. The only difference being, there were no on lookers, no scaffold or grind to cast a frightful look upon and no guards to hold him tight. Yet, it seemed as if his limbs were forcefully secured and he was going to crawl on his death bed to hide under sheets of white. The two hour walk had surely burdened him but the craving of coming to this place had hit the crescendo now – just five steps away was the place where the coveted answers to all his questions were lying bare.

The door was discouraging him. It was fastened. He knew the hour he had chosen to arrive unasked could be unwelcomed by the paganists inside. What if the door is not answered? What if he had to walk away? His hands, the second ones to defect after his feet, protested when he yanked them out of their slumber in the pockets. He brought his hands from behind up to the fore front, his shoulder blades cracked, another limb protesting. The gaze of his eyes upon his hands was interrupted by a bolt of lightning that struck somewhere and lit a spark. 'Fire? Is that a sign of being here?' The spark was beaten to death by the impish droplets of water from above. 'Rain belongs to God," he thought. Though the rain was persistent upon beating him down, he held his jaw and wasn't dampened.

Five steps, the five colossal steps were hard, so were his facial features. The only way to stop his teeth chattering like a sucker was to clench them tight. With shaking hands he lifted up a hand to thud on the door. Thud, not knock: to create more sound and wake up anyone inside, even Satan himself. As soon as his palm touched the brow beaten entrance gate, it creaked open.

This was a warm welcome which he had never thought of. He whimpered a sigh but could not tell whether it was reflective of relief or the appalling awe that had clutched at his heart like a tiny cold hand and had put the drumming rhythm of his heartbeat to a frozen still. Bewildered, he stepped inside the dark compound where the torpor of the boundary walls could match his present demographics. He kept walking till he reached the entrance of the ceremonial hall. He could hear voices inside. Human voices. He put an open hand against the door and it opened with the littlest of force. In the candle lit vigil he could not spot faces. The ritual was on and they people sat in a circle, holding each other's hands. There were about ten of them.

"Vikki?" he called out.

"Harry?" she replied, astonished.

He saw a figure move towards him, he had burnt out every last bit of his energy by the time she broke the ritual and came to him. He put his hands on her shoulders and found no words to say. He was out of breath, the occurrences of the past few hours had aged him and he looked old. His hands shook as he found support in Vikki but his legs could no longer carry the burden of his body so he dropped like a sack of grains on the threshold. Vikki gasped, and with the help of her fellow ritualists, she dragged him out of the rain inside the hall where he had once been before.

Epilogue

Maryam breathed the fresh morning air and a concoction of aromas filled her nostrils. Someone was brewing tea in the kitchen that led down the long corridor. Six bedrooms were lined up on either side of that corridor and Maryam shared one of those with Harris. There was the appetizing smell of fresh nan bread being baked in the family tandoor and the faint smell of jasmine flowers arose from every corner of the house. The reason for the last faint fragrance was the oldest lady in the house who woke at the crack of dawn and said her morning prayer in the garden at the back of the house which was laden with shrubs of jasmine and periwinkle flowers. The old lady, Maryam's maternal grandmother, would pick the fully bloomed flowers and make garlands out of them, hanging them on every door handle in the house.

No one was sure since when this ritual had been performed first but every morning, come hail or storm, the door handles were adorned with these garlands. Maryam smiled as she sat up in bed and was greeted with these heart warming aromas. She looked around and didn't spot Harris which brought forth another smile for she knew where he would be – climbing the steep hill two streets away that could overlook the local lake. It was frozen in the current weather but the condensation that arose from the frozen icy layer of the lake surrounded by stiff looking pinecone trees and coloured rocks made it look even more beautiful.

The sun was being lazy as it hid its full glory behind a blanket of clouds. The full moon of the night past was still visible in a faint shade of white and the sky was heavy with clouds. Maryam got out of bed and peeked through her door. She saw women running quick errands, waking up the kids, getting chores done or half done, instructing the house maids to perform their duties well and the men sipping the aromatic kehwa green tea, flapping newspaper pages, chatting all the while and kids running from one bedroom to the other. She spotted Harris among them.

She smiled for the third time and a few minutes later, joined the ladies, her aunts and cousins as they all gathered around the communal dastarkhwan – eating mat – and shared a cup of kehwa with them, munched on freshly baked nan and thanked the Heavens above for everything that surrounded her at that moment.

In the meanwhile, in another continent, a young school teacher had just received his mail on the threshold of his one- roomed house. It was Sunday, so the mailman had arrived a couple of hours later than usual. The recipient had smiled when he read the address of the senders – they were from Pakistan. "Lots of mail today, Malam?" the mailman said pleasantly and Malam

Yakubu smiled in return. Yakubu had understood his inner commotion the night Maryam and Harris had stayed with him. He understood his part in Maryam's life. Some people act as bridges in our lives. They help to transport us from one phase of our lives to another. They are sturdy, dependable and trustworthy. They appear in front of our eyes when the ditch seems too deep to be jumped over. Such people cannot be found out and dug up like pearls among sand. They can rather be waited for like carbon is waited to turn into a diamond. These people have the tendency to appear on their own and make the crossing-over more convenient. Malam Yakubu was one such man to Maryam and Maryam was one such woman to him. She helped him discover the greatness in him and he helped her find the strength in her.

Rustam Road,
Peshawar.

Dear Mr Yakubu,

Hello. I hope this finds you in good health. We have reached Peshawar safely and are well. I must say my memories of Lahore do not have as much similarities with this other city of Pakistan as I would have imagined but it is a decorous place to be. My maternal family – the uncles and aunts and cousins – seem to be taking turns to make my stay as comfortable as possible. I am already feeling like royalty!

Just so you know, Mr Yakubu, I shall never be able to repay for your kindness and your humane concern for Harris and myself. I wish there was a way to let you know how indebted I feel to you for your help while arranging for the air tickets and the departure. Harris's prized moments are the two days he spent at your house... he will treasure the memory forever, I am sure.

I have made a deposit to your bank account for the loan I took – monetarily – the support I found in you is immeasurable and unfathomable. Harris is having a good time, finding himself lost in a bigger family. I hope to send him to school as soon as the winter holidays are over here. Wish me luck, for things have changed quite a lot during this decade in Pakistan.

I will write to you as soon as I find a decent job. I think I have a chance as an art teacher. Did I ever mention, my father was a botanist and a professor at the state university?

I cannot thank you enough but for etiquette's sake, thank you.

Regards,

Maryam Ahmar

P.S.: Harris sends his greetings and regards too.

*

Cathedral School,
Peshawar.

Yo Obi,

I wish you could come here or I could come there. Hey, maybe when you go to America, you could stop by. I could show you so many places around here. I have been to the mountains up here, Obi! There are no bush lands, though, but the valleys and lakes and the woods with pine trees are pretty cool too. I was shown around by my cousins – I seem to have plenty of them. Twelve girls and eight boys. Finally, I got a bigger family than yours! All of them are older but all of them are nice.

My school is close to home and I still walk to school! There's just one problem – there's this local language Pushto which I am learning but it is hard! Well keep writing, say Hello to Malam Yakubu and tell him I am being good.

Okay, gotta go, you write back, okay?

Harris

*

Rustam Road
Peshawar

Dear Zainab,

Hello. How are you? How is Binta? I am fine here. It's a pity I couldn't say goodbye. But maybe we will meet up again. You are the best girl ever. Don't forget to take your English lessons from Malam Yakubu, he is great with good students like you. Also keep teaching Binta. She no speak bad English, anymore? Ha-ha. Tell her Mum says hi to her and sends her love. Don't forget to write to me. And hey, here's a picture of me sitting in a rowing boat at a lake near my house. Do send me a picture too.

Yours,

Harris

You are what you are;
Thus your likes and dislikes.
You are what you are;
Thus your faith and disbelief.

- Jalaluddin Rumi (Persian Poet 1207 – 1273)

ACKNOWLEDGEMENT

I am and always shall be deeply indebted to my loving mother who taught me to read, write, think, analyse, believe, question and have faith. To my beloved Dad, for encouraging me all his life to write and speak my mind, being my best critic and making me believe that there is 'a writer in me'. To Mumtaz, Mahnaz and Zara for being so patient with this project, encouraging me, supporting me and loyally questioning me like my personal editors – is it done yet? They are my sturdiest rocks. To my dear husband Amir Mir for his support and the inspiration, I am grateful. The deepest vale in my heart belongs to you. Tahira Munir and Bushra Munir, your contribution to this book and my spiritual uplift shall always be a debt unpaid, for being there to jostle ideas and give confidence throughout the perilous compilation of this book and for being staunch supporters, I thank you very much. Rafia Shujaat, for all sorts of co-operation one can imagine, for the critique and the moments spared to an over-burdened mind requiring a second perspective, for lending an ear every time a writer's block hit, I am indeed grateful. To Suhaira Hasnie for being a friend who believes and makes me believe in the goodness of human nature, I extend my gratitude, for this and everything else. Yasmeen Bilal Soofi, the person who taught me more than poetry, prose and drama at college – she is thanked and thought of every time I begin a sentence. Shujaat Ali, thank you for being the elder brother I never had! Never had! Hamid Bhaijan, your encouragement is indeed appreciated.

Last but not least, thanks to Adrian Kane, for being so cooperative during publication of this book. There were tough times and he helped me glide through them. I thank you Joe Anderson, for making the tedious process of editing a delight.

Printed in the United States
By Bookmasters